KT-563-377

THROUGH THE WALL

CAROLINE CORCORAN

avon.

Published by AVON
A division of HarperCollins*Publishers* Ltd
1 London Bridge Street
London SE1 9GF

www.harpercollins.co.uk

A Paperback Original 2019

First published in Great Britain by HarperCollins*Publishers* 2019

Copyright © Caroline Corcoran 2019

Caroline Corcoran asserts the moral right
to be identified as the author of this work.

A catalogue copy of this book is available from the British Library.

ISBN: 978-0-00-833509-0

This novel is entirely a work of fiction. The names, characters and
incidents portrayed in it are the work of the author's imagination.
Any resemblance to actual persons, living or dead, events or localities
is entirely coincidental.

Typeset in Bembo by Palimpsest Book Production Ltd, Falkirk, Stirlingshire
Printed and bound in UK by CPI Group (UK) Ltd, Croydon CR0 4YY

All rights reserved. No part of this text may be reproduced, transmitted,
down-loaded, decompiled, reverse engineered, or stored in or introduced
into any information storage and retrieval system, in any form or by
any means, whether electronic or mechanical, without the express
written permission of the publishers.

MIX
Paper from
responsible sources
FSC™ C007454

This book is produced from independently certified FSC™ paper
to ensure responsible forest management.

For more information visit: www.harpercollins.co.uk/green

To S, S and B, my team.

Prologue

Present

I sit, listening to the drip, drip, drip from a shower that only runs for a short time to prevent me from trying to drown myself.

There is a loud, unidentified bang at the other end of the corridor. A sob that peaks at my door and then peters out like a siren as it moves further away towards its final destination.

I slam my fist down on the gnarly grey-green carpet in frustration. Pick at a thread. Trace the initial that is in my mind: A. A.

A psychiatric hospital is such a difficult place in which to achieve just a few necessary seconds of silence.

Nonetheless, I try again, pressing my ear against the plaster and shutting my eyes, in case dulling my other senses helps me to hear what's being said on the other side of that wall.

It doesn't.

My eyes flicker open again, angrily. I look around from my position on the floor and take in what has now become familiar to me after my admission four weeks ago. The mesh on the windows. The slippers – not shoes – that are never far from my toes. The bedside table up there and empty of night creams, of tweezers, of the normal life of a bedside table.

And then I go back to trying to focus on what they – my imminent visitor and her boyfriend – are saying. Because it's too good an opportunity to miss, when I can hear them, right there.

'Both of them again,' announces the nurse as she flings the door open.

She looks at me sitting there on the floor, raises her eyebrows. I stand up slowly, move back to the bed. If she thinks my behaviour is odd, she doesn't say it. I imagine she gets used to behaviour being odd. Gets used to not saying it.

'Just sorting out the paperwork and then we'll let her in,' she says. 'He said he's staying in the waiting room again. Not sure why he bothers coming.'

But he does. Every time it's the two of them, in a pair like a KitKat.

I press my ear against the wall again, so hard this time that it hurts. But since when did pain bother me?

1

Harriet

December

I listen to them have sex, frowning at how uncouth it all sounds.

And then I think – what a hypocrite. Because here I am having sex myself. With a man who I *think* is called Eli. I wonder if the couple next door can hear us too; if they are having similar thoughts.

Over Eli's naked, olive-skinned shoulder I glance at the TV. I have no idea who turned it on but they have put it on mute, a breakfast news segment on turkey farming. What an odd juxtaposition, I think, to all of this sex.

As Eli finishes, I look away, embarrassed, from the poultry, then pull my dress back down over my thighs.

'I'd better head to work,' he says, no eye contact. I barely have the energy nor inclination to nod.

'Door's unlocked,' I reply, and he slips out without another word.

I exhale and reach down to the floor to pick up my glass then take a sip of amaretto and Coke. It's 7 a.m. but I haven't been to bed yet so it's not quite as bad as it sounds. Plus, it's there and I'm thirsty. The door slams.

I rest my head back against the sofa, look around. Half-full glasses, Pinot Grigio bottles, cigarettes stubbed out into old chocolate dessert ramekins. Crisps, squashed into vinegary

3

hundreds and thousands on a cushion. Student scenes; not what I had thought my life would be at thirty-two.

I turn the TV off and return my attention to the couple next door. I think they are doing it on their sofa, this couple, because intermittently the arm of their furniture is knocking up against the wall. Sorry, wrong pronoun: it's knocking up against *my* wall.

2

Lexie

December

'Tom, we need to do it,' I say. I have a provocative way like that.

He's sitting on the sofa in his T-shirt and pants, shovelling in a spoonful of porridge with one hand and scrolling through social media with the other. I pull off my pyjama top without waiting for an answer because the stick said to do it and we are slaves to the stick. Tom knows this is compulsory even though he has tired eyes, will likely now be late for work and really wants that porridge.

But he goes away tonight for three days, so it's now or not at all. Not at all – when you're thirty-three years old and two years into trying for a baby – is not an option.

Tom takes off his pants one-handed without removing his eyes from his phone. You learn, when trying to get pregnant, to multitask in ways you could never imagine.

I move the porridge to one side, being careful to rest it somewhere where it won't get knocked off. This isn't 'I have to have you now' sex so much as 'I have to have you now because the stick says so but we've obviously got time to move the porridge to one side because no one wants to get sticky oats on the DFS sofa' sex.

'Don't worry,' I whisper breathily. 'We can be quick so you're not late.'

Tom swallows a mouthful of porridge and waits until the last second to give up scrolling. Half an hour after he leaves I am still lying on the sofa, knickerless, with my legs up against the wall, hoping – as I always hope despite increasing evidence of its uselessness – that this gravity-boosting move helps to propel things along.

I was pregnant, once. It never happened again.

Now, I think of pregnancy as less of a yes or no thing, rather as something more cumulative. A spectrum, on which I am in a segment marked Unequivocally Unpregnant.

My underwear goes back on gingerly. Don't upset the potential embryo. Don't disturb the sperm.

I stand up. I can hear my neighbour, Harriet, moving around next door, ticking across her wooden floor in heels, keys rattling, front door opening.

I know I should feel embarrassed in case she heard something just now, but I'm so focused on my only current goal that I can't muster up the pride to care.

Plus, I swear that I just heard the sound of sex coming from her flat, too. Hot morning sex, I think, that they couldn't resist even though they were meant to be at work. The opposite of the type that we were ticking off on a to-do list through the wall.

3

Harriet

December

'I cannot believe how many *chain* restaurants are in this neighbourhood,' says Iris, using a tone for the words 'chain restaurants' that most people reserve for 'terrorism training centres for toddlers' and grinning widely through her astute observation. 'You know?'

I know.

I take a large glug of wine and feel my cheeks singe. She thinks where I live is embarrassing. She thinks I'm embarrassing. Everyone here thinks I'm embarrassing. I have been taking extra wine top-ups this evening and the room is starting to spin. I stare at her, try to bring her into focus.

Really, I think, Iris should be trying to bring me into focus. Because the truth is that she – they – have no idea who I am. What I'm capable of, what my real name is and who the real me is. What is at my core and what I did, nearly three years ago before they knew me.

Anyway, I think, flooded with rage suddenly as they speak around me: I *love* Islington. Take somebody socially awkward and place them in the heart of one of London's busiest areas and they will adore you. They will never need to make small talk with the butcher. They won't have a favourite restaurant because they have sixty within walking distance and when they do, it will change hands and become a pop-up Aperol bar anyway. You can know no one and that doesn't mark you out as odd: it's simply the way things are. You can have a secret, because you can hide away.

I recover from the insult quickly. A couple of drinks later, I am talking with unwarranted confidence about British political turmoil in the Eighties while intermittently chair dancing to Noughties pop music. I'm very drunk – I'm often very drunk – and I'm laughing. But it is an empty laugh because I don't know the people I'm laughing with.

Next to me on my sofa is a man named Jim, 'incredibly talented', gay, talks about being an introvert often and loudly. Opposite me is Maya, who has been nursing her glass of Pinot Noir for the last two hours, despite my best attempts to top her up, loosen her up, liven her up, something her up. On the floor, barefoot and knees pulled to their chests, are Buddy and Iris, who live in Hackney and were probably christened Sarah and Pete and who rarely leave the house without making sure a copy of Proust is sticking out of their bags. A Christmas hat sits joylessly atop Iris's shiny brunette bob.

I look around at all of them and try to feel something but there is nothing. Or there is worse than nothing; there is a low-level stomach ache that tells me I feel awkward and sad and that this gathering in my home is the opposite of friendship.

Merry fucking Christmas.

Last month, I met all of the people currently squeezed into my lounge for the first time. I am a songwriter, we are working on a musical together and I invited them over for Christmas drinks. For God's sake, I even wheeled out a box of Christmas crackers.

I do this with everyone I work with. We usually rearrange around four times and people's excuses are vague, but I am persistent. They all capitulate, eventually.

I'm still trying to find something that makes me stop craving the city's anonymity; something that claims me as its own, despite four years passing since I left my native Chicago. I'm trying, desperately, to be social. But sometimes I think the truth is that when you carry a history like the one I carry, you can never truly grow close to people. It's too risky. Too exposing.

I pull a cracker with Buddy and lose.

But still, I keep trying.

'So, Harriet, are you seeing anyone?' asks Introvert Jim, loudly, bolshily, butting in rudely to my thoughts.

I shake my head, top up my wine.

'No, Jim,' I slur, matching him for loudness as my drink glugs into the glass. I forget to offer a top-up to anybody else. 'I am single.'

Oh, I am very, very, very much single. Unhappily single. I am not content being me. I'm not joyous in my own company. I am awkward and I make terrible decisions and I want another half to make 50 per cent less me. I aim to dilute myself, like a cordial.

'Karaoke!' I say, fuelled by wine and the panic that people may leave, and Iris and Buddy find it ironic enough – like the Christmas hats – to join in. Maya slips into her denim jacket and slopes off, giving me a pitying look that sets a flare off inside me as she says goodbye. Jim can be persuaded once I find him a dusty bottle of tequila for a shot.

These colleagues may not be an immediate solution to my solitude, but perhaps one day it will come in the form of a man who one of them knows.

Plus my parties, alcohol-fuelled as they are, rarely begin and end at my colleagues.

It happens, always, as it is happening tonight. The door is propped open so that my guests can pop downstairs for cigarettes. I live next to the elevator and what I never envisaged – given how antisocial my neighbours are in daylight – is that late at night, people started coming in the other direction, too. Peering in to see what's happening. Hearing a song that they like. Grabbing a beer.

So it could be one of those, too; an unknown neighbour who comes for the alcohol but stays for me. I might not be perfect, but I have things to offer. Enough to hope that one day, someone *might* invite me back, might claim me.

There are hundreds of flats in our tall, imposing tower block, and most of them are inhabited by men and women in their twenties and thirties who don't have children and can get drunk on Tuesdays without much consequence beyond a hangover they have to hide under carbs the next day at their desk. If they live here even as renters then they are mostly paid well and work hard for long hours, so that their evenings take on a desperate quality. Enjoy it, make the most of it, drink it, snort it before you're back in a meeting at 8 a.m.

The building, with its modern feel, feels to me like it aids this. The sparse, airy lobby is an anonymous retreat, painted head to toe in magnolia with just a desk for the concierge and a sole plant that never wilts but never grows. Is it fake? When I stare at it, I can't tell. I wonder if people ask the same thing about me.

In the lobby is an unplaceable but specific scent that never alters. The temperature's always exactly what you want it to be, whatever the season.

At times it reminds me of an airport. People pass through, collect their parcels, take off in the elevator up to the eighth floor, and there are so many flats that you can easily never see them again. Occasionally, it reminds me of somewhere darker: of the psychiatric hospital where I used to be a patient. A coincidence? Maybe this is what I want from a home, I think. Utter sterility.

Now, my neighbours traipse into my home, three, four, every half-hour. They are on their way back from their work drinks or their dinners and they stick their hazy heads in to see what's happening. Someone – me, most likely – shoves a wine glass into their hand and the next minute it is 1 a.m., and a city banker in his early twenties who I've never seen before is kissing Chantal from the fifth floor and vowing to move with her to a hippy commune in Bali. Chantal, like me, is a rare exception in this building to the city-banker rule, but I'll get to that in a minute. By day, my neighbours are antisocial and aloof; by night, they are debauched and overfamiliar, revelling in their freedom. Happy mediums are not what we do in Zone One.

Did I make an idiot of myself? Chantal will message tomorrow, inevitably.

The message will come from her sofa, where she lies every day thinking about retraining as a masseuse. Chantal was made redundant from her job in marketing a year ago and from a distance, it is clear that she is in a deep depression, which isn't helped by the fact that her rich parents pay for her to lie still and be sad. She has no motivation to move. But at 1 a.m. Chantal is shining, lit by lamplight and Prosecco. At 1 a.m., Chantal and I are something approaching friends. At 1 p.m., we exchange awkward chat in the preprepared aisle in Waitrose.

'I'd better head to . . .' she will mutter, gesturing vaguely at some bread, or a door, or anywhere.

'Yeah, I'd better get on, too,' I'll concur urgently before ambling back to my sofa.

But meeting somebody is a numbers game, that's what my mom would say if we still spoke. If it wasn't impossible for us to speak, after what I did. It's a numbers game and I'm following that policy. Let the strangers in. Keep them coming.

The nights begin with wine offered politely and with small talk. And then they descend into strangers and a blurry chaos I spend most of the next day clearing up. It's worth it, though – the mess is comforting. It gives me a purpose.

Again, tonight, my flat is full of unknown or barely known neighbours and the last of my colleagues who are heading home now at 2 a.m., slurring. As they wait for the elevator outside my flat I hear them through the door that's been left, as ever, temptingly ajar.

'She's just a bit . . . much, you know?' says Iris, her voice loud because she is drunk on the alcohol that I just gave her, for free, while she hung out in my home. She is talking about me.

Buddy concurs, as the world always has concurred on this. I'm a bit . . . much. I'm not quite the right amount. Not on target. Not the level of person you would ideally want. If I were a recipe ingredient, you'd tip a portion of me out, or balance me with salt. As I'm a person, I can't be amended, so I remain a bit . . . much.

I sit against the wall behind the door listening to the rest of their thirty-second conversation on the topic of me before the elevator announces itself loudly. An hour later, when everybody else leaves, everything is quiet, and I hear a TV being switched off next door and the soft, kind padding of slippers on laminate floor.

I say goodbye to my next-door neighbour, Lexie, in my head. She never turns up at my parties, but I know her name because I have heard her boyfriend say it through the wall. And then I lie down on the sofa, mascara on the cushion from the start of tears that will go on and on and on until the moment that I finally fall asleep.

4

Lexie

December

I'm typing and deleting and at that moment, Harriet starts singing in a children's TV presenter voice that is too loud, surely, to be normal. Was other people's noise this irritating when I worked in an office? I've always loved sound; the radio on in the background, talking to friends over TV shows. Slowly though, I think, all the rules of me are changing. I throw a cushion at the wall.

I uncurl my legs from the sofa then head for the kitchen because I've been thinking about the flapjacks in the cupboard all morning.

I look down at myself, bottom half shrouded in Tom's pyjamas. My own strain at the waist too much now to be comfortable.

I eat the flapjack. And then I lie back on the sofa and think. Is it right that Harriet can get to me so much? Is it normal? My relationship with my next-door neighbour, to anyone living in a place that isn't a vast Central London contemporary apartment block with a concierge service that takes delivery of your online orders and helps out the lost Deliveroo driver roaming hundreds of identical corridors with a pad thai, would sound bizarre.

I know more about her existence than I know about most of my friends'. We are closely entwined. She is by far the person I spend most time with. I know about her boozy parties with

13

their Prosecco glugged into friends' glasses as they try to resist and go home but they can't – they can't because they're having too much fun.

I know about Harriet's love for karaoke as her friends laugh and groan that they have work tomorrow. But then the intro kicks in and they stay and there is whooping. More friends join them. The joy multiplies. And there is always so much *noise*.

Now, the piano. I put pillows over both of my ears, but her sounds – always there, competing against our quiet home – are impossible to drown out.

Harriet writes songs for musicals that thousands of people hum on the bus home from the West End. She's interviewed regularly for industry websites, sounding intimidating-smart. She is successful and rich, I presume, if she lives here. In this building, Tom and I are the exceptions with our normal salaries, and we can only be here because Tom's parents own our flat and they've let us rent it for way below market value.

I realise I'm googling her again. I look at the picture of Harriet on her professional website. She is tall, striking and handsome and she looks powerful. I like her mouth. I envy her smooth, silky blonde hair. At school, she was undoubtedly the popular girl; a person who wouldn't have sought me out as a friend as I battled my fringe of frizz and Play-Doh thighs.

In her flat, which doubles as a studio, Harriet writes and rewrites lines, her bare foot on the pedal of her piano; painted, unchipped fingernails flicking up and down before she scribbles down what she's created. Harriet is a creator, she creates, she is creative. Purposeful, she is often so lost in her work that she forgets her plans and is late as she dashes to meet friends for brunch. She picks up flowers at Columbia Road, to sit on top of her piano and make a bright home even more colourful. She knows her own mind and tastes, *never* decorating her flat with something generic from a chain store, and to men, she is the whole package: smart, buckets brimming full of fun and utterly gorgeous.

Oh, I've never met her, of course.

I *saw* her once getting out of the lift when I had taken the stairs during a low-level fitness drive. I've found her mail in our postbox and shoved it into hers, and sometimes, like now, I Google her name. And yet I feel, somehow, like I know her.

From my home-office, aka the sofa next to the wall, I see my next-door neighbour, Harriet's, existence happening, and it is plump and full and bursting.

Meanwhile, I have been here for three hours now with the start of back pain, flapjack on my chin and only seven sentences of my 2,000-word copywriting project on the page.

I wipe crumbs from my lap. I am no Harriet.

Just getting on the tube, says Tom's text, later. *Curry?*

As I reply, I notice the stain on my – his – pyjamas and mean to change, but then I get distracted looking at the Thai menu.

Curry is bad. Curry means my size 12 jeans will dig into my skin. Curry means that we are unlikely to have sex tonight, when we should be doing it any chance we get.

Our impromptu and erotic sofa sex didn't reap rewards and now almost a month has passed.

My ovulation sticks don't say we're in the window yet, but Great Doctor Google, alongside freaking me out about everything I do, have ever done and will ever do in my life, suggested that the more, the better is currently on-trend in medical policy. The idea that there is an 'on-trend' in medical policy is a worry if I think about it, so I don't and instead choose my side dishes. I add duck spring rolls to a list of things I worry are stopping me from getting pregnant. They have many, many companions on that list.

In reality, we have no idea yet why I'm not pregnant. We have no idea why I got pregnant once, miscarried, and why it never happened again. And why, two years later, we are still static, waiting to move on and realising that we were so sure that I would get pregnant again, we never even properly grieved.

With every month that passes, anxiety wraps itself around me more tightly as I convince myself that it's my fault. Despite trying everything. Despite following Tom, who works away sometimes making TV documentaries, around the country to have sex at the right time. Despite once buying a sexy nightie from Figleaves lingerie and staying in a Travelodge in Hull for a whole bloody week.

But beating myself up is something that's been happening more lately, increasing alongside calories and sleeping as I do other things less: see friends, pluck my eyebrows, wear clothing items without an elasticated waistband. Laugh.

Through the wall, to snap me out of my internal chatter, comes Harriet. She slams her piano in frustration and then I hear a phone ring.

'Yeah?' she says, brusque, like people who are busy do. I am not even busy in this, the week before Christmas, the busiest week there is.

It must be a delivery driver, because ten seconds later I hear her buzz someone up and answer the door, shrieking about the beauty of the flowers. An early Christmas present? From a boyfriend? A friend? Her mum?

I peel myself away from the wall and nestle into the sofa. I'm home so much now that I work for myself that Harriet constitutes a concerning amount of my human interaction.

I picture her in heels, phone snuggling into her palm, hopping into her taxi, running out to dinner, to lates at a gallery, to taste potent festive cocktails. And I'm reminded of the old me, the me before fertility worries happened and sprawled over my life.

I shuffle to our bedroom in my worn-out slipper boots and rummage around in the wardrobe until I find the box I'm looking for. It is, as they always are, an old shoe box, full of photos that were supposed to be filed away in albums that were never bought and now live sandwiched between thank-you cards and badges from hen dos and birthday invites and leaving cards filled with in-jokes and old ticket stubs.

Somewhere along the line I stopped being this person who inspired people to turn cards around and write up the sides, who brought on exclamation marks and capital letters and leading parentheses.

I picture myself in my old job at a women's magazine, where I had a reputation for always coming up with the best interview ideas.

'Lexie will nail it,' people would say, and I had the confidence to agree. I shared in-jokes, suggested new places for lunch. And then I shrunk. Now, as people sing Christmas songs outside my window and eat their fifth turkey roast of the month, I am alone, again, waiting.

I don't know how life became this limited little space. I don't know when I crammed myself into a box that was only just big enough for me, because I used to be a Harriet, too. And I am envious.

5

Harriet

December

I'm halfway to a work Christmas meal – the kind where I preordered my soup, turkey, tiramisu in October – when I realise that I've forgotten my phone and have to head back to the flat.

I nearly trip when I get off the bus, swear under my breath.

I'm too clumsy and tall for these heels, and I make a note to switch them for sneakers when I get home, despite the fact that I will never rock a trainer in the breezy way I've seen other girls do – in the way Iris does – that bares a chic, non-icy ankle. How are the ankles of all of these people not freezing?

On me, a sneaker–jeans combo will look as though it belongs on an awkward thirteen-year-old on a school trip, not a thirty-something who should have mastered her classic look by now. I look down at myself: far from it.

I swipe my fob against the screen and pull the door to just as someone is getting in the elevator. I curse my timing, because there is an unwritten code in this building that no one shares elevators, when I notice the man who has beaten me to it.

His hair is dark, curly, wildly untamed. He shoves it impatiently out of his eyes with each hand, alternately.

And I breathe like I am due to jump out of a plane in two

seconds because an alarm bell has gone off and is drowning out everything else.

It's not just this man's hair. It's his dark eyes, it's the hunching of his shoulders as he heaves his large rucksack onto his back and puts a takeout food bag on the floor. It's the sigh he does, so internal for an external noise. It's his long legs and his straight jeans and it's his nose, slightly too Roman for most but not for me.

This man and my ex-fiancé, Luke, who used to live here in this flat and get in this elevator with me, do not share a passing resemblance. Instead, they are doubles. Identical. Interchangeable.

For once, I climb the stairs and slam the door of my flat behind me. But like the Thai spices, the man from the elevator has crept in anyway. I know – rationally, I know – that it wasn't Luke, that it couldn't be Luke, that my ex-fiancé isn't here, in London, clutching his takeout in the elevator of my building. That after what happened, his former home is the last place he would ever come. But there is a part of my brain that the message hasn't reached and that's the part that is making my heart hammer into my chest, surely audible through the wall to next door, I think, as I realise I am leaning against it. I gasp for air.

After a few seconds I hear Lexie, her tiny voice quiet, gentle, the opposite of my own. A northern lilt, I sometimes think, though English accents are still not my forte.

'Tom?' she asks, raising her voice to carry into the kitchen. 'Can you bring me a . . .'

But the end of the sentence falls away. As ever, there's just enough wall between us to mask life's detail.

But Tom. Not Luke, Tom. Tom from next door. I must remember that, when my heart starts racing, when my mind starts racing and at 4 a.m. Especially at 4 a.m. I pour a glass of wine, down it and – forgetting to switch my shoes – kick the generic flowers that were delivered from a generic former

19

colleague to say a generic thank you out of the way and head out with my phone, trying to fight a feeling that Lexie from next door has stolen my Luke. That Lexie from next door has stolen my fucking life.

6

Lexie

December

'I miss Islington,' sighs Anais as I flick the kettle on and she yanks off a tan Chelsea boot in the hall behind me. 'Bloody Clapton.'

I've known she was coming round for a week now – she had a Christmas lunch around the corner – but still I had run around flustered for five minutes before she arrived. Endeavouring to put on eyeliner, remember how real people (I haven't really considered myself to be one of those since I started working from home) dress and shove piles of post into drawers. Tom's been away for a week now. I am flailing.

'Remember why you live in Clapton, though,' I say, brandishing a mint tea box and something ridiculously expensive from Planet Organic at her, and she nods to the latter, of course, because we are middle-class Londoners. 'You own your place. No chucking your money away on rent.' I sigh. 'We'll be here forever, because Tom's dad will never put up the rent and we'll never get anything better so we'll never have the motivation to get a mortgage.'

It's not just Anais; I say this to everyone, all the time. It's my only response to my self-consciousness over how lucky we are to have moved this year into a Central London flat that has its very own swimming pool in the basement.

It's still such a surprise to me, too; my own parents have barely lent me twenty pounds in my life – they're of the 'learn the value of money' school of parenting. I've been encouraged to be utterly independent. Which makes this whole scenario pretty ironic.

Now, for less rent than my friends pay in Zone Six hellholes, I live somewhere where there is no paint chipped in the communal areas but walls that are freshly covered in high-end magnolia once a year. Where cleaners spirit away dead flies or discarded ticket stubs with the speed of a five-star hotel and then fling the windows open so that the feeling is hospital sterility. Where every type of night and day life we could need is in walking distance.

Right now, Islington's anonymity soothes me. I walk out of my flat with nowhere marked out as my final destination and I wander up the high street past hipster thirty-somethings with children dressed in fifty-pound jumpers on scooters. At weekends, I clamber onto the bookshop on the barge on the canal, picking out piles of worn, second-hand classics. I smell the brunch that's being eaten in seven-degree cold on the pavement like we are in Madrid in July and I know that that wouldn't happen anywhere else in this country, but does here, because we are in a bubble. Nothing is real. Nothing gets inside.

Round here, CEOs play tennis at Highbury Fields with their friends like they are fifteen. In summer, I watch thirty-somethings charging around a rounders circle with friends. At the pub, there will be no locals but there will always be someone who is twenty-two and excited, who has just discovered that they can get drunk on a Monday and eat an assortment of crisps for dinner without anyone telling them otherwise.

On sunny evenings, we drink gin and tonics in overpopulated beer gardens that spill onto pavements. For Christmas, I have bought everything I need within the radius of a ten-minute walk from my flat. We are spoilt children and I adore it. It's not a feeling I've ever known before.

But by repeating my mortgage conversation on loop, it's become true to me. I've started to care about ownership and getting my hands on an enormous loan that will never be paid off. Whatever I had, it turns out, I would look over my shoulder to see what someone else had and want it, too. This is me. Perhaps it is everyone.

And there *are* downsides to life in this part of London.

We're transient because we know this isn't where we will settle.

It does happen: I look up at the family houses that surround Highbury Fields and like everyone, I wonder who could possibly have that life, that real life, living here beyond their thirties and becoming a family here, becoming old. But there are bins outside, spilling out with pizza boxes and wine bottles and toilet roll holders and nappies. It's real.

Most of us, though, will never be the 0.000001 per cent with their pizza boxes. If you're thirty-nine, Islington looks at you sadly like you've stayed at the party a *little* too long. Perhaps you could have a quick Sunday afternoon picnic on the green on your way out but then yes, it will be time for you to head off to the suburbs.

Anais is doing just that and building a life. Where she goes to sleep, there are old food markets and boozers and there are people who have lived there forever, who sell vegetables loudly and look at you blankly when you talk about brunch. There are new people, sure, but it's not like here. Here, heritage ebbs away every time a greengrocer's becomes a gin bar and a rental notice goes up in the window of the old pub. We are all to blame: I spend Sundays strolling in between market stalls selling lockets and trinkets and soaking up the feeling of it all, and then I spend my money in Waitrose. I am part of the problem. I am at its heart.

'Mortgages are overrated and I have no idea why everyone is so obsessed with them,' Anais says as she rummages in her bag for the box of brownies she's brought with her. 'Very much like babies.'

I bristle. She puts the brownies on the side.

'Salted caramel,' I say, reading the label and trying to distract myself from the irritation that's surging through me over her flippancy. 'Thanks.'

Since we were at university together, Anais has been vehemently opposed to procreating and didn't change her mind even when she met Rafael. He's Spanish; she's Barbadian. If you were the kind of person who wheeled out terrible clichés, you'd tell them they'd make beautiful babies.

I'm not and I don't. If struggling to conceive has any upsides, it's taught me emotional intelligence. I make promises to myself that whatever happens, I will never be one of those people who don't consider for one second that by proffering their opinions on your position on having children, they might have just ruined your whole week. You don't know. You never know.

Anais and I did our journalism postgraduate course together and while the rest of us only manage yearly get-togethers, Anais and I are still proper friends. Her: a political editor for a broadsheet. Me: a copywriter for various dull brands who pay me to produce words about their products. I'm currently writing instructions for a washing machine. This isn't how I saw it going when I turned up ten years ago for my first day at university, clutching a copy of *Empire* magazine and declaring my intentions of becoming a film critic.

But I left my last job at a magazine because I returned home four nights out of five stressed and panicked about something that had happened to do with internal politics. The sort that at the time seem like the centre of the universe and really are part of some distant solar system that no one should care about, ever.

And, mostly, because Tom and I had been trying for a baby for two years and, since the miscarriage, nothing else had happened. I wanted to alter something. I wanted to relax, get some work-life balance and go to Pilates at 2 p.m. if I fancied it. The problem was that I rarely fancied it. The problem was that being at home alone all day without the distraction of those internal politics and a 10 a.m. meeting to prep for left me depressed and so anxious that a two-minute walk to the post office felt far beyond me. I zoned in obsessively on the absence of a baby. As time went on I grieved more, not less, for that baby who didn't make it. I'm not saying that leaving my job was the wrong decision. But it certainly hasn't been a quick fix.

'It's been such a ridiculous run-up to Christmas at our place,' Anais says, taking her tea from me as she frames herself, beautiful, in the entrance to the kitchen. 'I'm still so jealous of you working for yourself.'

And I look down at my one Official Seeing People outfit, pulled on two minutes before she arrived and to be discarded one minute after she leaves, and glance at her phone on the side, lighting up with messages and urgency, and I think sure, Anais, sure.

'Working from home, all that flexibility.'

Then she comes up with a very specific example of this.

'You can bake a potato while you work.'

That's it. That's what I was after when I held that copy of *Empire*. Baked potatoes. While I work.

'You can go for a run at 3 p.m.'

Because I do. Often.

She pads in her tights through to the living room.

'Jesus, what the hell is that noise?' she says as she sips her tea. Something with fennel.

I head back to the kitchen.

'Oh, just Harriet!' I yell as I press my own teabag against the side of the mug and fish it out. I decant the brownies onto a plate then I follow her in and laugh, because she is stood, ear pressed to the wall, to listen to Harriet's latest composition involving chickens and a farm.

'Get away from there,' I stage-whisper, even though we both know she probably can't hear us over that level of farmyard-based noise. There is a chicken impression, in rhythmic form. We are folded, creased, with laughter.

When we calm down, Anais sits, doing a noiseless impression of someone earnestly singing an opera as she curls her feet under her on the sofa.

She leans and takes a brownie from the plate that is sat on our tiny coffee table.

'Does she do that all the time?' she asks.

I think about it.

Suddenly it seems weird that I have started to think this is so normal, this woman singing loudly about love, dreams, emotions and chickens. I hear her pound the piano in frustration. I hear her ARRRGGGHH out loud when something doesn't go well. And I live alongside it, like her cellmate.

'Yeah, pretty much. There you go, another downside of our Islington life. Successful music writers move in next door and sing weird songs about farmyard animals.'

We laugh, a lot, but then there is a lull.

'So, how are you?' I ask.

As I eat my brownie, she tells me about the new app Rafael just designed, a Korean place they'd tried at the weekend and the trip to Mexico they've just booked. And then, when I can't stop her any longer with my questions, questions, questions, she asks me the dreaded one from her side: 'How about you – any news?'

I mime a full mouth and take a second.

It's loaded, that question, once you get into your thirties. It means 'Are you getting married, having a baby, buying a house? Do you have an awesome, game-changing new job that pays you so much money you can buy in Notting Hill?' And if you don't, if none of those things exist, you feel like you have failed at news. Sometimes I think I want a baby partly so I can succeed at news.

'Not really,' I say before spinning some mundane work and a trip to the theatre with Tom's parents into news.

Because you can't actually have *no* news. We must be busy and rammed and manic and constantly doing, and no news isn't allowed. I dust brownie crumbs off my chin and onto a plate.

After Anais leaves I change back into my – Tom's - pyjamas and consider why I didn't speak to her about The Baby Thing.

Every time we've done this and I've omitted it, I've surprised myself. Because that *is* my news. That's my story. Anais is my friend and I am a sharer. And not mentioning it means I have a low level of nausea about the unknown elephant in the room every time we meet. I didn't even tell her about my miscarriage. Anais, my best friend, *doesn't know that I was pregnant*. Doesn't know about the biggest thing that ever happened to me. That seems crazy now but at the time I had hoped it would be a footnote to some good news, to the best news.

Not telling Anais what is going on in my head also means that we are drifting. I know it and she knows it; I can feel the chasm getting wider but I can't do what I need to do to close it. So why?

I come to this conclusion: once it's out there, there's no taking it back. Once you say you're trying, that's your thing. That's the 'news' they mean. That's the black cloud over my head that everyone will see.

'Are you okay?' Anais asked into my ear as she left, hugging me close. 'You seem . . .'

But I avoided her eyes, shrugging out of our cuddle and seeing her out with some paint-by-numbers thirty-something rambling about a busy week and work worries.

I eat the rest of the brownies, alone, leaning over the kitchen sink. It's a while before I hear from Anais again; definitely longer than normal.

7

Harriet

December

Suddenly, there is a loud giggle from next door that makes me jump. It's not Lexie, it's a woman who is less softly spoken, and I can hear Lexie replying, louder than normal to match her friend, and laughing heartily.

Tom has been away for a few days now, I think, so Lexie's spending some time with the rest of the people in her life. I am irked at her greed. A beautiful boyfriend who brings her curry and loves her and friends, proper friends, who share in-jokes with her and pop round for tea. Does this really happen?

'Just Harriet,' she shouts as I stop playing my piano for a second and jolt.

It is the incongruity of my name, heard through the wall where I thought that I did not exist. But like they exist to me, I exist to them. I look down and see my hand shaking. The spell is broken and I can't even focus on my piano.

Then they laugh again, loudly and together.

Through the wall, I am a person. They acknowledge me. They speak about me. They laugh at me. If there's one thing I can't take, Lexie, it's people laughing at me.

My heart is pounding.

It's been three days since I saw Tom/Luke getting into the lift with his curry. The hair. The shoulders. That nose. I shiver.

I can't sleep and I'm behind on a deadline for the score on a children's musical. The guy I am working for is getting twitchy and my usual desire to impress has deserted me. I don't care. I am focused on Lexie. I feel a surge of rage.

I can't even get it together to put the generic flowers in a generic vase. They finally made it off the floor, but they are limp now, lying on the table in their plastic, begging for a drink like a neglected puppy. What can I say? I'm not one of life's nurturers.

All I can do is Google. It starts innocently enough but then, of course, I search for Luke, even though I know that online he manages not to exist, in case the woman he was supposed to spend his life with sees news of a job promotion or the gig he went to last night.

I Google again.

Luke Miller, Chicago. Luke Miller, media companies. Nothing.

I slam my head back against the sofa and consider what he thinks I would do if I found him. See a social media food shot and book a flight to New York to queue up outside the diner where it was taken, in the hope that he came back for another rare burger and this time, I snared him? Or something worse? Something like last time.

I bang my laptop shut and sit, ruminating.

I should have been married now. Perhaps I'd have a baby, asleep in an upstairs cot somewhere in Hertfordshire. Or maybe Luke would have fetched my backpack and told me we were off, to travel around Europe. We'd come as far as the UK together from the US already, and we might have gone for a year of eating Comté cheese in France and devouring art in Barcelona. Whatever he had wanted, obviously. That's how it had worked.

I look down suddenly, realise I'm in pain. My nails have been digging so deeply into my hand that there is blood; I have pulled off cuticles and left skin red raw. It throws me. I didn't notice the harm being caused. I rarely do.

Perhaps Luke would still be all about London. It would only

29

have been four years and he adored it here. We earned good money, me as a songwriter for musicals and TV shows, and Luke in media sales. We – well, he – had a huge circle of friends. Thursday nights I would beg to come along to his work drinks in a fancy hotel bar near The Strand. Occasionally, he gave in.

There are tears now, threatening to jump.

Weekends, thankfully, were usually more private. We'd take our hangovers for chilly walks up Primrose Hill, Luke's sensitive teeth hurting from the cold and both of our ears pinching until we found a pub to serve us tea in front of a fire.

We'd defrost, pull off hats, flick through the supplements. I'd pretend to lose at Scrabble to avoid a row. I'd pet the spaniel across the bar and fantasise about a future full of dogs, and then Luke would frown and point out all the reasons why pets were a terrible idea. I'd realise quickly, of course, that he was right.

'Weren't you thinking of getting a pet?' asked my mom one day on the phone.

'Luke doesn't think it's a good idea,' I said, forgetting to edit.

'But what do *you* think, Harriet?' she said, gently but firmly. 'Sometimes I think you're so caught up in what Luke wants that you forget to ask yourself that these days.'

I hung up. Started calling less often.

In my version of us in the future, I would be better, too. The sort of person who didn't forget I was supposed to be dieting and order chips, and not the sort of person who wears the wrong-shaped jeans and has a haircut that 'seriously, you've had since 2003'. Thanks, Luke.

I am crying now, unstoppable. In February this year, one year after we got engaged, Luke left me.

I take out some nail scissors and start snipping at the ends of my long, dull blonde hair before realising what I'm doing with a jolt and going back to work. Trying to go back to work.

I Google Lexie again and this time I click the 'images' tab. It's not like searching for Luke. Searching for Lexie gives you

30

all kinds of information. She isn't a blogger showing off her life but she does elicit a hundred or so pictures, even for the general public, of which, I suppose – for now – I am still a part.

Lexie lying propped up on her elbow on a beach with her giant, wild, curly brunette hair loose around brown shoulders. Lexie at a laptop, absorbed in her words with a fresh coffee next to her and a Jo Malone candle lit on her immaculate desk. I roll my eyes.

A selfie of Lexie and Tom next to a Christmas tree in their flat. I peer at that one for longer, trying to work out where they are in the mirror image of my home; analysing the small amount of background that I can see.

Eventually, I move on. There's a picture of Lexie in heels and a pencil skirt with professionally done make-up looking steadfastly without smiling to the camera, one hand on a beautifully curved hip.

She looks incredible; a world away from the freckled girl on the beach or the Lexie in front of the Christmas tree. Online, Lexie is a changeling Barbie to me, and this is the Going Out version.

She goes out with confidence, she goes out with good hair, she goes out with Tom. There are pictures of her throwing her head back and laughing with friends, drinking bright pink cocktails on roof terraces and showing off tanned legs on holiday. She clutches her nephew close as he leans up to kiss her. Holds a mug like it is a tiny puppy with both hands in front of a raging wood burner. There is a theme: in all of these pictures Lexie looks loved, in-love and happy. Not tense. Not nervous. Not waiting for something to go wrong. Lucky fucking Lexie.

I slam the piano lid shut and go back to bed, forgetting, again, to drink some water. And I dream of Lexie, surrounded by her friends, smirking at me and laughing.

8

Lexie

December

I start looking up everyone I know who could potentially be pregnant and because this is the reality of what constitutes life in your thirties, half of them are rocking baby-on-board badges and bump selfies.

I Google the stats on getting pregnant after two years at my age and it's depressing, so I read about all the things I shouldn't be eating, doing, drinking, thinking and realise I am eating, doing, drinking and thinking most of them.

I shovel in eight chocolates that I've just hung up on the tree and hate myself, then Tom puts his keys in the door and it's obvious what's about to happen. Instead of immersing myself in my Maya Angelou as planned, I've spent the last hour in a Facebook tunnel of pregnancy announcements and baby pictures.

I pick a fight. I don't want a hug, I want to shout and for someone to make that legitimate.

'Oh, there's no dinner,' he says, looking around as though he expected a steak and ale pie to rise from the ashes of the wooden spoon holder. Excuse provided.

'What does that mean?' I bite. 'I'm so pathetic that you come back from your exciting life and all I should have been doing is rolling pastry?'

He cuts me off with a hand in the air.

'I wasn't being a dick, I just thought you mentioned pasta on a text earlier.'

Oh crap, I did mention pasta on a text earlier.

'So nothing is allowed to come up in my life? Nothing is allowed to happen? As it goes, I got some last-minute work and I've been chained to my laptop since, Tom, so no – I haven't had much time to make pasta . . .'

There was no last-minute work. If I was chained to my laptop, it's because I wanted to see what social media thought about the women on *The Real Housewives of Atlanta*. To torture myself with the bump pictures.

But I miss it, the kind of day I'm pretending I've had. That feeling of being important and needed and relied upon. Even the stress of it is superior, a far more glamorous stress than this one with its leggings and its ovulation sticks and its cheap festive chocolate.

'I do have a career, I do have a life.'

He runs his hand through his perpetually unkempt curls before pulling his jumper over his head.

'I'm going for a shower,' he says, undoing the belt on his jeans as he heads, sad-shouldered, out of the door. Then he turns around and kisses me on the forehead, and I'm reminded how much he's started doing this, making allowances because we're not equals any more. I'm the victim; he's the carer. He impresses in meetings; I sit at home googling 'ovarian reserve' and eating biscuits.

I bite my tongue so I don't cry until I hear the shower start, then I sit on the sofa and sob hot, heartbroken tears because he still loves me even though I don't feel much but disdain towards me any more.

I hear Classic FM turn on next door and feel the redness in my cheeks burn deeper. She must have heard that, Harriet, me shouting, Tom's pity, the tears that Tom – door closed on his long shower – will never know about.

I don't care if she hears us have sex, but I care deeply if she hears me cry. This is far more exposing.

I google Harriet again, through blurred vision. I stare at pictures of her on Twitter looking statuesque and confident as she poses with colleagues at the opening of a musical. I see her toasting it with a glass of champagne. I think of my old life when I would post similarly glamorous pictures. Now, Tom inevitably finds me here when he gets in, pyjamas and stains, unwashed face and lethargy. I look at Harriet again and think how it would be impossible for me to do those types of things now; I am not capable. I am not the right shape to fit into those places.

Harriet stares back at me from my screen. There's an oddness about London life that means you can live here, centimetres from another person, and never know them and that is okay.

Once, I cried on the bus after a bad day at work and a purple-haired South African woman with maternal eyes offered me a tissue.

It took me by surprise. My own mum isn't maternal. She's brusque and pragmatic and would have told me to get on with it – 'that's simply what the working world is like, Lexie' – as I pined for maternal coddling.

But when it actually came? I was horrified. There's supposed to be an imaginary wall around you in this city and it had been knocked down. And now I have the same feeling. I listen to Harriet hum along to Beethoven and think of her, hearing my sad life and wondering about me. Why doesn't she go out? Why do they never have parties? Why does he put up with her?

This, now, is too intimate.

9

Harriet

December

I hear him come in and I turn on the radio to listen to glib
Christmas hits, because hearing this man who is Luke, really, tell
Lexie next door that he loves her is too much tonight, when
I've not slept for a week thinking about the ex-fiancé who
persuaded me to emigrate then abandoned me. Thinking about
the fact that the Luke who used to live here, in my flat, has
gone. About how there is another Luke who lives next door
and a woman he lives there with, one who has taken my life
and is enjoying it, more happily, more successfully than I ever
could.

Tom, this other Luke, is still in his relationship; still wants to
be there. I hear him laughing. I hear him being content. Unlike
my Luke, this Luke has decided that this is enough for him.
Lexie is enough for him. I lean against the wall and dig my nails
into it so firmly that I chip the paint, and it's only then that I
realise what I am doing. Clawing my way to this other Luke,
literally.

Through the wall, Tom and Lexie are Luke and I, a couple,
together. And on the other side is new me, single, the remnants
of what is left of a couple, not even half but maybe a quarter.
I am too much, but then in other ways, I am not enough.

And then, my bad mood is exacerbated when I see an email

35

from my brother, David, 'checking in'. As usual, I suspect it was sent at the behest of my parents, making sure that I was alive. And, really, that anyone who was around me was alive. *So, my girlfriend, Sadie, and I have bought a house*, it reads, as though we caught up last week, as if I know who Sadie is.

Sleep has been difficult lately and I am suddenly exhausted, my eyes blurring at the screen enough to make me feel nauseous.

'How can I not know who Sadie is?' I say out loud and am shocked at the sudden noise.

I picture David, sitting on my bed as I packed around him to move to London. 'I'll miss you,' he mumbled, staring at the floor, and I looked at this teenage boy masquerading as a six-foot-tall grown-up who went to work every day and rented a house. I touched his blond surfer hair gently then kissed his head. It still blew my mind that he was no longer a child.

Luke was sitting on the floor, staring at his phone. He looked up, irritated that this was taking so long but mostly that this was taking so much emotion.

'Come and see us,' I told David, working hard on not crying, or on being distracted by Luke. Focusing all of my energy on a grin. 'We can go to gigs in Camden or take a trip to Paris for the weekend.'

David looked at Luke, who gave him a distant smile.

'We'll hook you up with some hot British girls,' Luke said, eyes already back on his phone. 'If that's what will persuade you.'

I zipped up a suitcase.

Luke had loaded his own cases the week before, everything ironed and packed with precision. He showed no emotion – as he didn't about most things – at leaving our life. He was matter-of-fact about it. Except for the long monologues about the job he already had and the myriad career benefits.

'I can really *go* somewhere in work when we're in London,' he told me. 'I'm going to make so much money.'

I cared more about my career than he did, there could be no

doubt about that. I earned more too, though we never mentioned it. But I was rushed into the move before I could find work and Luke never once asked what my own thoughts were on London's career opportunities.

I left the conversation alone. It was easier that way.

It was me who was most apprehensive about leaving my family, favourite takeout places and our life.

But Luke wanted it and Luke came first. Luke was more attractive than me, cooler than me, better than me. I would have chased Luke anywhere he went uninvited but incredibly I received invites. He wanted to move to the UK; I was moving to the UK.

David will never visit now and maybe that's better. Friends – colleagues, really – are simpler than family. Less emotional. Less history. Less transparency. Less reality.

And how is London? Work? the email continues.

I delete it so I can't reply to it maudlin and wine-fuelled at 2 a.m. when my latest batch of hire-a-friends has traipsed home.

But then to taunt myself I pull out old photos of David and me. Heads together as we lie on the sofa in new pyjamas on Thanksgiving morning as kids. Awkward teenagers with matching spots and matching grimaces on a family weekend to New York. Posing with illicit beers in our parents' kitchen. I can't cry this time because it is so confusing. There is so much happiness in these pictures that my face, against all instruction, is smiling ear to ear. *God, I miss you*, I think.

The only thing that cuts through my thoughts is Tom and Lexie. My new family, really, drowning out the old one. I do everything to drown them out too, taking a long shower, hammering at my piano, but they get through like they always do, and later, when I hear the door slam shut, I watch them out of the window, arms around each other and darting into a restaurant across the street to eat noodles and be together, still.

I open a bottle of wine and sit down at my laptop, googling

Lexie, Luke, my brother, but this time the one I return to is Tom, whose surname I know owing to a sloppy postman. I know, eventually, that I'm going to have to let Luke go, but I am an addict and cold turkey is too much. Tom can function as my methadone.

Image search is my favourite and opening the folder of pictures I have of Luke, I was right, there is far more than a resemblance between him and Tom. In the hair, the before shot in an advert for hair wax, in those lazy shoulders and those gangly, endless legs. And that nose. I could kiss it, gently on the tip, and swear that Tom would know me and know my kiss.

I zoom in on Tom's eyes. Take a screen grab of the left first, and then the right. I consider them, really look at them. These are the eyes of a man who I could love. And if I could love someone else but Luke and make a life with someone else but Luke, maybe everything would feel less dark. I would feel diluted again, like I used to feel. And maybe I could finally move on, too, from what happened.

I peer closely at my laptop, look at Tom's eyes again. And then I start to go through all of his pictures, one by one, zooming in on body parts and details. Screen grab, save.

Sinking the last glass of Pinot Noir, my brain is whirring. Lexie. Always Lexie. Why does she get to have this life, the one that I wanted, when I worked so hard for it? When I put up with so much? Why does she get to laugh at me, while I sit through the wall, lonely? I feel a searing rage, so I open another bottle and I begin, slowly, to type. She doesn't know what I am capable of, I think. She has no idea what I did and who really lives here, just through the wall.

10

Lexie

January

Tom isn't away for work at all this week, so I am forced to alter my routine. I don't want him to know that I rarely brush my teeth before lunchtime and only put on proper trousers if I'm going out.

I already worry what this version of me is doing for our relationship. So I make an effort. We eat meals together, I dab on foundation, I attempt not to talk relentlessly about having a baby. And one night, I heave myself up from the sofa and we go for noodles and a gig in our local pub, where we order gin and tonics and everything seems young and light and bright. By the end of the week, though, the bliss has abated.

'It's *offensive* that you put your clothes on the floor and expect me to pick them up,' I hiss, belligerent, as Tom walks past.

'I've not put my clothes on the floor,' he says. 'What are you on about?'

I march to the bedroom and return clutching a T-shirt.

'I dropped it,' snaps Tom, losing patience with me. 'But if I had put it on the floor, I don't think it would have warranted that nastiness.'

And he walks out of the flat, to the park maybe, or the pub, or to anywhere to escape me.

Maybe we're not used to this much time together in our tiny home, maybe we're too used to our own habits.

But then it shifts, again.

My period comes and we're close, he's my family again, because this is one loss we feel together, every month.

'I think we should go to the doctor,' I say tentatively when we're exhausted from the sadness.

I know he's of the mindset that we should let nature take its course and not panic – that it's happened once, it will happen again – but this time, he agrees. Though with a caveat.

'Can we leave it a few more months? I have so much on at work . . .'

And it's this that sets me off. I don't know my own fuse any more, it's different now, so unpredictable, and suddenly I'm ranting, sobbing, shouting about how he can possibly think that work is more important than this, and he's got hold of my shoulders.

'I never said more important, I just said . . .'

Then he stops sharply and he folds into the sofa.

I know he is close, the closest, to crying.

His breath is shallow. His face is a sheet of crumpled up paper. It's pressure on him, too, and I hadn't tended to that. Incredibly, it hits me. I just . . . forgot. In all of this I forgot about Tom, when Tom means the most.

'It's just,' he says, shoving tears furiously from his face. 'It's overwhelming. It feels like being a proper grown-up. And this is the first time that that's truly happened to me.'

He tells me that he thinks I am depressed, nervously awaiting my reaction, but I agree. Yep. Depressed. There's a relief in capitulating.

Now, I want help. I welcome it. I will ask about therapists and contact acupuncturists and invite the help from every corner where it makes itself available.

'Let's go to the doctor,' says Tom. 'You're right. We need to move this on. It's not doing us any good being in limbo.'

Later I lie awake, thinking about what I – or trying to have a baby – have done to him. I stroke his face, kiss his head, tell him I'm sorry, cling to this man who I love.

11

Harriet

January

I wake with a feeling so familiar that it has a regular, cushioned spot in my brain.

There is something to worry about.

I am responsible for it.

It is not right and it is not good but I did it anyway.

Last night I set up an email account, purporting to be a student called Rachel who wanted to make documentaries, and I messaged Tom. It wasn't smutty; I know Tom – Tom wouldn't like that. Tom has integrity. This is one of the reasons Tom will make a great boyfriend.

There was no pouty profile picture, no innuendo. I was just an earnest student who admired his work.

This morning I look over it again. It doesn't give a hint of my being drunk and it's only sent at 10.30 p.m., so I will get away with it. I do, most of the time.

I lose the day to email refreshing and by the time night – or the early morning – comes, my eyes are sore and I pass out on the sofa. Though, to be honest, that's how most nights end, whether I'm alone or next to yet another naked body that won't call me tomorrow.

The next day, though, a reply comes.

Thanks for your comments on my work, says Tom. *It's lovely to hear someone so passionate about what they want to do.*

He recommends a couple of websites, offers me a contact.

I take my laptop as close to the wall as I can get, listen for sounds of life. But if they're there, they're quiet. Or Tom is replying on a bus, in a café. I try to picture it but it doesn't elucidate. Tom could be anywhere, doing anything, and I wouldn't know because he's not mine.

Suddenly, I feel stupid. I consider never replying and simply continuing to be his neighbour. Someone who sneaks occasional looks at him getting into the elevator. A crush, existing without everything else that people think I am capable of. No danger. No violence.

Even if I do reply, I can't do it yet, so I need to distract myself. A colleague has invited me to drinks tonight and I make a last-minute decision to go. Rachel would. She'd be putting herself out there, young, excited, keen.

I've had a burst of Rachel energy. I'm running on Rachel.

Harriet's not all that different to Rachel; it's just that she's been screwed over. It's made her jaded.

Then, when I head from the bedroom into my living room to grab my purse, I hear her, losing it with him, loud and clear. I pin myself to the wall. This is the most I've ever heard, by far. He is quiet but she is still shouting, and though I can only get the occasional word, it's enough.

'Fertility . . . doctor . . . priorities . . . work . . . age . . . men . . . women . . . unhappy . . . baby.'

My palms sweat with knowledge and I stay there long after they've fallen silent. I'm used to suffocated noise here, the hum of buses, the barely audible sounds of Lexie and Tom living life. Anger and rage may sometimes drift up from the pavement outside in the booze-soaked early hours, but in here we live measured, muted lives. Listening to shouting through the wall feels like being back in hospital.

And then, there's the detail. It's not that I don't know that plenty of couples have fertility issues. It's just that through the wall their life sounds unblemished. And that now, there is a gap between them, just large enough to squeeze myself into.

12

Lexie

January

'Lexie!' goes the voicemail. 'Would love to catch up. Let me know if that freelance life of yours isn't too busy.'

I smile, wry. It's a school friend, Rich, who I haven't seen for six months. It's difficult to say why because my working days are short and erratic and filled with procrastination, and my evenings are bursting at the seams with Netflix and pyjamas and scrolling Harriet's social media. But somehow, I mimic busy. I have time to read a bulky Donna Tartt novel in four days, but no time to catch up face to face with people I care about.

Slowly, after I left my job a year ago, meeting friends took on the magnitude of a job interview, so I began to swerve them, telling myself that this was self-care. I had left work after a year of trying for a baby to be less stressed; though, ironically, my stresses simply sprawled wider. I stressed about everything from my work abilities to my friendships to whether or not I was eating too much wheat and whether or not *that* was what was holding me back from getting pregnant.

But I thought it was all okay, because I had Tom.

Tom and I met when we were at university in London. I was working in a nightclub selling super-sweet shots for a pound a go; he was on antibiotics so not drinking. I had to walk away from him to carry on flogging the alcohol.

'What if I give you twenty pounds and you throw the shots away?' said Tom, not cocky, just pragmatic.

I laughed, threw back three of whatever it was that claimed to be apple-flavoured and sat back down.

I was full of the bravado of being twenty-one, skinny in Lycra now my puppy fat years had passed and slightly drunk. My dress was tiny, pale blue and strappy, the kind that seems laughable these days when I view polo necks and knee-high boots as valid going-out outfits. This was the early Noughties, though; we warmed up with cheap vodka, not cashmere socks. We thought self-care was buying ourselves a shot with our Archers Schnapps and lemonade.

'I thought you were so out of my league,' Tom tells me now, often.

But everything about Tom was what I wanted. I had never looked for cheeky, or bad, or sarcastic, or mean.

I wanted kind and I wanted stable. I had roots but my roots spread wide. When I was sixteen my mum and dad – an airline pilot – moved to Canada and my childhood, already an almost-version of adulthood, was very suddenly over. This isn't a tragic tale; nothing terrible happened to me and I wasn't orphaned or abandoned at seven. But enforced adulthood leaves a mark. I wasn't ready, not quite. I was still battling that puppy fat and some high-level awkwardness in my own body, and I needed home-cooked meals and sofas that smelled of my mum's perfume to give me a place in the world.

When they left, it was with an attitude of having done their parenting years. Now, we speak on FaceTime and message but I think, often, *couldn't you have given me two more years?* Just to get me to the finish line instead of making me stumble my way through the last bit stunned and in shock that they had suddenly gone AWOL.

I did two years at boarding school then fled to London. At university, I was the only one without a 'home' to go back to in the holidays or for weekends. Sure, I could fly to Canada, but not for a two-day stint to fill up on macaroni cheese. Not to get my white washing done. Not to coddle myself in a blanket in my old bed and feel like a child again. Not to ask my dad sheepishly if he could look at my electricity bill because I didn't know what the hell it meant.

'You can come to me,' said my brother, Kit, but that meant a student dive at the other end of the country with five blokes and a pubic hair mountain next to the bath.

I loved him for offering. Not enough to brave that bathroom.

So what I needed from a partner wasn't chaos or abandonment or erratic behaviour. What I needed was goodness, reliability, someone to bring me toast in bed and book me a taxi home. It's what Tom and I have always done, both of us, for each other.

'I'm Tom,' he said as I set the tray of shots down on the table in front of us. He put his hand out and I teased him for the formality and his slight poshness.

I mocked his Surrey accent, laughed when he told me later that he kept a diary that he had written in most days since childhood and downed a pint mimicking something I had read about called a ladette.

Then, when he stayed around, I felt my body relax, and I ordered the drink I actually wanted and talked to him for four hours, until the lights came on, when he walked me all the way to my front door and even carried my shoes.

I introduced him to my friends three days later. A gaggle of girl-women at a birthday dinner. I was three glasses of wine in and just starting to believe I had passionate views on obscure Nineties indie bands, when I saw Tom having an in-depth conversation with my flatmate, Alana. I smiled, tipsy and happy. He had arrived and slotted right in.

After that it's as blurry as most things are after 9 p.m. when I was twenty-one. There was dancing, there were fifteen people all shouting the same song lyrics and there was kissing, kissing, kissing in Soho at midnight.

A couple of months later, I sat around his family's giant dinner table, his mum dolloping extra portions of lasagne on my plate and calling me honey, and my grin wouldn't take a break.

I glanced across at Tom, smearing garlic bread around his plate. I looked at his dad, nipping out to the kitchen for another bottle of Chianti in his slippers. I smelled melted cheese and scented candles and heard the sound of Radio 2 coming from the kitchen.

'You're lucky, you know,' I said later when Tom and I were squeezed awkwardly into his single childhood bed. 'Having a family.'

'You have a family,' he replied, adjusting his body in the tiny space.

But we'd have rather done this than slept separately. Sleeping separately would have felt like torture.

'Kind of,' I replied.

I hadn't told him much about my own family yet. But even in our best days my family hadn't been like this family. Tom's mum squeezed me tight as soon as she met me; I always had the feeling that my own mum was recoiling if I hugged her. Not that she didn't like it; just that she genuinely couldn't cope with it. Meals weren't a comforting event, they were functional: people did their own thing, turned up and grabbed a sandwich.

This version of family was the one I wanted, long term. Tom, tipsy on the red wine, nodded off next to me, and I lay there looking at him and thinking, I wonder if it's you I'll have children with? And wondering what our family would look like. Knowing, already, that it would look like tight hugs and lasagne and sheepskin slippers heading to the kitchen for another bottle of that Chianti.

Tom is still here thirteen years later; still, to me, incredible. But even Tom is just one person and one person can never be enough to carry a whole life. What a pressure I have been applying to him, what a heavy, heavy weight.

13

Harriet

January

I am on a 7.38 a.m. train out of Liverpool Street, because Tom is on a 7.38 a.m. train out of Liverpool Street. I shiver; the day is pure January. Dark, cold. This feels like 3 a.m.

I waited for the door to close as he left the flat then I took the stairs, quickly, as he jumped in the elevator, and followed him out. Half an hour ago, I walked behind him onto the platform, pulled my scarf tighter around my neck, saw the destination he was heading to on the screen and everything went blurry.

Of all the places Tom could be going to on location for work this morning, I was following him to Hunstanton, the pretty Norfolk seaside town. The place where Luke and I got engaged.

On the train, I sit four rows behind him and burrow into my scarf to conceal myself – although, worst-case scenario, I figure, there's no law that says a person can't get the same train as their neighbour. Coincidences happen all day, every day, everywhere. They're the basis of brilliant novels, and films, and stories. Look at my history with Hunstanton and how I am now heading back there, for starters.

I watch him and see the defeat in his shoulders. I see him sigh heavily. I see him stare out of the window for the whole journey, even though there is a book on his lap, even though it is barely light. There is a lot to be learnt from watching a person alone, doing nothing. I used to do it in hospital. It helped to pass the time: seeing if I could tell who were the dangerous ones, the violent ones. The ones, I suppose, who were the most like me. The ones who were capable of terrible things, as I was capable of terrible things.

I look around at the other commuters now, thinking what judgements they would pass if they knew about those terrible things. Could you tell what *I* did, if you stared for long enough? What would people learn, if anyone cared enough to watch me?

'I care, Tom,' I whisper to myself. 'Look how much I care.'

He stretches his arms above his head in a yawn, unknowing, oblivious.

When Tom steps off the train, meets colleagues and shakes their hands then heads off to work, I leave him to it. I can't follow further or loiter on the edge of their small group. But it has been enough. Just observing him. Gathering information for what might come next. Being in his company.

Before I get the train home, I swerve left and take another trip: it's down to the beach, takes me down memory lane, too.

What peace, I think, as I stare out to sea. The sand has that miles-to-the-water Britishness. You want to swim? Fine, but you'll have to earn it with a long trudge.

I look around. Beach huts the shade of party balloons have found fame since the social media bloggers turned up, desperate to tick off their daily dose of beauty. Hunstanton's beach huts didn't feel so ubiquitous when Luke and I were here. It made them quainter.

I walk on. Perfect tableaus are everywhere I look. A shaggy dog, braving the sea when all humans goosebump at the thought. Parents hugging hot coffee. Families taking out optimistic picnics. Later, their pictures will say they were happy eating the ham sandwiches; the reality was that they were happiest when they started speeding up the motorway towards their central heating and duvets.

I am watching all of them, nosy and cold with my nostrils the only body part I will allow out of my scarf. Things get hazy. I don't know which of these people are here now and which of them were here then, when he did it.

It is four years almost to the day since Luke rooted one knee into the sand, wobbled slightly then sniped under his breath at the man who walked past and said with a grin, 'I'd do it quickly mate, it's freezing.'

'Will you marry me?' he asked, the familiar phrase sounding faintly amusing to me although I knew I couldn't laugh: that wouldn't be right for this scene. Luke was still snarling slightly at the guy who had ruined our moment.

His hand was ice as I held it and my eyes squinted into bright January sunshine. I felt my whole body shiver despite it because it was still winter and I hate the cold.

A boy was crying for ice cream nearby and I knew Luke's teeth would hurt at the idea. Gulls squawked and waves crashed and everything smelled of sea air.

'Yes,' I said quickly before he said a word. I felt victorious. I felt validated that I had taken a gamble on him and moved away from my family and done all of this work to be better. And I felt, finally, like Luke *must* love me. That the charming, engaging man I had seen at the beginning *was* the real Luke. That he had just been under pressure lately, taking it out on me because I was closest. But he was still smart, still funny, still beautiful. The knowledge was as physical as the bracing wind.

Luke was on his phone twenty minutes after he proposed, looking at sports results, trying to buy some gig tickets from a friend, but mine stayed in my pocket: I didn't need any distraction. I just stood there in the biting wind, smelling the vinegar from the chip shop, feeling it all.

'What if we invite David over?' I had blurted out, my confidence peaking. 'Tell him in person?'

I missed David to the point that I felt it in my stomach, in my bones. He still hadn't visited. This would be the perfect excuse.

Luke looked up from his phone.

'Are you serious?'

I regretted my words already. This perfect tableau, ruined by my idiocy. I felt my body temperature shoot up like I'd just stepped off an air-conditioned plane into summer in the Mediterranean.

'After the way your brother's been to me the whole time we've been together. You don't think that would be hard for me? To have him stay in our home? Turning you against me?'

I wished desperately that I could go back in time, take the words back.

But still, I had no idea what he was on about. My mom and dad might have been wary of Luke, sure, but David? David saw the charm that a lot of people saw in Luke; David had idolised him.

'You'd probably break up with me by the time he went home.'

I gave in easily, desperately. I was horrified that I had started this conversation and wanted only for it to be over. I didn't mention David again and after that, I stopped contacting my brother so often, too. What if he *was* trying to split Luke and I up? Things were getting confusing. I couldn't really be trusted to know.

On the train journey home, Luke didn't speak one word to me, despite my stroking his arm the whole way and making unending, desperate small talk.

Later, I messaged my parents to tell them our news but ignored their calls in response. I knew that hearing what they had to say about us being engaged would bring me down.

But the voicemail did it anyway.

'Just checking though, Harriet – you are sure, aren't you? You are really sure?' said my mom after the obligatory congratulations and a pause. I ignored and deleted her message and after that, the distance that had manifested itself since I emigrated stretched even wider.

I didn't tell Luke what my mom had said. He would blame me for painting the wrong picture of him, for somehow *making* them feel that way, and he was being frosty enough with me anyway after our row about David. Until, suddenly, there was a surprise trip to Copenhagen booked and the dial pinged to the other side: I was forgiven.

'Let's celebrate our engagement!' said Luke, euphoric, high.

See, I thought, see – there's the charming version. There's the man who sparkles.

I nodded, grinned, kept quiet about the inconvenience to my work schedule and to everybody I was going to have to let down, since I hadn't been consulted on dates. I just felt relieved that he had thawed.

In Denmark, we left the hotel to the shocked faces of reception staff, who believed we should stay indoors. It was minus thirteen, while the hotel had fluffy cushions and a sauna.

'It's so cold, though,' said a concerned manager, shaking his bald head and shivering at the thought. 'It's so cold. Even for Copenhagen.'

'We'll survive,' said Luke sharply.

I winced. But I kept quiet: the one time I had brought up his rudeness to strangers, we had had a huge row.

'Because I stand up to people when they don't do their jobs, Harriet?' he had said. 'That's not rudeness. That's just not being pathetic.'

At the Little Mermaid, a bronze statue coated in white snow, we paused for twenty seconds, ticked it off, walked on.

'It's so cold,' said a passing tourist to us amiably. 'Even for Copenhagen.'

The man held his partner's hand. I reached for Luke's but he shook me off, told me it was too awkward to hold hands in gloves.

We waded back through wedges of snow to the café that served hot chocolate as real chocolate on a stick, melting into your milk, making the powder we stirred into water at home look like an abomination.

I took off my scarf, ordered my drink.

'It's so cold, though,' I said, faux-serious as we sat down. 'Even for Copenhagen.'

But Luke wasn't laughing. My stomach lurched.

'Can I ask you a question?' he said, playing with the packets of sugar.

Our order arrived.

I looked deep into the sludge of my drink as the milk darkened. I picked up my spoon to stir and saw my hands shaking. Had I done something? I tracked back desperately. It had been going so well, but evidently I had messed up. Idiot. I steeled myself.

'Do you want children?'

First, the relief that it wasn't something bad. But then, the question itself. I was young and I was in love with Luke and with my job. Did children sleep through pianos playing at midnight? If I had a child, would I have the energy to compose in the evenings, which was when I worked best? Working was what had made London feel doable. I was turning down job offers, gaining a strong reputation. I was working on more lucrative projects; being approached for big-name musicals.

Luke had complained about it, how 'obsessed' I was with my job these days, and I wondered sometimes if that was making him snappier. Maybe it was my fault and I was neglecting him. So I had agreed on this holiday to put an out of office on and ignore work calls, despite the short notice. But it was hard. It was a part of me and I was happy. I wasn't sure about placing limitations on that.

I knew, too, that I was prone to depression. I knew that in life I wobbled and wasn't sure I had the stability to hold up others.

But at that moment, holding onto Luke's arm with one hand and drinking pure liquidised chocolate with the other, I felt like I was being shored up by love and sugar and as stable as I had ever been.

Perhaps, I would feel surer too, in us. I panicked, always, that Luke would leave me. I looked around in restaurants and saw that woman, that woman, all the other women who would be better suited to him. I glanced and saw him looking, too.

If Luke wanted children with someone like me then someone like me should be grateful. I should have all of the bloody children he wanted, grow them in my womb immediately. I should shut up, as he often told me, and stop thinking and agree.

'Yes,' I said tentatively, but he didn't hear the hesitation.

Instead, he was immediately manic, gripping my hands and describing this huge family, four or five kids, all of us travelling together.

'Imagine it!' he grinned, that intense eye contact that people found so beguiling. That I had described to people when I first met him. That was one of the many things that made me feel so adored, at first, so important. 'Swimming in the ocean and skiing down the slopes in this cute little line.'

This idea bedded into my mind until it became the clearest, most perfect thing I could imagine. This would make us whole; make us too busy for the bad times.

In October that year, with Luke in agreement, I took my last pill and we started trying for a baby.

I told my mom, surprising myself. But it had been so long since we had something to pull us close together. I longed for my parents, despite my attempts to block the feelings out. The idea of a grandchild, I thought. That might change things. Do something more tangible than an engagement. Reset mom's thoughts on Luke and me. Glue my family and me back together again.

'Luke and I have decided to try for a baby,' I told her in one of what were now our very occasional phone calls.

'Well that's lovely,' she said, but I heard the tone in her voice and regretted my words already. There was a long pause and I could hear her debating. Should she say it? Keep quiet? Was she pushing me away further, if she said what she really thought? 'But I thought you were definite on not wanting them? Have you changed your mind?'

I stayed silent, furious, on the other end of the phone. Because I knew what she was getting at.

'You mean that you think Luke pushed me into it, right?' I hissed. 'Why are you always, always having a go at Luke?'

She was silent then, for a second.

'Because I don't think he's kind to you and I don't think he's right for you,' she said gently.

I put the phone down on her then, not for the first time. After that, I began to ignore most of her calls.

Then Luke and I started trying for a baby here, in this flat, where I now live alone, next to a happy couple and their happy life. And what do you know? They are trying for a baby, too. They live my old life and I live my new one.

Before my flat was empty, it was full. Before it was lifeless, we lived life, planned life, hoped, here, to make life. We cooked joints of beef, sent scents out into the hallway that said 'We are here, we are popular, we are rich and full and greedy.' We chose colours together, put up pictures. We put plants on the window-sills that are dead now, withered.

Whatever our imperfections were, whatever anyone else would have judged them as, I could live with them. They were worth it for what was presented to the outside world. For my value, when I came in this package. Isn't that what matters now, anyway? Behind closed doors can be flawed, as long as Facebook says joy.

Luke and I planned to turn one of the rooms in our flat into a nursery, as Lexie and Tom will soon. Luke presumed I would give up work and I presumed that I would do whatever he wanted, so we left it there, even though the thought of not composing made me feel nauseous and unanchored.

Sometimes I thought of how much our children would miss out on in grandparents and my heart hurt. Luke wasn't close to his family and, I had to admit to myself now, neither was I any more to mine.

Luke had no interest in trying to have a better relationship with my family – even when I had spoken to them more regularly, he would leave the room when they popped up on FaceTime – and Luke was the focus, so I created more space between us.

I didn't think it mattered, anyway. Until I took a wrong turn and became one, we were two, set to become three, four, five . . . I pictured that ski trip. I had all I needed.

After Luke's proposal, my confidence surged. I stopped doubting my worthiness with Luke quite so much and work was soaring. I started speaking up. Questioning. The difference was noticeable. Luke started to comment on it, called me 'arrogant', 'difficult'.

In December, we landed back from a trip to the German Christmas markets and headed straight out to West London for tapas with some friends of his. I complained. I was tired, cold, lugging a giant bag and I wanted it to just be us. Us was always enough for me. Simpler, easier, less likely to end in a row.

'Why do we have to be with other people all the time?' I sulked on the Stansted Express – exhausted enough not to edit my thoughts before they became words.

'Because friends are important, Harriet,' he said lightly, typing a long message that was hidden from my view. 'One day you should get some and see.'

He spent the rest of the journey on his phone. I spent it staring at him, nervous. It's just because we're tired, I thought. Don't panic.

I sat through dinner with one foot mentally wedged in the door of the train home. I smiled politely through a chorus of Happy Birthday. I listened patiently to a woman called Francine tell me about her love-life woes. Luke ordered dessert and I bristled because seriously, how much longer?

'You look stressed out, Harriet, everything all right?' said his friend Aki, dark fringe hanging in eyes that peeped out to mock me.

Later, Luke would deny that she was anything other than concerned but I knew. She was one of the ones I thought would make a 'real' girlfriend for Luke.

Aki – single, too – met the eye contact of another friend, Seb, and I saw it in that second: they talked about it – how odd I was, how peripheral to the group, how I made everyone else feel tense, even as they speared olives and toasted their friend's thirtieth birthday with the obligatory bottle of cava. I glanced around, paranoid.

Over tapas, the night got worse – drunker, blurrier – and Luke leaned in close to Aki, brushing her hair out of her face and whispering to her. I wasn't in the toilet or outside. I was simply sitting next to him. This was an old move of Luke's. He didn't try to be subtle. He didn't need to, because he knew I wouldn't react.

Finally, we left.

And this time I did react.

'Were you flirting with Aki?' I dared to ask, drunk enough.

'You know what,' he said, fixing his eyes on me, hard. 'You're so obsessed with flirting that it's probably you who's shagging someone else, not me. Are you cheating on me, Harriet?'

From then on I went back to biting my tongue so often that it must have been scarred.

Meanwhile Lexie, I hear her, shouts and speaks and argues and *still* gets to live out everything I want, just centimetres away through the wall. She and Tom make meals, the kind that Luke and I used to share before dinner became a chore for one. They curl up on their sofa and watch films, as we did, and make plans, as we did.

And I listen to the life I should have had, and am expected to exist alongside it. I sit as close to the wall as I can and I listen to them laughing, and I know something purely and clearly: I cannot let Lexie and Tom have a happy life. I cannot let Lexie steal my happy life.

I think of what happened before. I think about how, when someone steals my life, I am capable of doing anything to get it back.

14

Lexie

January

I smear lipstick on then panic that lipstick isn't in any more. Is gloss back? My reference points stop in time when I stopped in time. It's one of the reasons I need this.

I need to snap myself out of my rut, so I am going on an official night out.

I need to leave this box. I can't exit the one in my brain, but the front door of the flat is easy to open when you make yourself do it – and when you take your pyjama trousers off – and that's what I have to remember.

Tonight is a leaving do for my former colleague Shona and I am on the bus, heading to a cocktail bar in Dalston.

Tom does a low-level whistle at my pencil-skirted bum as I walk past.

'You're just trying to make me feel better about looking fat,' I say, embarrassed.

'Untrue,' he says, shaking his head firmly and looking back at the TV. 'You look hot.'

I have been edgy about going out all day, my hand shaking when I made a bad attempt at doing my eyeliner.

Mostly, I'm going so I can tell myself a story of my existence as the kind where I go on nights out – sometimes I feel I need to justify the fact I live in Central London and see so little of it – but also because I know it's the kind of thing I should do to network.

How, I wonder, did I end up in an industry that revolved around contacts when I am this antisocial? Or am I? Is this new? The worst thing about current me is that I genuinely have no idea. I am so lost, I can't even remember where I started. What's new, or a problem, or fertility-related, and what's always been there. I have no courage of my convictions, no decisiveness.

Then as I go to leave, I hear a baby crying next door. There is no baby next door. Is there? Could Harriet have got pregnant and had a child without me realising any of this was happening through the wall? Will I need to hear that every day, a baby growing into a toddler, giggling and needing milk and talking?

'Did you hear that?' I ask Tom.

'Hear what?' he asks, and I try to forget it, hope – or dread – that I am imagining things now, hearing children where there are no children. It is suddenly possible. Again, I am flailing.

When I cross the road I pause and look up at our apartment block.

I crane my neck but our flat, on the fifteenth floor, is anonymous, out of reach and far away.

A few floors up I can see a lamp on, a window slightly ajar. On the ground floor, a man sitting on the windowsill smoking a cigarette and shouting, furious, into his iPhone. The flat next door to him oozes Nineties pop music and shrieking laughter. The couple above them have lit a candle and are framed in the window – he is kissing her on the cheek like a motif.

All of these people, I think, suddenly outside my bubble, living these lives in such close proximity to me and yet, I have no idea who they are.

They are below me and above me, side by side. They are kissing, fighting, sleeping and dancing. Are they ill, in pain, feeling sad? Did they have good days today, or bad days? Did they have life-changing days? Have they broken up with their first love today, fallen for someone, or just been to the supermarket to buy some frozen peas? I stay there for five minutes, wondering what *my* life would look like from this perspective. Wondering who I am to people on the outside; what questions I inspire. In my mind, every single one of those people in there is like Old Me, not New Me. Not feeling their hands shaking, dabbed with sweat, as they put their phone back into their bag, simply because they are going out for the evening.

A few minutes later a bus comes and I am caught up in a wave of other people, swiping and taking our seats.

This used to be my day to day; now, I flinch when people move close to me. I look down at my hands and see that I shake, still.

On the bus I am next to a mum who is staring out of the window, her child talking to himself in the buggy in front of her.

I pull tongues at the toddler.

'I like your giraffe,' I say to him.

He blows a raspberry.

I stick out my tongue again and I smile.

When the bus begins to move, I look across the road and see Harriet coming out of our building. I stretch to get a better view, but the bus moves before I get the chance.

It's been a few days since I lost my temper over the doctors and Tom broke down and, finally, I'm starting to come back to life. Right now, the sun's toasting me through the bus window on an incongruously warm January day and some positive feelings are finding a gap to make their own way in, too.

I get off the bus with the hint of a grin and walk the few metres to the bar.

'Lexie!' bellows a man I used to work with who has definitely had at least three beers.

I order a glass of red wine and a few more and refuse to feel guilty about fertility advice not to drink. We have a plan now. This is my last hurrah.

'Pitch to me!' says my old editor.

'I will,' I promise, and I mean it.

And you know what, I think, as I look round the bar full of men with their ties pulled off and a waiter walking around asking anyone if they ordered chips, no one else is perfect, either. I am okay. I am going to be okay.

'You've been so off radar, Lexie, we've missed you,' says Shona as she squeezes me in a one-arm cuddle.

And because we're on our own at the table, everybody else standing, I make a snap decision.

'I'm so sorry,' I say, one-arm cuddling her back. 'I've had some fertility stuff going on. I don't think I've been dealing with it well.'

I hold by breath. I said that out loud, I think. I did it.

'Oh, bloody hell, Lexie,' she sighs. 'I wish you'd told me. Me, too. That's why I'm leaving work, to be less stressed.' She pauses. 'And that's why . . .'

'You're drinking Diet Coke,' I fill in, laughing. 'Oh God, the booze guilt is the worst, isn't it?'

'Only beaten by the sugar guilt, and the wheat guilt, and the 'are you having enough sex' guilt,' she replies, eye-rolling.

I'm laughing harder than I have in a long time and it's that easy not to feel alone. You confide and you're confided in and you empathise, and you find the comedy in the awfulness. Why did I imagine some invisible rulebook that said I had to keep this to myself? That no one wanted to be burdened by my problems? That it was kind of . . . tacky to bring it up?

A psychologist would probably track it back to my childhood. I think of my mum, flitting into a room and out again, and my dad, heading away for work for two weeks at a time, and I think – there were no windows. There were no windows available for people to ask for help or to analyse. Was that deliberate? Did my parents – the children of postwar stoics – avoid leaving any windows open, so that things didn't get too emotional?

'I hope things get better for you soon,' I say, still squeezed into her, close. 'You'd make such a cool mum, even though I know it's crap when people say that.'

She cuddles me, tight.

'We should meet up soon,' I say to her, mid-hug. 'I'll go nuts and buy you an elderflower pressé.'

I feel her shoulders shake and I don't know if she is laughing or crying, but I tighten my arms around her, just in case.

I am not the only one here living this, consumed by it. They're everywhere, the other mes. I've just been so wrapped up in my own narrative that I haven't seen them. But I want to. I want to help them, and bond with them, and cuddle them. I hold onto Shona, even more tightly.

15

Harriet

January

I am in a bar, watching Lexie. Similar to when I followed Tom, I just want to know how she works, what she does when she has a moment alone. But Lexie doesn't have time alone; she makes sure of it.

Lexie is laughing and sipping wine and I am drinking wine too, faster than her, and I am not laughing.

I am not worried about Lexie seeing me because it is dark in here and busy, and she is surrounded – of course – by friends.

So I am able to sit at this safe distance and stare at her as she touches her hands to her hair and face, pulls at the side of her skirt. Nerves, Lexie? Thinking about that YouTube baby you heard crying before you left the flat? I see her drinking and I judge her. From my now extensive online research on fertility issues, I know that alcohol is a fuel to them. Tut-tut, Lexie. Does Tom know you're throwing away your baby chances with every sip of that large red? It's almost like you don't deserve it anyway. It's almost like you don't deserve your whole lovely fucking life.

'Want some company?' says a man who is too small for me anyway but pretty.

I examine his clothes and I can tell: he isn't someone who people would view as cool. I steadfastly ignore him, fixed stare in place. He goes to say something but he can't think what and

65

he simply retreats. A little smaller now, a little less sure. Briefly, part of me feels guilty. But I need to focus.

I see Lexie having a deeper chat than the others, a personal one. I tilt my head to one side thoughtfully, trying to read Lexie and the girl's facial expressions and work out what they are saying. The other girl sips Diet Coke. They hug, at a certain point, like one of them is dying.

When Lexie goes to the toilet I go along – like girlfriends do! – and slip into the cubicle next to her. I stay in there while she washes her hands and reapplies her lipstick, humming to herself happily.

'How's freelancing going?' asks the woman next to her.

'It has its ups and downs,' says Lexie plainly. 'But mostly I'm glad I did it.'

Something we have in common actually, Lexie. Perhaps we could be friends. If I wasn't about to ruin your life.

She continues. 'Nice to keep your own hours but a bit lonelier than the old office.'

'No Thursday crisps for dinner club?' her friend asks, spraying musk perfume that drifts into my cubicle.

Lexie erupts in a guffaw.

'No Thursday crisps for dinner club,' she laments. 'Oh God, I miss crisps for dinner club.'

I go back to my spot at the side of the bar, where I pick up my bottle of wine and top myself up then carry on watching Lexie.

Lexie leaves at 11.30 p.m. and I slip out after her. She stops at the corner of the road and swaps her heels for ballet pumps. I'm close enough to hear her sigh of relief as her toes yawn into the shoes.

We even take the same bus home. I'm a few rows behind her, face buried in a scarf, but she wouldn't notice me anyway. Her own face is buried in her phone.

I look at her social media as she updates it and see comments on a selfie telling her she looks good. She did. I glance up. She does. But I log into the account that I've created under a new name and tell her she doesn't. Tell her the opposite. Tell her that she looks hideous, and old. I watch her shoulders fall and I know, even from here, that she is reading it. Glass, Lexie, thin glass. Smashable, which is convenient.

She gets in the elevator and our night together ends. I loiter outside and head up a few minutes later.

When I get home I can hear him, playing computer games and speaking to drunk, drunk Lexie in a tone that sounds concerned and gentle. Not annoyed. Not furious.

'Really, Tom?' I say out loud. 'You're not even a bit pissed off that she's drunk when you're trying for a baby?'

I think of how Luke reacted when I got drunk. He never liked it. Compounded my hangovers by telling me how embarrassing I had been. Whereas drunk Luke was popular and hilarious, according to him, according to his friends.

I throw my handbag at the wall.

When I've calmed slightly I sit on my sofa and write my reply to Tom.

Thanks so much for your advice.

That's all I have. I'm wary of anything that sounds too flirty; I suspect Nice Tom would run a mile. But I need to make sure I don't kill the conversation. I need to know him better. The sounds through the wall aren't enough and the likeness to Luke is driving me crazy. This is the closest I can get. It's why I played the baby noises. Just a few things to tip them over the edge, make the misery greater than the joy. And then things can reset. Lexie can move on; Tom can be with me.

Plus, ever since I heard Lexie's voice, raised and ranting, and Tom's, bleak and beaten in response, I've wondered whether things are as perfect as I thought they were anyway. Or was I hearing something unreal?

In hospital, my therapist would have said that I was projecting

Luke and me onto Tom and Lexie, I'm sure. Seeing them as more perfect than they were, as I used to do with us.

But we'll never know: I decided to stop seeing my therapist despite her repeated insistence that we have a lot more 'work' to do. Despite her suggesting that I had been a victim of abuse. I stopped seeing her. I didn't like her being mean to Luke.

I hear something bang down on a table. A beer? A laptop? Is Tom checking if he's heard from Rachel? I tell him I'll order the book and that the work experience contact would be great. And then I add some drivel about passion.

I am making myself feel nauseous but still, I send it and get no reply, which irritates me because all he's doing is watching some non-event 0–0 draw; I know the result because I mute my TV and then watch what he's watching, for insight.

He updates his social media too, some football-based joke with an image from his TV, metres away from me, and I feel a surge of anger that I – Rachel – am low down on the priority list.

Then, despite the fighting the other day, I hear him and Lexie chatting normally. Fuck them and their eternally happy relationship. I throw the remote control at the wall.

I go to bed and make sure I slam my door, and I think about Tom, but when I think about Tom, it is hard not to think about Luke. I'm drifting again, the two of them merging.

Luke met me when I was at my lowest ebb. I had broken up with an ex-boyfriend, Ray, six months ago because I knew people thought he was uncool. Because I wanted them to think I was better than that.

But I missed him, that man with jeans that were too short for him, whose ability to make me laugh was obscene.

Ray had moved on, though. To someone who was proud of him; who was confident enough in herself, most probably, not to care what other people thought. Since then, I had been all over the place. Tried on some different crowds. I played at being artsy, picking up baggy patterned trousers and talking loudly about my love for the playwright Joe Orton before landing on something that was easy to pick up: party girl. This one was brilliant, because you didn't need to learn a hobby for it, or acquire any accessories. Unless a hobby was chucking liquor down your throat most nights until 2 a.m., when you vomited in an unknown sink and your accessory was cheap vodka.

I slept with anyone, everyone. I missed Ray and I disliked myself, and I was trying, even back then, to dilute me.

Then one night I was drinking sherry at the home of a pretentious mutual friend who had just got back from a gap year in Europe and become obsessed with everything Spanish.

'No one actually likes this stuff though, right?' a guy at the party had asked bluntly with a grin. 'It tastes like *mushrooms*.'

I was horrified. I wouldn't have ventured anything other than polite agreement and awe at her sophisticated drink choices. The friend was new, someone from work, and I was trying to impress. Or rather, not to offend. Are they the same thing?

Either way, I thought this man was fearless and impressive with his honest sherry feedback. Everyone laughed and slapped him on the back; he was popular and down-to-earth. And handsome, I thought with a jolt as I looked up at him, so handsome.

Luke's confidence soared even more as he drank and I listened to him take on somebody's views on bullfighting and somebody else's thoughts on Rioja. He put arms around people's shoulders, nudged them playfully in the ribs.

Then he turned his attention to me.

'Have you ever tried any English wines?' he said out of nowhere, focused in my direction. 'They're making some really good stuff down in Sussex.'

He placed his hand on my waist, steered me to a sofa in the corner next to the back door. I hadn't even thought he had seen me. I was shaking.

I muttered an intimidated no, sneaked a glance up at his messy curls.

The idea of *dating* someone like this man, Luke, with his wine knowledge and confident views? This was a world away. This was what I had been looking for. But I knew there was no way he would be interested in me.

Except then when our friend turned off the music and started to read aloud from Hemingway like a primary school teacher introducing the class to Roald Dahl, Luke whispered 'Shots?' in my ear and took my hand.

The crowd big enough for our friend not to notice, he led me out of the back door and down the street to the British pub in town, making me cry with laughter at his impressions of the Hemingway reading as we walked. I had drunk enough now to stop being quite so mute.

'I wish all American bars were like this,' he said, two notes too loudly, as I looked around, confused, at the snooker table. I had never been in a British pub before. I could see why.

He ordered us some drinks and it was only as we sat down that I realised just how drunk he was. Conversation became hazy and nonsensical and we got up to dance, though it wasn't a dancing vibe and, really, I felt too self-conscious to move my limbs.

'Come on!' he said, twirling me around in a different beat to the music. 'You're too beautiful not to dance! Dance, dance, dance.'

It was almost a chant. My protests were ignored and half an hour later, my mouth was full of yeast and hops as he kissed me, forcibly and deep. I was sober enough to be aware that like it wasn't a dancing kind of bar, it wasn't a kissing kind of bar either, but I tried to block that out. His Roman nose knocked against mine. I had my hands at the nape of his neck, just at the start of his dishevelled curls.

'Shall we go back to mine?' he slurred.

I wanted to go home to sleep and he was barely coherent enough to be company. But I went home with him because he was beautiful and he wanted me and he had fixed his eyes on mine, and we had brief sex that felt like a one-night stand.

Until two days later when he sent me a message.

I've found a place that stocks English wine. Come and sample with me?

It felt glamorous and clever and new. It felt like being in my twenties should feel. It felt fancy and impressive. Luke wasn't just a boy to drink beers and have sex with; he was sophisticated and a grown-up, clutching a fresh white from the British countryside.

Minutes later, a message pinged in from our mutual friend.

Saw you leave with Luke the other night. He's a charming guy but just . . . be careful, okay?

I rolled my eyes – how novel, someone being jealous of me – and didn't think about it again. Instead, my thoughts for the next few months were taken up with the French restaurants Luke took me to and the plays he booked. With the way he stared at me so intently and told me I was beautiful. With the books he lent me and the movies he recommended. With his height, with his curls, with his long arms steering me into his car or into a beautiful hotel room with a deep, plush bath.

I didn't think about what our friend said for six months or so when – to my utter shock – my presumed one-night stand Luke and I were together, an established, long-term couple.

It took those six months for Luke and I to move in together with four of his colleagues. I longed for us to have our own place, but that would come in time, he said. It was a statement of fact; not the start of a discussion. In the time we had been together, things had shifted. I had already learnt that this was how things worked. I had done what he wanted that first night; now, a precedent was set.

What we also didn't discuss was how much I longed for

Frances, my best friend and former flatmate, who had said that Luke could live with us with barely an increase in my rent.

Frances was solid and she solidified me. I got funnier when she found me funny; cleverer when she found me smart. I pictured us, dressed up as we were in a framed photo in our living room. Before Luke and I met, Frances and I had thrown a Christmas party. In the photo, our faces are squeezed together, a tiny bit of eggnog on Frances's chin.

The morning after the party, hung-over, Frances climbed into my bed and we watched already-old *Friends* episodes on TV. We'd giggled loudly over the dance battle that had taken place in our living room the night before, the rhythm shifting every twenty seconds as another drunk person had a great brainwave and pulled up a different song on their phone.

'Can we make it an annual thing?' I asked, my head on the pillow next to hers, throbbing. 'It was so, so much fun.'

'Well, as long as we're still here,' said Frances.

'Whoa, bleak.'

'I didn't mean dead, you idiot,' Frances laughed, and we got the sort of giggles that come from that very specific combination of sleep-deprived, hung-over, happy and young. 'More that we might both fall madly in love and head for the suburbs to procreate.'

I had laughed like it was ludicrous, but we had only squeezed in one more Christmas party before I did meet a man and I did move out. There were no suburbs, though; just that bleak houseshare a few roads down from where Frances and I had lived, where I was expected to do six people's washing up.

I still didn't know why Luke had said no to Frances's offer for him to move in with us other than maybe Frances might have started to see too much of our reality.

For the duration that she saw him, Luke had enough charisma and charm that she didn't know that reality. Didn't know that after the early weeks of foreign wine and dinners and compliments, things had shifted. And that now there were subtle digs, comments, seeds sewn. I had become good at lying, dressing up, glossing over, even to Frances. I clung to the early weeks, wrote a narrative that was led by them and that buried the other. A narrative that shifted time and spun and twisted. I was convincing, even to Frances. Even to my own mind.

Mainly, though, I think Luke didn't want to live with Frances because it was what I wanted, my idea. And as time went on, I was realising that that wasn't something he would put up with.

But that was okay. I felt, the whole time we were together, that Luke was out of my league and that I had to work harder, try more, be better to make up for it. We would get back to those dinners, to those stroked cheeks over English wine, if I just worked that bit harder. He would laugh, very occasionally, and I would catch that glimpse of the early weeks and become more determined.

'It's weird,' Luke said to me, on one of our earliest dates. 'I'd been thinking on my way to that party that night that I quite fancied having a girlfriend.'

His comment hung in the air and I thought: What? So you picked me up like a packet of cookies?

But really, it confirmed what I thought. I've always believed that no one could actually love me. It would just have to be serendipitous timing. A bit like when the man you want is living next door to you, at the very moment that he is having relationship problems.

16

Lexie

My good mood passes as quickly as it came. I pitch to the editor who was enthused about me writing for him last night, and he doesn't reply. I am hung-over and my insides feel rotten, and I get the fear that drunk me told sober Shona too much.

In the afternoon it's worse when I check the mail and find fertility clinic leaflets jammed in there so it's full to bursting. What the fuck?

I log on to social media absent-mindedly and my stomach lurches. My accounts are filled with cruel messages from unknown, faceless accounts that are trolling me, like the one from last night.

Ugly bitch, says one.

Why would you post selfies when you look like that? says another. I switch tabs. Different network, same nastiness.

I feel disproportionately sick. Given these messages are from faceless people with no context, how can I care? But maybe that makes it worse. Why would they target me? What have I done?

The baby cries again next door and I am gasping for breath, suddenly. I feel like I am being attacked on all sides or losing my mind and I am not sure which one is the worse option.

74

In the evening my anxiety is worse again, speeding up and threatening a panic attack, and Anais texts me.

You're doing that thing where you go off radar. Phone me x.

But I can't reply. I need to be happier before I reply.

In her world, things are the same and this is one of the things I struggle with the most. For me, there is no stopping this, stepping off and rejoining the old party. There is guilt in wine, envy in other people and the knowledge that I have opted out. That I want something else.

But the something else is out of reach for me, too. The crew I've decided to join have no place for me. My mum friends from childhood do an annual trip to one of those family-friendly holiday parks together. I am never invited.

'Oh you wouldn't want to come,' goes the refrain. 'It's all kids.'

They are right, of course, but not for the reason they think.

They are so removed from my reality that they picture Old Me, sipping cocktails, dancing behind VIP ropes and eating ceviche on rooftop terraces. They see me throw my carefree head back and slick on more lipstick. That me wouldn't have wanted to go on the camping trip, they're right. But that me's a very distant memory.

And now, if I tried to go back to hanging out on that roof terrace, I would stick out there too, clearly over that phase of life and stuttering with my newfound lack of confidence.

I am in thirty-something limbo and I don't belong anywhere. Except here, on this sofa. I get a biscuit.

Then my phone rings and it's Tom.

He shouts hello and sounds drunk, and I know I shouldn't be annoyed with him but I am. Because I tried to call him earlier, to tell him about the messages. Because I have cried in shame for the bulk of today and though he couldn't have known that, I'm still angry.

'I've got good news!' he yells, clearly walking down a street as there are people shouting in the background. 'We need to go to Sweden next month for this documentary. And the best bit is that they've said you can come out for a bit too, free flight.'

But if I'm honest, I'm mostly furious because unlike me, he *can* still be in the old world. He's not gone to the pub nervous and shaking or spent half the night talking about fertility issues. He's just been drinking with work colleagues, nothing new, nothing unusual.

A few years ago I'd have loved the idea of the Sweden trip. I'd have boasted about it on social media, booked restaurants, bought expensive boots, made plans. Now, I am so irritated I can't speak.

The messages pop into my head again, too. Why would someone target me, unless they have something against me? Unless I have done something wrong. Or unless I have something they want.

'So?'

Could that thing be Tom? That's how these things normally work, isn't it? Love rivals and vengeance?

'Mmm?'

'What is it?'

He sounds, suddenly, trepidatious. I am now a person who can make him trepidatious.

And he's right to feel it, because now I have to bristle; tell him what the problem is. In I come to ruin everyone's mood and make it all about fertility again. I am so tired of this role that I barely have the energy to speak.

'We said we'd go to the doctors,' I say, deadpan. 'I don't want to go on holiday. I want to go to the doctors.'

He's quiet.

'But it's only a month. We can fit the doctors in before we go or . . .'

'Plus that means we probably won't get to try at the right time. I can't stay for the whole trip, can I? It's going to be hard to make sure I'm with you on exactly the right days.'

76

We are silent for thirty seconds and I consider, or try to consider, what it would be like to forget babies. To enjoy the rest of life. It would be so easy, to step off this trajectory. But I know it in my fibres – I can't.

'It didn't even cross your mind,' I say quietly, sadly. 'And it's all I can think about.'

Because there is so much pressure, being the one doing the planning, calculating, moderating, bleeding. I am exhausted. We haven't even started any of the truly hard stuff and I am spent.

'Well, you know what, maybe you need to think about some other stuff,' says Tom.

I put my head back on the cushion and close my eyes.

Tom does something with his voice that is akin to putting a 'hold fire' hand up, were we in the same room. 'Just for a month. Think about some other stuff and then when we come back we'll go full steam ahead with the hospital.'

I hear someone shout his name and my eyes spring open.

'You're not *with* people having this conversation, are you?'

'No, no, someone just came out of the pub and shouted me, but they can't hear anything, I promise. I'm going to have to go but we'll talk about it later, okay? I'm sorry. I love you. But Sweden!'

I sit, mulling over the conversation we have just had and wishing that logic and patience still existed for me. Wishing one month was what one month used to be, instead of a ticking, looming period of time in which we cannot have a baby, which may mean I never have a baby – a waste, a throwaway month, a month that pushes us down the list. The small becomes huge, the inconsequential becomes life-altering.

In another universe, Tom is right, but my brain won't receive the message. My brain just hears *delay*, *delay* and works out how many months until I turn thirty-four. And it stews on the fact that Tom, when asked about going to Scandinavia, hadn't thought for one second about the doctors when it would have stamped itself as a headline across my thoughts. I thought he was my teammate on this. Some of it though, the internal figuring out, there's no denying that I am doing alone.

But *Sweden*! I think of the leaflets I picked up earlier that seemed to fill our postbox. Fertility clinics and IVF success rates. Had the universe – or the marketing part of it – uncovered my secret and was now targeting me at home? Or was I reading too much into a coincidence? They do happen.

Then, I think about the messages. What am I considering when I link them to Tom? Cheating and lying and angry other women? How can I possibly be serious? My Tom. My loyal, honest Tom.

It's only then that I realise I didn't even tell Tom about the messages, when they are why I've been desperate to speak to him all day. This is how much fertility issues dominate: when you're talking about them, a part of your day that is so huge can become nothing, less than nothing, in seconds.

Later, I ignore Tom's texts and curl up in a ball on the sofa, wishing that I could feel better as Harriet sings some sort of classical reimagining of a Take That song.

'Fuck off, Harriet,' I mutter. 'Just fuck off.'

17

Harriet

January

I'm making small talk with Chantal in the preprepared aisle in Waitrose when my phone beeps to say I have an email. It's an odd thing, to feel colour, but I know the second that my face turns pale.

'Are you okay?' Chantal asks, seeing the change, too.

'Yeah,' I say, distracted. 'I just have to . . . deal with something.'

I walk quickly towards the entrance of the supermarket, dumping what's in my basket in the wrong places as I go, annoying middle-class shoppers as I barge past them with no apology.

But it's only when I get outside that I feel like I can breathe. I stop and lean up against a bus stop under a screen that's flipping from page to page to tell me when buses are expected – two minutes, one minute, due. I try to remember the tips from the mindfulness app that I've been using erratically for a few months, but my breathing won't steady. There is ice on parked cars, but I feel no chill. I shove my phone back in my bag.

I think back to Chantal, standing there next to the baby corn. She's probably relieved anyway, I think. No one wants to get stuck speaking to me when they're sober.

On the way in to our building I glance at Tom and Lexie's postbox. It doesn't look too full. One of them must have picked up those leaflets I dropped in. Just a reminder, Lexie, I think. Just a hint that someone knows things aren't as perfect as they seem, a suggestion that one of them is breaking ranks.

I take the elevator upstairs and open my door with a shaky hand. I lie on my sofa, shoes still on, sneakers and visible white socks dangling over the edge.

The message was sent at 9am US time.

Does that mean my parents were thinking about it overnight? Discussing it before bed? I know one thing: this is a direct response to me not replying to David last week.

Before now I'd ignored my parents but kept up enough occasional contact with my brother so they knew, at least, that I was alive.

Harriet, it begins, and my stomach lurches as though I have been disciplined by the principal. I usually delete her emails before I open them.

Since when did my polite, traditional, sixty-something mom ever not begin even an email with a 'Dear'?

David says you didn't respond to him last week and that made us worry such a lot. Are you feeling well?

I can sense her awkwardness. If I'd ruptured a lung, she'd shove some Oreos at me and fetch a blanket.

Mental health? I don't get cookies. There's no need for a blanket.

All she wants to know is that since I was in the psych hospital, my mind has been dusted, polished and vacuumed to make it as good as new. She wants to know she won't be shamed again; that I'm not running around the world leaving smears. She wants to know that what I did once, I won't do again. We'd all like to know that, Mom, I think. Me more than most.

Let us know. We think about you often. Mom and Dad x

I think about messaging Chantal, telling her everything that has happened, and her coming straight round with her Waitrose haul and plonking it in the hall in her rush to hug me. And then I feel embarrassed. How ridiculous. Chantal and I barely know each other. Chantal and I bond only when we are paralytic and lonely. And if I told her the truth and confessed what I did? Gave her my real surname and let her sit down on her sofa and Google? She would run a mile – and even that sliver of friendship that we have right now would be over.

So instead, I cry alone as usual. Because this is the twentieth message, or the twenty-fifth that I know I will ignore from my parents when before, we were close.

I'd go round to theirs and we'd order Chinese takeout and play board games. In summer we'd sit outside and chat until the early hours, tipsy on Californian rosé. But after the first few times of enthusiastic bonding, Luke – at the same time changing how he behaved with me, too – began to swerve those nights.

'I don't even like the place they order from,' he'd say sullenly when I occasionally pushed. 'So what's the point?'

But I'd remember the man who would book plays he knew that I would like; turned up with cheese that he knew was my mom's favourite. He's just having a bad day, I would think. Everyone has a bad day.

But it kept happening.

'We don't see much of Luke any more,' laughed my dad awkwardly. 'Does he not like us or something?'

And I would make excuses and hate it, always being the one in the centre. Feeling like it exposed me, too.

David, though, we still saw. He would pop round to our place after a night out, filling Luke and me in on his evening, so Luke found him harder to avoid. I would sit up with my brother and be able to be as sympathetic or amused as he needed because look at me! I didn't have these dramas. I was in love. Okay, I'd have liked for Luke to be closer to my parents, but still – no one had it perfect, did they?

I was smug, until I wasn't any more. What is the opposite of smug? Is it bitter? Something worse?

I run over the last time Luke and I saw each other, when she took his hand, her finger shaking, terrified of me after what I had done, and I saw a tiny, almost imperceptible squeeze, and the tears roll out again. But this time, they are angry.

18

Harriet

January

Lexie, social media tells me, has gone away to her brother's house. Meanwhile, Tom has gone to get drunk like he has the hangover resilience of a student and the funds of a Russian oligarch. I know this because I am sitting in a pub reading a book and watching him. I am quite the pro at this now. Unlike at my actual job, for which I have an inbox littered with warnings and queries and complaints. I'm behind on dead-lines, letting people down, failing, ruining my hard-fought-for reputation.

But how can I focus when I need to keep watch on Tom? I have read a lot of blogs on fertility issues, including on the impact on men. The pressure of knowing that there is something Lexie needs to make her fundamentally happy and that that may not be possible can't be an easy thing to deal with.

Tom's friends order food but Tom doesn't want dinner. He doesn't want to nurse a pint like it's midweek and he is in his thirties, both of which are things that are true.

He goes to the bar to get his round.

'Double JD,' he adds at the end of the order, and I watch as he drinks that drink alone, in a second, before he returns to his friends with the more sociable pints.

Between rounds, he flags a waiter and orders separate vodka

83

and Cokes. When his glass is nearing empty he looks around, twitchy, as his friends drink too slowly.

This morning I followed Tom to where he was filming on the South Bank and waited patiently, book or phone in hand at a distance, all day. One thing having being in a psychiatric hospital teaches you: how to wait it out, how to keep sitting, sitting, sitting.

And then, when he packed away his equipment and headed to the nearest pub, I decamped here, too.

Occasionally, I see a look of questioning in the eyes of the friends that he has met as they say no to the shots because they have an 8.30 a.m. meeting or a toddler who shouts about Cheerios in their face at 5.30 a.m.

They're wondering what it is. Whether he has had bad news or has been fighting with Lexie. If someone in his family is ill.

I know, because I have drunk those drinks and I have seen those faces. This is why people turn up and drink like this. His friends might not know specifics, but they know it's out of character and so must be needed, and so they humour his odd Thursday-night behaviour until midnight when really, they'd have liked to be back in their Surrey suburbs at 10 p.m.

'I'll stay with him for another couple,' I hear one say to a third friend at the bar. 'You get off if you need to. I won't leave him alone in this state.'

'Lexie, do you reckon?' the friend, tall, bald, asks.

'God knows,' his friend replies. 'But whatever it is, it's not good.'

That is kindness, I think, melancholy for friends I no longer have and kindness that I was not shown when it was me who was suffering.

'You could try a smile, love,' says a man waiting for his pint at the bar.

'Nothing to smile about,' I say, but I take the drink he offers to buy me anyway. I look at his face and it is okay, and I consider having sex with him, but then I remember that I need to stay on track.

Tom walks home idly, despite the January chill. He is in no rush to get there. Me neither, Tom, me neither, I think as I follow him. What a shame we can't go for a drink together. And then I have an idea.

The next night, as I predict, with Lexie still away, Tom follows the same path. After-work drinks and more pitying faces, I presume, as this time I don't see them. Because I am at home, setting the trap.

Tom was drunk enough last night to follow any party he could find, but when his friends left, there was no party to follow. Tonight there will be. When he comes out of the elevator, the party will be easy to follow; in fact, impossible to ignore.

My door is ajar and Tom pushes it open as my kitchen clock flicks to 12.01 a.m. I smirk, laugh aloud. Predictable Tom, carrying my plan along.

'What's so funny?' says the guy I have been making small talk to for an hour now at the door to my kitchen. He smiles awkwardly.

It obviously wasn't a comedy moment in his monologue. I'm not sure any of them have been, despite what he believes.

'What?' I say vaguely. 'Sorry. Tell me that part again about your issue with feminism.'

And then, as he lectures me, I get back to Tom. Tom is wearing an old T-shirt that began life as navy. He's in jeans and dark trainers, and his hair is overdue a haircut; even more overdue a haircut than usual. His forehead is slightly sweaty and as he turns around and takes his coat off, I see a hint of damp coming through on his lower back, too.

Between Tom and me is a dense crowd that is making me look sober enough to chair a meeting. Tom, too, looks out of it and unfocused. I suspect that he hasn't even computed that he is at his next-door neighbour's flat, or that underneath that giant throw is what constitutes my life – my piano – and what would be the giveaway. Right now, it's just a dumping ground for empty glasses and rogue crisps.

Tom closes his eyes for a second, just stands there. When he opens them he looks dazed. Then it's like he wakes up.

Suddenly, he has recalibrated and his eyes are everywhere. On Chantal, dancing alone in the centre of the room with her bright scarlet hair spinning around her face. On Steph, passed out and cuddling her wine bottle like a teddy and on a man whose name escapes me snorting coke off my piano-table. Remind me to give that a good Dettol before I start composing in the morning. The same man has done this at four separate parties. He speaks to no one while he gets high but clearly he is craving company in a strange form. Just to be there, in the background, and feel comforted by the noise. I get it. When I see him at the bus stop in the morning he utters a sheepish hello, thanks for the party, I have to head off now, as most of them do.

I pretend to engage in the conversation I am in and watch Tom. Leave him though, I think. Just observe.

But then the man I am speaking to – Aaron? Andy? – lunges at me, tasting of the hops and yeast of my first kiss with Luke, and of so many other kisses, but I am recoiling.

'What are you doing?' I yell at him, and a woman across the room looks vaguely over her shoulder.

'Kissing you?' he laughs. 'This is often how this goes. We chat, we get on, we kiss?'

I glower at him. I am furious at this distraction.

'I literally can't even remember your name,' I hiss. 'Your chat was boring. What did I possibly say that suggested we got on? Don't come near me again.'

He leaves, laughing in apparent disbelief at the level of my anger, and I go back to watching Tom. Searing with rage that I missed a few crucial minutes with something so pointless as

Aaron, or Andy, or whatever the fuck his name was. There is nothing I hate more than wasted time.

But Tom. Back to Tom. As I stand, pretending to look at my phone, what there is to observe is a man with sad eyes who doesn't touch drugs but drinks everything he can see. Even more than the parasites who usually come to my parties. The dregs of a bottle of whisky that someone left on the side. Beers that people put in his hands. Vodka and Cokes that he pours out for himself in my kitchen as though he lives here. I allow myself to fantastise momentarily that he does. Put some coffee on while you're in there, Tom. Shall we make a risotto?

I consider being offended that Tom is in my flat pilfering things that I bought and without even acknowledging my existence, but it's overridden. He's here. This is an opportunity.

Someone hands him another beer. There are twenty-five to thirty people here in my tiny flat and Tom spends twenty minutes talking to a young, smiley set designer named Ian who lives way down on the first floor about the didactic theatrical style of Bertolt Brecht. I stand close by, taking it all in, waiting for something useful. But the pretentious drunk small talk keeps coming.

'How did you end up here?' Tom asks him. 'If you live all the way down there?'

Ian looks surprised.

'The parties on this floor are legendary,' he says.

'Bloody hell, I feel like someone's grandpa,' slurs Tom. 'Yours, possibly. We *live* on this floor.'

'And you don't hear anything?'

'We hear music and noise and parties but we didn't have a clue that this was something that our *neighbours* joined in with. We assumed everyone was as anonymous as we are.'

We, we, bloody we.

'To be honest,' he adds with a smile. A sad one? There's certainly some sadness in there; in his face. 'We're also happier in front of a film with a bowl of crisps. We're in our thirties now, we're pretty boring.'

'I just hear the noise as I get near the building then get in the lift if I've been out and I don't feel like going home,' chirps Ian. He whispers, hammy: 'And also . . . free booze.'

A fair point, Ian.

They get another beer and get back to Brecht.

The verb 'rattle' is normally reserved for five-bedroomed homes and old, widowed grandparents, but I rattle around this tiny flat and some nights that is unbearable. Even in hospital, there was more company – sure, some of it was in the form of disembodied noise from someone being restrained down the corridor but still, it was something.

Now, I need to fill this silence, and in the absence of friends and family, I do that with anyone I can in the only way I can, by offering them something for free. For most of them it's wine, for the occasional man it's sex.

There is the potential, of course, to have sex with Tom, too. But no, I think. I need to play a longer game.

Watching him, still, I head over to Chantal.

She grabs my arm, swings me around for a dance. I am happy enough, unusually, to join in. We twirl and we laugh and we drink, the whole time. I lean in close to her. 'See that guy over there?' I whisper.

She looks at Tom. Tries to focus.

'He's going to be my next boyfriend.'

'That's amazing,' she hisses, slurring a Prosecco spray at my cheek. 'You deserve a boyfriend. You deserve *all the boyfriends*.'

And then she pulls me in close and sways with me until she says, teary, that she feels like she might vomit, then shuffles to the door, carrying her shoes.

At the door, she leans in close to me.

'I know I'm probably about to be sick,' she says, gagging. 'But I am still so excited about your next boyfriend.'

She kisses me on the mouth.

When a couple of hours later, Tom falls asleep on my sofa, I sit next to him and touch his face as gently as if he were a newborn. I move close to feel his sleep breath on my cheek. I touch the end of his curls, rubbing the tips between my fingers, and lean close to inhale his scent. Beer and sweat and hair gel.

Then I take out my phone and loll my head on his shoulder, snapping a selfie of us. He doesn't react, still passed out. I am one more body in a sea of bodies and it's 3 a.m. I see his keys, they have slipped out and are just next to his pocket on the sofa, and I make an eighth of a second decision to slip them into my own.

Shortly after that he wakes, looks like he may be sick, too, and then stumbles through the crowd the few steps to my front door.

When he has left, I touch the indent from his head that is on my cushion on the sofa, the place where I usually Google his name and turn the TV to mute so I can hear his relationship woes.

I watch him return moments later and search pointlessly for his keys before stumbling home again. Oh Tom, I think, as I pat his keys, safe in my pocket.

And then I go to bed while I still have party guests, which means my door will be unlocked all night and my belongings open to strangers. Whatever. The night – though it may have consisted of people I don't know drinking all the alcohol in my house with barely a thank you – has been one of the best I've had. Beautiful Tom and his curls. I drift off with a smile on my face and a plan forming in my head. I sleep holding Tom's keys. I've been nibbling on the dregs of their postbox and their social media. The flat key gives me access to a Tom and Lexie buffet.

19

Lexie

January

I FaceTime Tom from Yorkshire, my nephew, Noah – desperate to speak to Uncle Tom with me while his dad cooks us pasta – sitting on my lap.

Tom appears on the screen and I can see that he is guzzling our adored Noah up, but he looks pale.

'Why aren't you at work?' I ask. 'I told Noah we would try you just in case, but I thought the most we'd get was a quick thirty-second hello. You look awful.'

'I have food poisoning,' he says quickly.

'Didn't you go out last night?' I ask. 'Is food poisoning code?'

I nod at my nephew.

'It's okay,' I say. 'He understands hangovers. Noah's dad's a Yorkshireman.'

'I'm serious,' he snips.

I ease off.

'I had a burger. Rich is feeling rough, too.'

I raise an eyebrow, but then Noah demonstrates to Tom the toddler yoga he does at nursery and I am focused on the tiny bottom stuck up in the air that's making me laugh until I can't breathe.

It's only when I look up that I see Tom isn't laughing. He is looking away, distracted, elsewhere when normally Noah consumes us both.

'Lex, on your way back can you stop at the key place and get a flat key cut? I lost my keys last night. The porter had to let me in.'

'Shit,' I say, then check Noah didn't hear. 'Should we get the locks changed?'

'No, I've got my wallet, so there's nothing anyone could get our address from. Just a stupid drunk mistake.'

I laugh.

'Ah! so you *were* drunk? But I thought it was the burger.'

He doesn't even smile.

I get home the next day and the night passes into history, for now.

Something hangs between us, though. I think about how close we were when we started talking about starting a family. I see the us from then and the us from now. I think of the times we fill silences by both blurting out something inane at the same time and then politely withdrawing, to let the other speak. I think of the extra few centimetres between us in bed at night. At the lack of touch. Of the slight tilt of Tom's diary – no longer a source of amusement to me but part of our routine, part of our calm – away from me now as he writes while I read, as we do.

I think about how a hug we shared the other day reminded me of the ones I get from my parents. Hanging back. Not quite invested. I think of how it's rare now that we get tipsy together slowly and speak about being teenagers, or politics, or any other conversation that meanders its way through a bottle of wine. I try to remember the last time we kissed, just kissed, without it being about trying for a baby, and I cannot. Alone that night in a bed at the other end of the country, I feel very distant and suddenly, very sad.

20

Harriet

January

It's an odd thing, walking into a flat that is a mirror image of your own. Everything is filtered, not quite right, and Lexie and Tom's flat feels half the size of mine as there is stuff, the stuff that makes up a life, at every turn. Mine has the air of a place that has been cleansed and purged so that it looks bigger in the AirBnB pictures.

I waited for my moment. Social media told me that Tom was away. Then, I heard their door slam and watched Lexie run across the road and gesticulate wildly at a bus before zooming away to give me space. Thanks, Lexie, I think, much appreciated.

I peruse, first, like I am at an art gallery or enjoying a Sunday afternoon at a museum. Contemplate, muse.

I should feel nervous, I think, but then I have done worse than this. Far worse.

I walk through the living room with its corner sofa squished into this tiny space. Lexie's make-up bag is on the side with lipstick blotted onto a tissue alongside it. I touch the colour so there is a trace on my finger. I hold her Pantone mug, cold now with a mouthful of leftover tea in its bottom, between my palms. I see a birthday card, half written, with a long, heartfelt message from Lexie. I run my fingers along the radiator and feel the leftover trace of warmth.

In the kitchen, a chalkboard on the wall says the words BROCCOLI NOODLES ICE CREAM WITH THE MARSHMELLOWS IN IT. There are biscuit crumbs on the side, a bottle of red with two thirds gone. A life.

They could do with emptying the bin though, I think, sniffing the air and grimacing. I walk into the hall and stroke my finger across the wall as I decide that this flat really does need a second coat of paint.

But they are, of course, not the most interesting exhibits.

First, sitting on Lexie and Tom's unmade bed, an iPad. No lock code on it, perhaps as it always lives at home. Email is too dense to bother, a sea of marketing and mailing lists, but there, as easy as that, are Lexie's personal notes. I find one entitled 'Work ideas'.

'Think about whether there is any future in writing/making enough money AT ALL,' it says. 'Retrain???'

Lexie isn't happy in her work. Needs more of it.

I move on.

Photos don't grab me – I've seen enough of those online – but an old handwritten school diary that I find buried in a drawer does, for too long almost, as after all, I have no idea how long Lexie will be and I do need to get on.

You'd think the diary would be Lexie's, wouldn't you, with her being a writer, but it's Tom's, wedged there and peeking out from underneath his socks. One has a hole in. Both letting yourselves go, I think. Bad relationship form. Gaps, gaps, gaps.

I scan to the date I'm looking for. A diary, huh, Tom? Maybe I'm sexist but that seems like a pretty odd hobby for a thirty-something man. But oh, what a convenient one. I arch an eyebrow and begin to flick through.

It was in a flat I thought was next door (Harriet's), though I was drunk enough already by then that it's hazy. And I don't remember seeing Harriet.

93

So maybe not, he writes and my face flushes with pride. I'm in his private, hidden diary. I reside there, under his socks.

I flick a few pages back.

> Fertility issues are taking their toll. I don't want to be that man wishing the pub was open an hour later so I can drench my sadness in the acceptable male coating of beer and ignore the real issues. But it looks like I am that bloke.

I could sit here guzzling this up all day. How quaint. How sweet. How *exposing*.

And then it is time to go. I take out what I brought with me from my bag and I shove it in the same drawer as the diary before locking the front door behind me.

21

Lexie

January

There are two versions of today, I have decided, there is a coun-
terfactual.

There is the version in which I sit on the sofa muttering
about Facebook friends who post endless updates on their kids'
toilet-training.

And then there is the other version, where I have been out
at a meeting and welcome Tom back from his work trip to Leeds
with a homemade risotto.

In version two, I am happy. And I'm making up to Tom for
the last three days, when I've been frosty and passive-aggressive
in all talk of motherfucking Sweden.

I put old Nineties tracks on and dance around the kitchen,
singing badly to Sophie Ellis-Bextor. I pour two glasses of Malbec
and place them next to the organic mushrooms. I look around.
It's the scene of something we have not been for a long time.
But it's so convincing that I'm almost feeling it. Maybe this is
how to make us happy again, copy the old us and hope they
reappear.

'Woo-woo,' Tom whistles, opening the door and taking in my
dress and make-up. 'Hot.'

He takes his trainers off to the soundtrack of our life, Harriet
at her piano.

'She's off again,' he says, rolling his eyes as he puts his slippers on and sighs a contented sigh. He's home and he likes being here, and I am part of that. We have that. I hand him a glass of wine.

'She's been at it all day,' I tell him, laughing. 'At least, when I've been here.'

Because we're in version two here and in version two, I didn't sit through the wall seething at Harriet's jolly singing all day and resenting someone I haven't met.

This is my brain now. Fury, guilt, self-loathing.

I know how resenting other people's happiness is a force for bad. We have Instagram inspo quotes. We have #goals. Women are supposed to champion each other, to want success for each other, and yet . . . here I am.

Over dinner, Tom tentatively brings up the trip again. We book my flights to join him and then agree to book an appointment at the doctors for when we get back.

'I'm so excited!' I say, smiling.

I'm trying to make it feel genuine but it still doesn't. I still don't want to go to Sweden; still hate the delay. He looks at me oddly and I wonder if I have overdone it with the fake joy. We're jarring, lately. Misjudging. Not quite meshed.

At 9 p.m., we are watching a film when I think I hear the baby crying again.

'Can you hear that baby again?' I ask Tom.

He stares at the movie.

'Probably just a mate of Harriet's brought her child over,' he says, barely registering.

'At *this* time?'

He just shrugs.

I will sound crazy if I go on about how often I hear it, fixated.

So I wait for Tom to leave the room and when he goes to make tea, I leap up. I put my ear to the wall but it's stopped. Or it never started?

And then my feet are cold, so I go into our room to the place that holds the best selection of socks, Tom's drawer, but something catches my eye. Not his diary, which I know is in here and would never touch, but a flash of red, a familiar branding.

'Tom, why have you got condoms in your drawer?' I ask, marching into the kitchen before I can stop myself.

'What?' he asks, pouring boiling water into mugs.

'Condoms. A brand new box of condoms. Why would you buy condoms? Why would you buy condoms *now*?'

He tells me he didn't and looks back at the tea because he doesn't think this is important. But it is important. Because I am doubtful and he now gets drunk and lies about it, and there are things, aren't there, that if I'm honest have felt strange. I got in the other night and the flat felt different. Like someone had been here. There's a possibility that I'm going crazy, but there's also a possibility that I'm not. The last few months have been hard for Tom, too. What routes do people take out of that?

But what else do you say?

I have no idea what I think but I sit back down, grip his hand and I try to hold on to something.

22

Harriet

January

It's there, a message from Tom in 'Rachel's' inbox. The stomach flip that seeing it there gives me makes me miss dating, romance. I bask in that feeling before I open it.

Here's the email address, he says. *Let me know how you get on.*

Brilliant; it requires feedback. Except that I can't apply for work experience with his friend because I'm not me and I don't work in his industry. Ah.

I decide to deal with that detail later and enjoy this, for now. I'm relieved, too, to be distracted from the email from my parents.

I know what happened last year was wrong – drilled into me through three months in a psychiatric unit and the reaction of my shamed family – but how could they not excuse it? How could they not see that when you follow all the rules, then the person you have done everything for changes their mind anyway, that that's not a normal thing to experience? If anyone would listen, I would like to explain just once how that altered me.

I'd woken up late, to Luke sitting up in bed, staring at me with an expression that I had never seen on the face that was more familiar to me than any other. It was a few months since we had started trying for a baby; less than a year since we had got engaged.

'I've been having these thoughts,' he'd said, earnestly, like he was auditioning for an arthouse film, not ruining my life. I had known, even if I never would have acknowledged that thought then, that Luke loved the drama. Heavy pause. 'That maybe this isn't right.'

I could see brochures for wedding venues on the bedside table.

'Forever's a big thing,' he had gone on, sighing, auditioning. 'It's made me question everything.'

I had tried to zone out. Tried to block out a memory of my mom, after I had gushed to her once just before Luke and I moved to the UK about how smart Luke was, how *inspiring*.

'You do know that you're just as smart as he is, don't you, Harriet?' she'd said, focusing her eye contact on the tea towel.

I'd looked up from the suds. Dried my hands.

'Why are you saying that to me?' I had snapped.

'I just wanted to make sure you knew,' she'd said and then walked away.

Perhaps, I thought for the first time as he wheeled out these clichés, she had been right. Had I placed Luke on too much of a pedestal? But the thoughts had disappeared quickly, as the reality of what was happening hit me.

Luke had hugged me like a lame apology and I'd thought of my phone and how the last ten messages had to do with our wedding – appointments with potential photographers, messages to Luke himself just a day earlier about what kind of bloody cake we would have.

A massive doughnut ring, I had suggested, only half kidding. *A nod to our American roots?*

Luke had dismissed it.

Traditional afternoon tea platter, he'd told me. *A nod to our British future.*

I knew, as a bland statement of fact, that I would always love him and need him and had wondered – practically – how that worked. I knew I should fight it, reason with him, show him

99

why he was wrong, and I had tried, but I was too desperate to sound appealing.

And yet, Luke did change his mind. In retrospect, probably another way to toy with me, since Luke never normally changed his mind on anything. But he went out and I sat in a ball on the floor, already knowing the loneliness of my new life. I had seen the photo of us at Land's End in Cornwall, wrapped up in long woollen scarves, out of the corner of my vision in the living room, and had made my hands cover as much of my face as I could, to block out as much of the world as it was possible to block.

And then Luke had put his key in the door and climbed down onto the floor with me.

'I don't know what I was thinking!' he'd said, a huge grin on his face. 'Let's forget it.'

Forget it? I'd thought of how twenty minutes earlier I had felt like I was dying. How I had looked at what else there was in my life and saw that aside from work, there was nothing. My family had become increasingly distant every time they criticised or questioned Luke so that by now, we were hanging on by a thread. I no longer had friends; even Frances was barely in touch. Luke didn't like me seeing people without him. But I had been all right with that: I had only needed Luke.

'Okay,' I'd said. 'Thank you.'

The relief had felt physical, zooming through my insides.

'That's okay,' he'd said, magnanimous. But not sorry, never sorry.

'Did I tell you about that exhibition I wanted to see at the National Portrait Gallery?' he'd then said suddenly. What?

Then he sighed like he was in love. 'God! I adore this city.'

He had moved on. This one might have been particularly extreme, but I was used to these turnarounds, used to flipping my emotions back and forth and being ready to do happiness, even when it followed so closely behind sadness. Used to playing whatever role he needed me to.

Once you start breaking up, though, you can't stop breaking up, not any more than temporarily, and it had happened properly two weeks later as we watched a film in bed.

'I'm moving out, Harriet,' he'd said and if the last version of Break-Up Luke had been drama school over-actor, this one was robot. No emotion, no flicker of doubt. 'It's not been right for a while.'

I'd sat in shock as he slung clothes in a bag and made toast to take with him, carefully spreading his Marmite for what felt like hours.

And while some break-ups might knock someone left field for a few weeks or propel them into a trip around Asia, I'd known for me that it was done. That life would grind to a halt that day he left our bed. How the hell would I start again? Who would want me? My life was over and he was asking for the phone number of our reception venue so he could cancel our wedding, as though it were a pizza we'd waited too long for. We're pissed off. The pepperoni was due at 7 p.m. and now it's eight thirty. We've had to have beans on bloody toast.

I'd stayed in bed until the evening. I watched bad TV and I didn't cry until finally, I did and I couldn't stop, and I sobbed myself to sleep. And this time, Luke didn't reverse out of it; didn't change his mind.

I'm jolted out of this familiar trip down memory dead end with a booming noise from next door. Movie night at Tom and Lexie's. I kick the wall then wince. Tom and Lexie and their eternal fucking togetherness.

The noise brings me back into the present, reminds me to act. I open up my laptop and slam my fingers on the keyboard. This time I am not Harriet, and I am not Rachel, but I am . . . Leo. Why not?

Hi Lexie, I begin, listening to the noise of the film through the wall and feeling the rage again, that swell. You have no idea what I'm capable of, I think. You have no idea what I did.

I work for a media agency and might have some copywriting work to send your way. Good rate and regular hours. Let me know if you'd be interested.

The address is gmail but I don't think she'll care. From that list on her iPad? Lexie is kind of desperate.

After that, there doesn't seem much point waiting up, so I get an early night, going to sleep dreaming of a Tom–Luke hybrid lying with his feet in the cold, cold sea on a beach in Norfolk and laughing, like Lexie did, in my face.

23

Lexie

January

It's when you have a meeting at a nice hotel that you realise all your clothes are too small and of a shape last featured in a fashion magazine a decade ago.

So I splashed out. Anais in tow, I bought a jumpsuit and today, I head to a salubrious hotel, check my coat and scarf into the cloakroom, and tell the maitre d' that I am meeting someone for coffee. He takes me to my table but I see a man, mid-thirties, alone and looking like he is waiting to meet somebody, so I head over. Take the lead, I think, dredging Old Me up from the past. This man wants you for work. Remember that you're good.

'Leo?' I say with a smile.

'Nope,' he snips and looks back at his iPad.

I sit back down, burning red, and pretend to be engrossed in my phone while I wait, looking forward to proving that there is a Leo and that he is coming to meet me.

But twenty minutes pass. My coffee arrives. And another ten. There may in fact not be a Leo, here at least. I have finished my coffee. My face flushes when anyone comes near my table, or whenever I look up from my phone. This is the reality then: Old Me isn't back, after all. It's tragic New Me who's turned up today, again. It's her we're stuck with now.

Hi Leo, sorry to bug you but just checking I have the right time and place? I email. *I'm at the hotel and it's 9 a.m. No worries at all if you're just running late, though! Lexie.*

As soon as I've sent it, I am embarrassed by New Me once again. Why am I sorry to 'bug' someone who hasn't turned up to an arranged meeting? Why is it no worries if he is running late but hasn't told me? Why did I put in an exclamation mark, like the whole thing was fun really, not a problem to me? I am sweating, though it is five degrees outside.

I ask for the bill and sitting in my taxi home, I estimate that altogether, Leo has cost me a hundred and fifty pounds. But more than that, he has cost me my pride when I tell Tom that the meeting I had built up as so important didn't even happen.

I feel disproportionately crushed. I found a small, possible use and it turned out to be non-existent. I had held on to today as evidence that I was needed, that I still had a role to play.

How did the meeting go? messages Anais. I'd built it up to her too, of course. What sort of idiot buys a new outfit for a barely anything meeting that was too unimportant for the other person even to bother to show up to?

I ignore her message.

24

Harriet

January

I watch her from across the room. I have been here for half an hour, to get settled. I enjoyed some granola and yoghurt, then treated myself to a pastry, crammed with juicy raisins, which I stuffed into my mouth hungrily. I am halfway through a juice, made from beetroot and ginger, and I am reading a broadsheet for the first time in a while. In truth, I've had a lovely morning.

Lexie arrives and she's wearing a navy jumpsuit that I am envious of and I think: Oh Lexie, what a shame that there is no meeting. What a shame that your outfit is more coveted than you are.

And then I see her stand up and head over to a man who shakes his head at her before she heads back to her table. Nice shoes too, Lexie. But oh, the embarrassment. I lick a tiny bit of pastry crumb from my top lip and keep watching as Lexie types on her phone. I see her wait, and wait, and I order coffee. I see her wait longer and I start on the newspaper supplements. As Lexie leaves, looking close to tears – oh honey, no need to overreact – I treat myself to a bellini.

25

Lexie

February

I'm sitting in an airport lounge drinking a (slimline) tonic with lime. Tom and I are going to Sweden and we are having a celebratory start-of-the-holiday G & T, except that I want a baby, and booze and fat are the enemy of embryos, so I am having a G-less & (slimline) T. One shot of a clear liquid, it's all it is, but somehow it kills the whole point.

'To the holiday!' says Tom brightly, but I've already checked out. I'm thinking about coming home and getting on with hospital appointments, and this drink, the flight, Sweden, all they are now are obstacles, things to get out of the way before I can get where I want to go.

It is February now and this is *our* year. This is it. I have been stagnant and now I want to go, go, go like the easyJet plane that just left the runway.

'Lexie?'

I'm staring. That's me, that giant orange flying vehicle, taking off after a massive delay but determined to still get to Malaga.

'Mmm?'

I am snapped out of my shit analogy.

I am irrational now too, so I have fears of air strikes, ash clouds, anything that can keep me away from the hospital. I dream nightmares of battling my way to somewhere and I know

106

that while in the dream it might be the jungle or the super-market, really it's the reproductive medicine unit. I need this to move on. We both do. Off his own back, Tom got himself tested before we went away – 'I thought it might be one thing we could easily tick off,' he said, shy – and came back with the all clear; good sperm.

The plane soars and I look at Tom.

He looks like he's about to say something but stops himself. 'What?' I say.

I'm on high alert; convinced always that something terrible is about to happen. This charge of anxiety has started to sit in my chest lately, thrusting itself upwards to my throat with the slightest nudge.

He looks shifty.

'What?' I demand. I'm horrified and suddenly sure he's going to confess that he doesn't love me any more in front of a stag party chanting about a man named Gavin in Wetherspoons in Gatwick Airport.

'Nothing. I was about to ask if you wanted some crisps,' he says, looking flustered and like he needs to reassure me quickly. 'But—'

'But you suddenly realised I was supposed to be healthy. I'm not allowed crisps on the holiday I didn't even want to go on,' I mutter, necking my (slimline) tonic and remembering once again that it's in a state of ginlessness.

Tom rolls his eyes but stays silent.

But after a few minutes he cracks.

'I'm going to go and buy a book,' he says. 'But when I come back, can we start again and try to make this a nice break? You never know, it might be the last one we have before we're parents.'

The thought – even in my negative, defeatist brain – makes me smile.

'In that case . . .' I look up at him but he's nodding already.

'Yes,' he says, 'I'll get you a gin.'

We order a gin each on the plane too, as it's a tradition on all flights we go on, and now that we've officially imposed the maximum fun, minimum limitation of things related to fertility rule, we're sticking with it.

We make a toast.

'To hopefully the last holiday where a flight isn't a total nightmare,' Tom says.

'To hopefully the last holiday where we don't have to stay sober to be responsible parents,' I reply, faux-seriously. I squeeze Tom's hand tight. I have had alcohol in the daytime and I can feel its joy and its novelty in my bloodstream.

'To hopefully the last holiday where we have time to have ridiculous conversations like this,' Tom adds, and this time we clink our plastic glasses then drink.

I put my glass down and my head on Tom's shoulder and I am sleepy, but a seven-hundred-page novel is more relaxing to me than sleep, so I reach down by my side for the Margaret Atwood I've slotted between me and the edge of the seat.

'To definitely the last holiday when you get to read a tome like that on the plane,' he says.

'Never, never, never,' I whisper, smiling sleepily and opening up to my bookmark.

A few hours later, we are in a four-star hotel getting ready to sample Sweden's nightlife.

Tom is on his laptop finishing something for work and I am lying in a deep bath with bubbles under my chin. Music is playing from my phone on the floor and I'm singing quietly to myself, smiling.

This is what it's like to be young and carefree. My new jumpsuit is getting another outing. I want a long, expensive cocktail. I want to laugh. I want to be with people who don't know me.

My phone beeps next to me and I strain over the side of the

tub to pick it up, grabbing a discarded sock to dry my hand with first.

It begins innocently and I am doing my 'Will this hurt me?' calculation, as I do now at the start of all contact. Even an engagement announcement can do it; I know that you're just focused on your ring now, but you'll be on to babies next and that will still probably all happen before I get pregnant.

I think this message can't punch me but then terribly, it does.

I tried to call you but couldn't get through . . . erm, I'm pregnant. I know – weird, right? Still getting my head around it (and it's very early days and obvs total accident – whoops!) but am happy xxx

I throw my phone on the bathmat and hope that it breaks. I put my head under the water, stay under a second too long and come up gasping.

I feel my heart hammering and I hope that Tom doesn't come in because I need to get myself together before I speak to him. Because while those texts bruise every time, this one is worse.

Anais, my friend who pretends to vomit when people mention children, has at some point while I have been weeing on ovulation sticks, googling fertility diets and giving up on books because they have mention of pregnancy, had spontaneous sex with her fiancé and got pregnant.

I'm angry with her even though I know it's illogical, because – the word is stuck in my head, 'whoops' – she is complacent about it, breezy, and I am so, so bitter.

My ears echo under the water.

I no longer like myself, I realise, sharply. I used to think I was kind. Caring. I felt joy when I heard other people's good news.

But now . . . who would like someone so resentful? Who would like someone who reacts to their friend's pregnancy in this way? I cannot garner one tiny flicker of joy for her. Nothing. It is all about me. It is all anger and sadness.

If other people I knew struggled to get pregnant it would probably make them start a support network for childless people.

They would become wellness gurus; yoga teachers. They would make the most of their lives without the limitations of children, opening a school for the underprivileged in Sudan or writing a screenplay.

They would be able to sip champagne at baby showers without it feeling as though their insides were being put through a spiraliser.

So what's wrong, then, with me?

Why am I the one who can't cope?

It turns out that I am not a good loser and that is a terrible thing to realise about yourself.

For once, I manage to hold it in for a short time, at least. I get out of the bath, pad out to the bedroom with a giant dressing gown trailing around my ankles, dry my hair, and though Tom comments on me being quiet, that is all. He's still at his laptop and his eyes haven't rested on my face yet. He directs his comments at his screen.

An hour later we sit opposite each other in the nicest restaurant we have ever been to, to eat a taster menu that is the best we have ever eaten and will be paid for by his company.

In front of me is a duck consommé that everyone around me is telling me is delicious and that I feel too sick to taste.

The other downside is that we have to share the meal with strangers to me, Tom's colleagues. There is Executive Producer Sue, his fifty-something boss, and cameraman – sorry, Director of Photography – Dan, who has brought his wife, Marissa. I'm usually on high alert when we meet newly married people or, indeed, any couples in their thirties, but tonight I'm distracted, still thinking about Anais.

And then in the buzz of the table, something rises above as Tom goes to pour the wine.

'Not for me,' says Marissa, opposite me. 'I'm pregnant.'

She gives her stomach the subtlest, lightest touch and from then on, I'm not there. I can't engage, I can't joke. I'm under the water again.

I want my glass of wine and yet I resent that, too. I don't want to be able to drink this. I want to be banned. I want to have a higher purpose that means the Pinot Noir is off limits to me. To be asking questions about the menu like Marissa is, to make sure no unpasteurised cheese passes my lips. I think about my short-lived Brie ban last year and my stomach tips further.

Tom and I told no one but my brother and his wife about the miscarriage. They're common, this early, I told myself. It happens to so many people. Another baby will come along and I'll move on. But no one told me that it doesn't always happen. No one told me that a miscarriage isn't a blink-and-you-miss-it thing, even in the early stages. No one told me that it is physically gruelling. No one told me that afterwards comes grief, in its own right.

I glug the end of my wine, as everyone around me finishes their consommé, and top it up again.

'What about you two?' asks Marissa absent-mindedly as she dives into her soup. 'Do you have children?'

I know I can't win a war against the tears springing up in my eyes. They're powerful; I am weakened, again. I should have spoken to someone about my miscarriage, I think. Now, it just feels like it's too late, but it stays there, undiscussed, unpurged, and then at moments like this it sweeps over me.

I shake my head, which is all I can manage, and shove some homemade rye bread into my mouth, miming towards it to show that I can't elaborate right now, much as I'd love to.

Even the bread is making me gag, but better that than the pâté that is just arriving. Or the lobster that I know is en route.

I curse Tom for being in an easy, mundane chat with Sue about work, helping himself to the pâté and missing the eye contact that I keep trying to send in his direction. I gag, again.

'Can you Google pâté?' says Marissa to her husband, topping up her fizzy water. 'I'm pretty sure I can't have that.'

Tom is still oblivious, leaving all this coping to me. The wine is the only crutch available to me and so I drink, drink, drink more, ignoring Marissa's question.

Later, as the long meal draws to an end with a plate left barely tainted by food in front of me, someone suggests we all have a digestif.

'Except you, Marissa!' I slur loudly. 'You can't have one because since you mentioned a *few* times, you're pregnant, aren't you?'

She is silent, staring at her (decaf) coffee. She smiles awkwardly.

Suddenly, Tom is round at my side of the table and whispering in my ear.

'Oh, so *now* you notice me,' I say. 'It only took about twelve hours.'

'You're really drunk and not making much sense and you're being a bit offensive to Marissa,' he whispers. 'We should probably leave.'

He starts to pull my chair out.

'But shouldn't we be "making the most of it", Tom?' I shout loudly, and I catch a glimpse of Marissa looking away from us, uncomfortable. 'We have to "appreciate this time", see, that's what *everybody* says.' I look at Marissa again. 'Look!' I announce. 'Poor Marissa has to have decaf coffee now. We should make the most of it. Let's get *espressos*!'

I boom the last word into his ear and feel him go slack. I see his boss, on his other side of the table, subtly take out her phone and pretend to scroll.

And suddenly I'm furious, once again.

'You don't want to do this tonight, right?' I hiss at him. 'No problem! Just let me know the timescale and I'll schedule in when I get sad because my friend, who doesn't even want a baby, is having one and the whole world's pregnant. I'll put it in my diary for six years' time, when I'll probably be too old to have a baby but *who cares*? Because it works well for you with your bloody job.'

The entire table is looking at us. Tom tries to give his boss some cash but she waves him away.

'We'll sort it out tomorrow,' Sue says quietly. 'Just get her back to the hotel – honestly, it's fine.'

I crumble then into sobs, and Tom scoops me up and shuffles me out.

'I'm so sorry,' I say repeatedly because I know already that tomorrow I will be mortified but I can't yet grasp hold of the feeling. I am too precarious myself to grip onto other things tightly.

We walk out into the freezing air but I can't hold onto that, either. I shrug off Tom's attempts to put on my coat.

'I don't need a coat,' I mutter, twirling around. 'Look at my lovely jumpsuit. Leo never saw the jumpsuit. What happened to Leo? I wonder.'

'Anais?' he asks quietly. 'Anais is pregnant?'

I sit down on the kerb and cry like this is grief. Which it is, in many, many different ways.

'I miss the baby, Tom,' I cry and it all comes out then, what should have emerged to a counsellor, or a friend, or a mother, and to Tom, of course, but long, long before now. It comes out in sobs, at the side of a road in Sweden. In tears rolling down all the way onto a new jumpsuit. In fatigue, a deep, deep fatigue that I can't ever imagine lifting.

'It's okay,' he whispers, parental. 'It's okay, it's okay, it's okay.'

His arms are my coat and he clutches me tight until I feel my sobs start to dissipate.

'I don't want this to be me, Tom,' I whisper as he holds me. 'I don't want to be this person. This angry, defensive, bitter person. I want to be myself again. How can I be myself again?'

He loads me into a taxi, where I sit silently, spent, thinking.

He tucks me into bed as I'm muttering about how I feel left out because 'everybody in my life is a *mum* with their *mum blogs* and their *mum friends*.'

And Tom, who has stroked and coaxed and tended until then, snaps.

'No, you're not,' he says. 'But you know what? I'm not a dad either and I'm still trying to enjoy my life with you until I am. It would be nice if you could do the same.

'And it would be nice if you hadn't done that in front of my work colleagues. I have to walk into work with those people now and they know my entire fucking business.'

And that is the last of my memory.

Next, I wake up fully clothed and full of self-loathing. Then I remember why and it's terrible, not just because of Tom and his work colleagues, but also because that is what I really think of myself.

Once more, I wish I had the strength of character to stand up for what I believe in. To practise what I say I believe: that I see motherhood as only one version of womanhood. That womanhood is a varied and eclectic construct. Something that doesn't have to involve being a parent and that still has value, even if you don't have fifty-five episodes of *Peppa Pig* downloaded onto your Sky planner. Instead of drinking too much wine then shouting about being left out by the mummies.

Tom has gone to work and I am left with the awfulness of a day alone, hung-over and paranoid.

26

Harriet

February

I am sitting up in bed in the early hours of the morning scrolling through Tom's social media, when a new email pings in. I click on it, because who emails at 1 a.m.? Answer: Tom. Today, Tom emails at 1 a.m.

How did you get on with Sam? Hope it went well x

Just that.

But is 'just' the right word? Do you 'just' email a girl you don't know, in the early hours of the morning when – according to the internet – you are in Sweden?

I think Lexie is with him too, because I heard them heading out of the flat together a few days ago and it's been silent through the wall since.

So he's abroad, working hard, with his girlfriend, and at . . . I work out the time difference . . . *2 a.m.*, he emails an unknown woman with a message he has no obligation to send? He had done his bit, shared his contact, there was no need for the follow-up.

If Tom is testing the water, I need to make it clear that I am not closing him off. I rewrite my reply five times before I decide that it will only sound off the cuff if it is off the cuff.

So I down a rum and Coke in the kitchen then climb back into bed and type quickly.

Not had chance to connect with Sam yet – having a rough time with a break-up so been distracted. Will do soon though and thanks again for your help. Can't believe you are so up for helping – reassuring to know there are good men out there . . . xx.

Probably a little much, but then so was following up my email in the early hours unnecessarily. He had upped the ante; I had just followed.

And then, seconds later, I get a reply.

You're probably too good for him anyway xx

I go for off the cuff again.

Blushes

That was it. But it was enough.

If you wanted, we could meet up – I could give you an overview about the industry, pass on some more advice – and maybe flatter your ego a bit more too . . . x

I sit up, eyes blurred, heart hammering.

The next morning I am sanguine as I pick up my post, thinking of all the things Tom and I can do together, how quickly he can leave Lexie, how Luke will feel when he hears the news about my new English boyfriend.

There is a new future, and it's Tom.

I walk down the stairs with a bouncy tread.

Lexie and Tom's postbox is spilling over and there is a letter with a hospital stamp and Lexie's name on it.

I am too curious and high – non-medicinally, I've taken a big hit of Tom – for legalities.

I whip it out of the top, slipping it between my own post and heading inside.

Then, suddenly, someone appears behind me. A flash of bright red hair. Big smile.

'Hey!' she shouts.

Chantal.

'Oh, hi,' I redden, clutching the post close to me, though she could never know.

'You okay?' she asks.

I nod. Don't ask me about the boyfriend, I think, remembering what I said to her at the party. Don't ask me about the boyfriend.

But then I remember how drunk Chantal was – how drunk Chantal always is – and know that she would never remember either that conversation or Tom's face. I back away, anyway, make the usual excuses that end in ellipsis.

'Sorry, I've just got to . . .'

Inside, I flick my sneakers off and stick the kettle on for an instant coffee.

Then I stand, holding the letter. I debate doing something TV-like with an iron and a penknife but then I decide screw it, everyone knows post can go missing, they'll just get someone to resend it and that will be that.

We are pleased to confirm your consultation at the fertility unit.

So, here are the facts:

1. Tom and Lexie are trying for a baby.
2. They're not having much luck.
3. Tom and Lexie have been arguing.
4. Tom is flirting with someone else, while on holiday with Lexie.

The kettle boils, though I don't remember boiling it, and I absentmindedly return to the kitchen to make the coffee.

Then I sit down to my iPad and ponder.

What's the best thing a man in the midst of all of that could hear?

I think about the blogs I've read.

Fun. Lightness. No pressure.

I leave the coffee on the side and pick up my phone, sitting down on the bed to write.

Sure – up for some mutual ego flattering over a drink or three. Mine's an amaretto and Coke ;)

27

Lexie

February

I step out of the taxi and haul my case out behind me, swiping my fob on the gate as I enter our building. I feel the relief that I always feel in here. Outside is the chaos of Zone One. Inside is the calm neutrality of a chain hotel. No bright colours, nothing to shock. The occasional artwork on the wall is generic. Notices to residents are inane. It's reassuring.

Tom, as was always the plan with work, is still in Sweden.

The post is gushing out of our box and I shove it under my arm as I get in the lift and head up to our floor.

As soon as I put my key in I can hear her, singing loudly, sounding even jollier than normal, I swear; though maybe that's just because she often becomes a reverse mirror to my own mood.

And I am feeling so low that it is difficult to find the energy to turn the key in the door. I can't imagine being able to get my clothes out of my case.

It doesn't come over me often, but I crave having parents who I could call and cry and receive a virtual hug from.

I'm surprised. I thought this was something I was used to and didn't have it in me to miss. Even in childhood I would go to Kit or to school friends if that's what I needed. So why am I missing it now, this thing I never had?

Because, I think, I've never needed it like *this*. Never flailed so much. Never needed shoring up. And because I've never felt so distant from Tom, who, more than anyone, for my whole adult life has been the one to take on that role.

I shake my head to snap out of these thoughts. I am genuinely amazed that I have just moved my feet enough times and made contact with enough people to travel back from Sweden to my home. Surely it was only doable because I knew that when I got here, I could stay still for the foreseeable future.

The day after the row, Tom came back from work early and he and I made up. But since then, exacerbated by one of those thirty-something anxiety hangovers that won't quite shift, I've started to panic.

I know external poisons can come in and wreck things. My lack of self-confidence has made Tom and I unequal. I think I'm being clingy, then I say sorry for being clingy, then I cringe at myself for saying sorry so much and suddenly that worry re-emerges: we're not quite right. What if this poison has come in and made us toxic?

I want to be an equal partner who drinks Pinot Noir with him through joy not pain. Someone who makes him laugh and impresses him. If I am not those things, how long will Tom wait? I check on the condoms. They are still there, unopened. I think – again, the drip-feed – about why someone would be posting cruel messages on my social media, why I would be relevant to this faceless stranger. Could Tom have done something that prompted this kind of revenge or malice? Is it outside the realms of possibility that in the midst of all this, Tom has cheated on me?

I throw the post on the table, lean my case against the door then sigh onto the sofa. I think about the last time I was here and how odd the flat felt, and a shiver runs through me that is not only from the memory of the in-flight air-con.

But what now? It will be two weeks until Tom gets home and until then, I have two choices: I can sit here waiting for him to get back, or I can live my life and start to get some of me back. And something seizes me that is so dominant it even drowns out Harriet.

I write a list of things I want to achieve this year. Having a baby is of course on there, but it's not at its heart.

At its heart is a sense that I have lost myself. And if I feel like I've lost myself then I need to go and reclaim myself, fast. I message Shona, suggesting that we meet up for that elderflower pressé.

Sorry it's taken so long. I've been in Sweden with Tom for work.

The truth, too, is that instead of seeing her as a comfort, as time had passed I had worried about being around her. What if she announced a pregnancy? How would I cope? Then in a moment of clarity I remember the support, how it felt for someone to understand. How good that hug was, for both of us.

I redo my CV and email five copywriting agencies I've always been intimidated by. I book to go to a talk by novelist Chimamanda Ngozi Adichie. Swiftly, a message comes back from Shona.

Yes to the boring drinks, she says. *I've actually just started treatment so could do with the distraction. This Friday?*

Then I belatedly reply to the message from Rich that suggested a catch-up.

Dinner it is, he says. *Mexican? If I remember rightly your dancing after margaritas is impressive so we must have those.*

I laugh, genuinely, because it's easier to remember the old me when someone else paints the picture.

A house party, a few years ago, in Edinburgh during the festival after watching our friend Gabe do stand-up. I can remember the happy pain from laughing in my stomach and the potency of that tequila. I felt human. Rounded. I must try harder to hold onto those things.

I eat soup then check my email and have a response from one of the agencies, suggesting a coffee.

Suddenly I'm buzzing so I go for a run, picking up some sort of green kale horror juice on the way home and vowing that my other mission for the year is to get healthy. To feel like I can take on anything I might need to in the next year. Right now, I feel like I can.

I power walk home and run up the stairs to the flat. I FaceTime Tom and he answers straight away, half a second passing before I fill him in on work, and running, and my night out, and my list.

'You've been busy,' he laughs. 'You only got home a few hours ago.'

He's grinning and I pull my mass of hair out of its ponytail, laughing, too, and drowning out Harriet, who's reaching a high note. The thoughts I had before now seem ridiculous.

'Oh God, I can hear her from *Sweden*.'

'I'm pretty sure the one about the chickens would make it to Venezuela,' I whisper in response.

We smile, relaxed.

'I'm sorry again about the other night . . .' he says, going over the same ground. 'What I said. I shouldn't have got angry, not when you were so sad. I was just so frustrated that I couldn't make it better. I was just so angry with everything.'

'I know,' I say. 'And I'm sorry again, too. I'm so sorry about doing that in front of your colleagues.'

Harriet hits an even higher note and the connection drops so we leave it there. I am sure I can hear that baby, so quiet but so piercing, in Harriet's flat again, but when I put my ear to the wall, there is only – as ever – a piano.

28

Harriet

February

It's only after I send my reply that I realise the insurmountable problem: there's a strong chance that Tom, my neighbour, if I sat in a bar with him drinking amaretto, would recognise my face.

But in the end, he sends another message anyway. It comes while I am in the middle of hosting a dinner party, a little respectable warm-up to the part where people drink to forget until 3 a.m. and vomit in my toilet.

I fork some ready-prepared microwave vegetables for five people I'm working with who are currently sipping G & Ts in my living room. One is loosely playing the piano and another is laughing uproariously about something funny that happened in rehearsal today that wasn't funny at all.

In the kitchen I am lonely and check my email to delay going back in. I'm not really expecting to hear from Tom. After all, the next move is mine. But I do.

Hey, Rachel, he starts and immediately, I think, formal.

Sorry about that last message. I think I gave you the wrong idea. I have a girlfriend who wouldn't be happy with me going for drinks with you, even in a work way. Good luck with it all though, Tom.

Kisses are absent and so is suggestion. Another one follows one minute later.

PS. Could you delete these messages too? it says, which seems a bit OTT, but I guess he's paranoid.

He doesn't strike me as the kind who cheats — maybe talk of drinks with me on email is the nearest he's ever come.

I stab the fork into the buttered leeks and shove it in the oven, the door slamming harder than my chest as someone shouts from the living room to ask if I'm okay, do I need some help.

'Fine, thanks, will be in in a minute!' I yell to her and despite all of the strangers sitting around in my flat acting as some semblance of company, suddenly I am the cheese on top of the ready-made lasagne, bubbling, steaming, spilling over.

I stab the fork into my own hand this time to distract myself from thinking about Tom, ending this embryonic thing that we have, and Luke, ending the bigger thing we had, and my family and the police turning up and how it made me feel, and who I am now, at this minute, in this kitchen.

Does Tom have any idea what can happen when people walk away from me? When they refuse to come back?

Blood runs down my wrist and onto my pushed-up sleeve as I pour myself a large amaretto, no Coke, and down it. Whether it's the booze or the adrenaline of the pain, I decide that no, it's not over, not just because he says it is. This was the first good thing that had happened to me in ages. I had seen a way to move on. And then he simply shuts it down? No. No.

That's a shame, I reply, not caring about the blood on my phone. *Googled you and thought you looked hot.*

I am cringing at me, but I am so used to cringing at me that it barely registers.

I bandage my hand, make excuses about cooking accidents, and sit through the roast chicken and the small talk. Instead of letting it descend into chaos though, I turn the music off and start tidying at 10.30 p.m. so that I can see everyone out early, declarations of how much fun they've all had coming thick and

123

fast as I think: you idiots. You haven't had fun, you've had booze, why can't anyone see the difference?

But I'm in a fog myself, the large amarettos I was drinking alone in the kitchen in between socialising hitting me hard now. I shut the door, grab the bottle and my empty glass, and lie down on the bed, picking up my phone. Nothing. How dare he! He started this, I think. He upped the ante. Him, him, him.

In the dim lamplight of my bedroom, I take my top off. I turn the camera to selfie mode, being careful to omit my face and just as careful to include my best feature: my 34E breasts.

'But still, if this doesn't appeal . . .' I say and I send the picture.

He's a man who's swapped a regimented baby-making routine for no sex alone in a hotel room in Scandinavia. I heard someone in the flat earlier but I know Tom's still away from his Twitter feed. So I wait and I see. And I pull my jeans off and the duvet over me before I pass out in my bed, which is too big for one tall, still bleeding, drunk person.

29

Lexie

February

I am out of my comfort zone, literally, as I sit on a school assembly plastic chair in a therapy session.

I am an adult. I comprehend therapy and its role and I have multiple friends who have gained great things from it. But for me, it has never felt necessary. An early night rereading a classic has been enough to cure the majority of ills. Nancy Mitford is my therapist, Daphne du Maurier is my counsellor.

But now I need more than Daph and Nance can give me and I am here.

It was on offer and I have taken it. I welcome claiming back my mind against conspiracy theories, doubt and paranoia. I welcome help, and positivity, and someone to tell me how not to be such an utter bitch.

That's a starting point.

'I just want to feel like less of a bitch,' I say to this woman with kind eyes whose name is Angharad.

'A bitch?' she says. Welsh. 'Go on.'

Or maybe I remember it that way because therapists always say 'go on' in films.

Either way, I go on.

They said to be brutally honest, so here I don't fake-caveat. I don't say that I resent all pregnant people 'even though I am obviously happy for them'. I just say that I resent them. I don't say 'I'm sure they do appreciate how lucky they are but it sometimes doesn't seem that way.' I just say 'None of them seem to appreciate it at all, as much as I would. They just moan about their swollen ankles or their sleep deprivation and I would kill for those problems.'

It's a release not to temper my words.

Except, suddenly, Angharad moves and I notice something, a tiny dune under her loose-fitting dress.

She sees me look.

'Are you pregnant?' I say, incredulous, before I have thought about manners. Or respect. Or professionalism. Or tact.

She is the fertility counsellor. Surely this isn't allowed? Although, I will think retrospectively, what probably isn't allowed is screening for hires on the basis that someone may become pregnant during their tenure.

'We aren't here to discuss me,' she says and puts a protective arm across her middle.

Another one.

I scan back through everything I said about pregnant people.

From then, I am as mute as it is possible to be in a room where the sole task is to speak. In its darkest corner, my brain is processing 'even your therapist is pregnant' as yet another reason to feel badly treated by the universe.

I deliver one-word answers and watch the clock like a child, then fail to make a follow-up appointment.

30

Harriet

February

Tom and Lexie have headed out and I am at their place, again. I'm taking a risk, I know, as I have no idea how long they will be or where they have gone, but what is life without risk? I know that more than most.

I sit first on their sofa, to rest. I'm starting to feel quite comfortable here. I put the TV on and imagine I am Lexie.

'Hey, Tom,' I say quietly, imitating that chirpy northern lilt. 'Stick the kettle on.'

I smile and stay there being Lexie for a few minutes. I search the TV planner for her recent shows and flick between them. Then it's time to move, so I get up, put the pillows back – then change my mind and mess them up again – and I pilfer. I take a T-shirt of Tom's. Some underwear. I snap pictures of myself lying on their sofa. I take aftershave from the bathroom. I stand and stare at a large, imposing image of a British postbox that dominates the walls in the living room, and I think *fuck, how did I end up here*? I am living next door to these people, in a flat I never chose, a city I never chose, a life I never chose. I didn't covet an existence surrounded by these iconic London images. I didn't romanticise Buckingham Palace or adorn my walls with red postboxes. I can take or leave Borough Market. I don't gasp at Tower Bridge. I think of when I told my parents I was moving to London, staying over at theirs as Luke was away. Exactly where was hazy; he didn't like it when I quizzed him.

Dad was in bed; Mom and I were in the sitting room drinking red wine. My palms were sweating. People in my family don't emigrate. They live around the corner and invite each other over for pizza.

I saw the clock hit midnight; today, Luke and I would be looking at flights, at apartments. I downed the last of my wine and blurted it out.

'Luke and I are moving. To London.'

'What?' said Mom, holding her empty wine glass. 'Why?'

I was defensive.

'What do you mean "Why?" Why not? We're young. It's something Luke and I have thought about.'

My mom made a scoffing noise.

'And that means . . .?' I snapped.

'You've talked about going to California. You've even talked about going to Asia. But you've never mentioned Europe, especially not England. You hate being cold, Harriet! But you know who loves England? Luke. Luke, of course, loves England.'

I stayed silent because there was no denying it. And yes, Luke loved English football and British beer. He had visited once and spoke regularly about how desperate he was to go back. He wanted to become a Londoner, at least temporarily.

'Well, what's so wrong with that?' I snapped. 'Luke's my boyfriend. I can think about what he wants, too.'

'And what about work?' she asked.

Just that week, I had experienced my own songs being performed on stage for the first time and it was mesmerising, that feeling of pride. I sat there beaming and looking down, watching people's feet in the audience tap to music I had written, my mom and dad on either side of me squeezing my hands intermittently with grins as wide as their faces. Luke couldn't make it: he had a colleague's leaving do.

But for once, I didn't care what Luke was doing. Watching that musical was a natural high I'd never known and I think in retrospect, what was known as happiness. But I could get that again, couldn't I? In London. Probably.

'I'm heartbroken that you're leaving, of course I am,' Mom had said the night I told her. 'But if you were going to follow a dream, that would be one thing. You're not.'

I'd flinched and lied, like you do when the uncomfortable truth is levelled at you.

'We've been talking about it for a long time. Together.'

'Seems unlikely,' she'd said, wine glass still in hand.

I'd known the drink had given her confidence and it made me disconcerted; normally, we could avoid rows about Luke with omissions and gloss.

'You know the truth? Everything you two do is decided by Luke. The area you live in, the holidays you take, all those London pictures and British paintings in your room. And it worries your dad and me. You used to be independent, Harriet, go your own way.'

I'd laughed.

'Go my own way?' I'd said, nasty. 'You don't want me to go my own way. You want me to go *your* way. Turn up at church every Sunday. Visit Grandma every Wednesday. Never break the mould.'

I saw her hurt in the lamplight but adrenaline was flooding me now. She had attacked Luke and that, to me, was licence to say anything I wished, to anyone, whenever I wanted.

'You know I was bullied at school?' I'd said spontaneously.

I saw the shock on her face; I had never told her for the reason many children don't tell their parents. It would have hurt her too much. Worse than it hurt me. I could handle it; she couldn't.

'Every day,' I'd said, quieter, less aggressive as I felt tears flooding my eyes despite the fact that I started this conversation. 'Every

129

single day. I did go my own way, for many years, but it wasn't the right way — it was a way that made me a target and a laughing stock. Being with Luke has changed everything for me. I have friends. My life is unrecognisable.'

She'd sat down. We'd stayed on the sofa for ten minutes in silence, her still holding the stem of the empty wine glass tight then finally putting it down and taking my hand instead.

'Or maybe,' she'd said quietly, 'finding your confidence has changed everything. Finding a career that you love and that you're *made* to do. Maybe it's not Luke, Harriet, maybe it's you.'

I'd snatched my hand away and refuted it then gone to bed.

In the morning, Luke and I had booked flights and I'd edited my website to tell potential employers that I would from now on be based in London. Luke, despite my leading questions, still hadn't even mentioned my work or asked what I would do. We talked about his plans daily.

My mom and I never revisited the conversation, but it didn't leave my mind and it was one of the things that contributed to the distance between us. On some level, I blamed her and my dad for what happened — like they had sabotaged Luke and I and our future with their negativity from the very beginning.

31

Lexie

February

The baby crying next door is getting under my skin. I think about my lack and it is a visceral reminder of someone else's luck. I think about Tom lying to me, being something other than Tom.

I sit on the sofa and am not sure I can ever get up. When Harriet starts singing, I feel like I need to stifle her, quiet her. The charge of aggression scares me.

Tom and I had been together for over ten years when we started trying for a baby, more than two years ago now. Friends were doing it; babies were entering our realm and dribbling all over it.

'I think I'm ready to be a dad,' Tom said to me through a mouthful of sashimi.

We were out for his birthday in a Japanese restaurant that was fancy enough for its Michelin star but tasty like Nandos on a hangover.

And now my stomach was flipping too much to eat. He knew how much I wanted a child; I had been ready for a while, waiting for him.

'I'm thirty-two now and I can picture it,' he continued.

'Is this a ruse, Tom?' I asked, faux-sharp. 'To get more sushi because I am too excited to eat? Because it's worked. Have the tuna. Eat the bloody salmon.'

I paused. Wiped my forehead. Then I looked back at him.

'Are you serious?' I smiled.

'Deadly,' he said while doing a rudimentary impression of a shark.

The first time we had unprotected sex we talked afterwards about baby names. Naive optimists, thinking that was all it took.

But two weeks later, my period was late.

I took a Prosecco at a barbecue but pictured a tiny embryo saturated in alcohol and swapped it for a Coke.

'I think I *have* got a metallic taste in my mouth,' I told Tom on the tube home, grin crossing a face that had been buried in my phone, googling pregnancy signs.

I bought the first pregnancy test of my life. At the counter I felt fifteen, panicking someone would tell my mum. My brain hadn't caught up to know that we were adults and the 'yes' outcome was the good one.

And the 'yes' outcome was the one we got. I was pregnant – that easily – and we celebrated and we talked endlessly about this new life that awaited us. About this person, growing.

I stopped eating Brie and stayed twenty metres from white wine at all times. I called Kit.

'Are you telling Mum and Dad?' he said, grin nearly busting out of the FaceTime screen. 'Or is it a bit early?'

Unsaid, we knew that Kit was the centre of my familial world – that he had the parent role – and that my actual parents were secondary.

'A bit early,' I said, being sensible without really believing I needed to be. 'I just had to tell you. But let's wait until the scan for everyone else.'

But a couple of weeks later, as quickly as it stuck, it unstuck.

'It'll happen again,' said Tom as I sobbed in his arms. 'This happens to lots of people, but the good thing is that you can get pregnant easily.'

I nodded. Underneath my sadness, I knew that, too. We just had to get through this part.

Except fertility doesn't work with order and precision. What I learnt afterwards is that there are no rules or logic. A book would say I should have been able to get pregnant again; a body decides differently.

And after that my period turned up every month; the unwelcome colleague who everyone hoped wouldn't rock up at after-work drinks but always did, eager to make their unwanted presence felt.

Now, I heave myself up from the bed, because that unwelcome colleague is here, again. I go to get a tampon from my underwear drawer and freeze. Because in there are knickers. They are not mine. They are the Marilyn Monroe of knickers to my sensible M&S. They are the worst thing I have ever seen, for everything they symbolise, confirm and everything I know that I am now going to have to deal with.

32

Harriet

My parents are polite even when they are disapproving and so despite my mother voicing her thoughts on my relationship with Luke, they did what they believed parents should do when their child is emigrating. They dropped me off at the airport. They told me to eat vegetables. They wept when I peeled myself out of their hugs. They made me promise to text when I landed.

'Look after her,' said David to Luke in the arrival hall.

'I'll look after myself,' I said, mock-outraged but then glancing at Luke quickly, in case that sounded like I was dismissing him.

Luke was too distracted by his phone to have noticed. I exhaled.

I didn't know, then, quite how much I could look after myself. How far I could go. That actually, rather than the one who should be scared, I was the one to fear.

'You can look after yourself most of the time,' David quipped, 'I'm talking about when you get drunk.'

I started to tease him about a drunken night out he'd had the week before that was far more extreme than anything I had done recently, but Luke talked over me, mid-flow.

'We need to go,' he said, brusque. 'Get through security.'

I saw my mom note the interruption.

It was left for David to give the whispered last-minute aside into my ear.

'I am here,' he said, holding my head in his hands. 'Any time, whatever time zone.'

He kissed my forehead.

I nodded, unable to speak because I was so overwhelmed by how much I missed him already. How could his scent cross the Atlantic? How could a look, a shared eye-roll at our parents? How could just being together, silently, like siblings are? I was trying so hard to hold in my sobs that I gagged and he held me tightly.

But later, I laughed, too. What would I, a together grown-up travelling abroad with a partner, need my naive little brother for?

The next time I saw him, he'd have flown halfway across the world to pick me up from a police station.

33

Lexie

February

I am lying on my bed working out how to speak to Tom. Trying to muster the energy, even though, conversely, my heart is racing. I touch my skin. I pinch my knee. Am I the same? Is there anything about this Lexie that resembles the old one? Can I blame Tom, really, for any of this?

In retrospect, I think, when I left my job behind, I left myself behind.

I handed in my notice, breathed a sigh of relief that now I would relax and get pregnant again, and headed out on my leaving do. It was like a hen do. A final hurrah to my old non-mum self.

I danced to Nineties pop music on a square of dance floor in the corner of a bar and between us we drunk forty-five half-priced strawberry cocktails that somebody's contact had 'sorted out'.

'Just *do not* drink any more,' Shona told me. 'Their cocktails are normally fourteen pounds each.'

'How many have we had?' somebody shouted when we went to the bar to order more.

Twenty-five. Thirty-six. Forty-two. At forty-five, the fifteen of us who were drinking switched immediately to cheap white wine. Life in journalism: feast or famine, if famine is the house Pinot Grigio.

I drunk fast and happily and didn't leave until I realised I couldn't remember what happened three minutes ago or which bus I was supposed to get home. And so I got in a cab, texting Tom that I was en route.

I'm growing up, I thought, nostalgic for this moment already as I fought the urge to vomit out of the taxi window. Now, the next stage of life would start. I pictured myself visiting my former colleagues in the office, my baby strapped to me in a sling, breast-feeding in the meeting room, a face from the past to them already.

I stumbled out of the taxi clutching a bag of leaving gifts with a soppy, drunken grin on my face.

I stopped on the pavement to send an important message to my colleagues.

I LOVE YOU, I wrote. It took me ten minutes.

WE LOVE YOU TOO, Shona replied. *Though leaving your own leaving do first is shit.*

But I got away with it. I had been the last woman standing at most other nights out until recently. I was the first to sign up for an after-work wine and if anywhere had an inch of dance floor, I was usually in the centre of it with my hands in the air trying to get the attention of a DJ regarding the immediate playing of some Destiny's Child.

Now, though, things were different. I had told Tom a couple of months earlier that I wanted to go freelance. It had been nearly a year now since the miscarriage and nothing had happened. I wanted to make a change, to get a better work-life balance and be more relaxed. He said he would support whatever I wanted. Thanks to his parents' generosity with the flat, we had few financial pressures; we were free to make these choices.

But still, I was bereft. My colleagues and I had the camaraderie of people who spent ten-hour days side by side then went to the pub with each other to dissect them. We were more comfortable in each other's company than flatmates; we had an ease that I had never known with anyone but my family and Tom.

This is the right thing, though, I told myself as I missed them over the coming weeks and months. A baby is the priority now.

I set myself up as a business, writing and – as I failed to get pregnant and depression kicked in – moving further away from that funny, smart woman surrounded by friends in the middle of the dance floor with her hands high in the air. And now, I lie here on my bed, and not for the first time I sob with loss and grief for everything that I was, that I was going to be, and everything that I cannot imagine I can ever be again.

34

Harriet

February

On social media, Tom has posted an old picture of him and Lexie to celebrate their anniversary. In it they are windswept and beautiful on a beach in Scotland. They are joyous, smiling so widely that they have lines around their eyes. But they don't care, because this is happiness, the modern version – see, happiness is not caring that you have crow's feet, even if you have put three filters on your picture and made it black and white.

Tom has added a comment: *Here's to the next fifty years*, it says, smug, unbearable.

How can this be happening? I've been to their flat five times since the first visit. It's easy, once you've crossed the line. And it's odd what can become normal. I think of my months in the hospital: how eventually, it started to feel like home.

When I go to their flat I plant things, take things . . . sometimes I just roam. After I leave, I drop leaflets, play baby cries. But *still*, they seem happy. Tom and Lexie, and their perpetual fucking happiness.

I turn my music up to an unsociable volume just to piss Lexie off and to ruin her anniversary. I set up a new social media account and send a single message to her, mocking her appearance. She blocks the account and then I hear sobbing. Lexie is the thinnest glass, so easy to break if you feel the urge come over you. And I do, actually. Often.

35

Lexie

February

I am on social media, without noticing that I have logged on to social media, and there is a message. I thought the one I had the other day telling me how ugly I was had been upsetting. This, from a girl named Rachel, is worse.

I've been swapping pictures with your boyfriend, it says. *Ask him. Or just ask yourself if he's been acting differently.*

Does this happen? In real life and not just to Z-list celebrities or nineteen-year-olds? Then I realise that I am not dismissing it. Ask yourself if he has been acting differently. I ask. I get an affirmative.

Minutes later, and my brain has taken me to a worse place. Is it, I think, even *just* pictures? I think about the condoms. About the weird feeling that someone has been in the flat. About the fact that somehow, I am burying the moment that I found someone else's underwear in my drawer.

I need to think, through the fog that now makes up my brain. Tom is central to my life and Rachel could be a robot, for all I know.

And yet . . . Things are adding up, they're making sense.

If Tom did this, I think, then I would have to make decisions about my relationship at a time when that relationship is a constant I really need to stay on course. I know how weak it sounds. I know how weak it is.

While I'm online, I read Tom's homage to our anniversary and I scoff. And suddenly weakness is superseded by blind rage. What sort of victim finds someone else's underwear in her drawer and doesn't push it? I accepted his dismissal. I buried it. I vibrate, suddenly, with everything I should have shouted and screamed and emitted, until he had told me the truth.

Tom is still in Sweden and has posted a picture taken when we used to go on spontaneous weekend breaks and talk about life goals and joining the Labour Party and what we could do about global warming and where we might want to eat Thai food next week. A picture from the easy past, delivered from the complicated present.

Before I know what I am doing, I am FaceTiming him.

'Happy anniversary!' he chirps, face giant in my laptop screen.

'Are you cheating on me?' I ask and he laughs, but awkwardly. Adrenaline surges.

'What?'

'That's what people say to these questions when they need to buy time to think, Tom.'

'Or it's what they say when they're confused,' says Tom, sounding a little annoyed. 'Where the fuck has this come from?'

'A girl called Rachel says you've been swapping sex pictures with her. There are knickers in my drawer that aren't mine. The condoms. Sex isn't exactly fun for us at the moment. So I'll ask again. Are you cheating on me?'

In the midst of every ounce of awfulness in this conversation, I am a tiny bit relieved. I thought I was too weak for this; it turns out I'm too angry for anything but this.

And then, our reception goes and Tom cuts out.

I sit on our bed simmering until he calls me back.

'Who the fuck is Rachel?' he says, no pleasantries. 'Send me these messages. I want to see them. Let me speak to her.'

I curse the lack of nuance on FaceTime. Is he red-faced? Are his hands shaking? How can I tell if he's lying to me when I can't reach out and touch him?

He sighs then, though, and he's more real. Nearer to human. He speaks more calmly.

'We can't do this properly over a laptop, Lex, but I promise you, I swear to you, I'm not cheating. I don't know who this girl is but we'll figure it out, okay? She's just some weirdo. I'm not cheating on you. I want you. I want a family with you. I love you.'

I sit silently for a minute.

'Happy anniversary,' he says quietly, but I just say a quiet, emotionless goodbye.

When I turn my laptop off, I realise I am sweating and that now I am late to meet my brother, Kit, who will be waiting for me at King's Cross station.

I see a call flash up from my mum.

Call you back another time, I text, instead of answering. *Just in a rush.*

It's the fifth, sixth time I've done this.

I am too fragile at the moment to cope with the sharp questioning that I've managed all my life from my mum. To brush off the 'Where is your life going?' or the career digs. I am too emotional to deal with the pragmatic nature of my dad.

I can hear him now, if I ever did tell him I was struggling to get pregnant.

'Well that's just the world,' he would say. 'If it's not meant to happen, it's not meant to happen. There's no point wallowing in it.'

The world is divided in two now, I think on the bus. There are the people I can enjoy being around and the ones who I cannot.

The first lot aren't necessarily my closest friends. The second lot aren't necessarily people I don't adore in other circumstances.

143

But the first category have soft edges and I never suspect that after we have spoken, they will say something cutting about me.

In the same way, I cannot appreciate sharpness or laugh at cruel wit. Last week in a coffee shop I saw a former colleague, Liv, who works for herself now, too.

'Stay for a latte!' she said, hugging me tight. 'On me. Let's catch up. Freelancer club.'

My heart was hammering. Liv is bitchy, sharp. I'd be expected to keep up and to participate, and that was too much. I made excuses and fled, clutching my coffee like a fire alarm had gone off.

Give me the soft people, though, and I will squidge up against them.

My brother has always been one of the soft people. Kit is thirty-six, married to Lucy, and three years ago they had Noah. His disastrous love life might have been a joke to a lot of people before that but not to me. My heart broke every time his did, because all that my brother has wanted, since he was twelve and overweight and bullied, is kindness and love.

'I just want a child of my own to tickle on the belly until they shriek,' he told me, drunk, late one night after a break-up with a long-term girlfriend. 'I just want to eat tuna bloody pasta with someone I love.'

At the time I couldn't fathom these tiny ambitions, as I threw everything into work. Now, I get it. These ambitions: they aren't small at all.

I don't resent Kit, despite him having a child, because he is so deeply entrenched in my team.

Luce is going away next weekend, his text said. *Noah and me thought we might come and stay?*

Kit's company, I think, as I stand at King's Cross waiting for them, is like a human cookie. He slows my breathing; he is like my head being stroked gently as I snooze. I need this now. I need this right now.

'*Auntie Lexie*!' says a tiny voice from the other end of the platform and Noah is running, Kit following closely behind with a bag falling off his shoulder and being shrugged back on with every step.

'Noah, hold my hand!'

They are a car crash. The happiest car crash you could see.

'Slow down!'

The other passengers are looking. I'm looking, proud.

'Noah, there are train tracks here! Noah!'

Noah lands in my arms, so warm despite the cold day, and I heave him up into the air.

'Are you still my best friend?' he asks.

'Absolutely,' I say into his ear as someone slams into my calf with a wheelie case. I wince.

Noah wriggles down too soon, like always, when I want the cuddle to last fifteen, twenty times longer. I am still inhaling him when he moves.

Kit catches up and engulfs me in a bear hug.

He's still massive; just now, his height has caught up with his belly and the smile on his face says he couldn't care less.

'You okay?' he whispers, one of each of our hands holding Noah's, and my eyes fill, as I knew they would, with tears.

He's walking love, delivered to me on the train when I'm at my weakest, and now I am crying into his chest so that Noah, hand tight in mine, cannot see.

'Everyone is pregnant,' I sob. Oh, the relief not to hold back what I'm feeling, his brotherly role secure whatever awfulness I throw his way. 'I'm still not pregnant and it's not fair. And I think Tom is cheating on me.'

He keeps me close, squeezed between his bulk and Noah's tininess, and I am spirited into a cab, into my sparse, familiar building, upstairs in the lift and onto my sofa, a pizza delivery following closely behind without me even knowing when or how it was ordered. Right now, I want to live in Kit's spare room in Yorkshire forever, where he will bring me tea and Noah will cuddle me, and everyone will have their soft edges.

Later, Noah is on a makeshift bed made of pillows in my bedroom, and Kit and I have glasses filled to the rims with Merlot. Kit is of the belief that a wine glass filled one third full could only ever be a sign of pretentiousness, because what other reason could there be to top your glass up three times when you could just do it once?

An empty pizza box lies on the floor. From nowhere, there appears to be a pack of Hobnobs. My stress levels have reduced by around 40 per cent in the last hour. 'Thank you,' I say. 'I needed this.'

'But Tom's not cheating on you? Not really?' he says, knowing Tom, trusting Tom.

'I don't think so,' I reply honestly. 'But I don't know. There are so many weird things, and I never seem to know what's reality and what's in my head. I don't trust my own judgement any more.'

I tell him about Rachel. Then about the knickers, the anecdote making me flush red.

'He is so adamant that they are nothing to do with him that I feel like I can't doubt it, but at the same time, where the hell did they come from? He says they must be old ones of mine, but I swear, I never owned those. Maybe I'm going insane.'

'Have you talked to Mum and Dad?' he asks. 'Not about the knickers. About fertility stuff. Tom.'

'No,' I say, defensive. 'I can't burden them. They're a long way away, they'd feel helpless.'

Plus, there are financial worries, a house here in the UK that won't sell, a retirement fund that really needs it to. They don't need this.

'I know what they're like,' says Kit thoughtfully, 'But if it was Noah, I wouldn't give a shit if I had no money and I was begging on the streets; if he was sad, I would want to know. And it was okay, wasn't it? The last time you saw them?'

I raise an eyebrow.

Last Christmas, Kit was at his in-laws and Mum and Dad spent it with Tom and me.

It is no exaggeration to say that I spent about 50 per cent of December on Project Proving to My Mum I am Doing Okay. I might not have a staff job or a baby or a wedding certificate, but I had Christmas-baked goods, grown-up tree decorations. I had presents wrapped with bloody ribbons in a tasteful colour scheme.

I messaged her, a day before they were due to fly over.

Got your room ready! I said. *I'm excited.*

I don't often admit an emotion to my mum but it was true – I was excited. This was new, a fresh stage for us, and maybe this was the one we would excel at. Real adults, doing real Christmas.

A reply pinged in.

Oh don't worry, darling, we're staying in the hotel, she said. *Sorry, thought I mentioned.*

I was a bit gutted but hey, I could definitely live with the space – except then I noticed the pronoun.

THE hotel? I replied. *What hotel?*

The one we're eating Christmas dinner at, she messaged back. *That we booked back in September.*

I never told her that I had thought I was cooking. That I had thought we would be peeling potatoes together while Wham played on the radio. That I had thought we could get drunk on Prosecco while we watched crap Christmas TV in our slippers after we'd stuffed our faces with mince pies.

Instead, I just cried, quietly, to Tom, who didn't understand why it mattered so much.

'We haven't bought much stuff,' he said. 'We haven't got the turkey.'

'But *other people's* families get to do this,' I muffled into his jumper. 'I don't get any of it, all year, any year, and just once I

147

thought it would be like normal family stuff. Except that I would be the grown-up.'

I had really, really wanted to be the grown-up.

In the end, my parents arrived and we ate meals together, pulled restaurant crackers, met up at the cinema to watch Christmas movies. We dragged them to an ice rink. But then we said polite goodbyes. Nobody fell asleep with a paper hat on their head. No one got angry over the bids for Bond Street in Monopoly. We simply met up again the next morning, ordered eggs and avocado, made more small talk.

I had wanted my parents – living abroad the rest of the time – to be in *my* home. Just to *be*. I had wanted them to check the gravy with me, and congratulate me on my stuffing, and drink a Baileys on my sofa, and get up in the morning in their pyjamas. I had wanted to lend them shower gel and towels and to make their beds. I had wanted something more real than the hotels that we stayed in when we visited them. I had wanted this to be the new normal.

But Kit was right. It had been *okay* when I last saw them. Digs about my job and my life choices had been there but they'd been fairly minimal. Nobody fell out. The hotel turkey was moist.

'Yeah,' I sigh. 'It was okay.'

'I can't sleep,' says a tiny voice from behind the door. 'It's very noisy in London. Can I have a biscuit?'

And I let him under the blanket while Kit tells him not to tell his mum about the late-night Hobnob.

36

Harriet

February

I have been laid face down on my bed, sobbing, for an hour now. Nothing is more likely to do this to me than the closeness of a sister with her brother.

Lexie, I know from a social media post, has her brother to stay in her flat. They speak in quiet, companionable voices that mean I cannot catch a word, but their laughter comes through with the sounds of a little boy, giggling too and shrieking.

I think of David and how he never came to visit me in the UK until he picked me up from a police station. I think of him moving in with somebody called Sadie and if they will have a baby. If it happens, will I know that child? Will I love it? Will I tickle its little belly after I change its diaper? I think about reaching out to my brother and how much I miss him, but it feels too late now, like it is impossible to come back from.

The sobs are overwhelming me and they are not, as people often say they do, making things feel better. I am not purging, I am cultivating. I click on David's Facebook page, where he is living his life with friends I don't know, sporting facial hair I don't recognise and espousing political beliefs that I didn't know he had. There are now people in his life who are so periphery and yet, are closer than me. Meanwhile, Lexie sits back and wins, yet again, laughing with a brother who is tangible and real and sitting on her sofa.

The worst thing is that it is my own fault. Despite their horror at what I did, my family tried to keep me in their life. When I finally allowed David to tell them what had happened, my parents – never before having left the US – sorted out passports and travelled all the way over to see me in hospital.

They walked in as I lay prone on my bed, staring at the ceiling. I had no phone to browse, no comb to brush my hair. I couldn't be trusted with even such innocent items.

The door pushed open.

While Mom rushed to me, Dad held back. When I refused to put my arms around Mom and carried on staring in silence, she returned to him looking confused, shaken.

'It's your fault,' I said when I finally spoke. Not how are you, not how was the flight.

I hissed a chasm between us.

'All of this. Look what you did.'

The family who had come thousands of miles to see me and love me didn't mean anything; all I wanted was Luke.

They were silent, utterly shocked.

'You never liked him. Luke never felt like he could be part of our family. That's why he left me. Now look what's happened.'

'Harriet, you can't blame . . .' began my dad, wide-eyed and pale at my response and at this environment that none of us had ever thought we would find ourselves in.

'We just want to help,' interrupted my mom, softly, with a hand on his arm.

I knew she was trying to bring the whole conversation down a level, to calm a hysterical toddler.

'Why?' I snarled, looking up and meeting her eye for the first time. 'You sabotaged my life. You pushed Luke out. No wonder we had to move abroad in the first place.'

They stood, framed in the doorway. A moment passed. My dad, I saw, still taking in the room in its starkness and its lack. My mom failing to blink away tears.

'You abandoned me,' I continued, eyes back on the ceiling. 'Now I'm abandoning you.'

They left then but tried to visit again every day they were in the country. I refused, repeatedly, to see them. Their return ticket delivered them back to the States two weeks later.

Towards David, I was a little gentler. My brother had decided to stay in England for longer, with some mates who were here on a gap year.

David was always my Achilles heel and made me comprehend what people felt when they talked about having your own child. I'd jump in front of a bus for David. So I let him visit.

He sat alongside my bed every day, before he went to a gig or a pub or a party. Sometimes I was silent; sometimes we would chat. Music, TV, mutual friends.

Then one day, a few weeks after I was admitted, he moved from his usual chair, sat on my hospital bed and took my hand in his. He thought I had had enough drugs and therapy to be spoken to more honestly. I steeled myself.

'I know you were heartbroken about Luke,' he said gently. 'But can you try to explain to me what happened? I just can't believe you're capable of *doing that* to somebody.'

I couldn't face a lifetime of knowing that David was disgusted by me. So I attacked, pushed away.

'I don't know why you care,' I sniped as a nurse handed me some meds. 'You hated Luke anyway.'

He looked shocked.

'For starters, I didn't hate Luke,' he said. 'I don't know where you got that from.'

I raised a sulky, weak eyebrow. Luke had told me. It had to be true.

'But anyway, that's kind of beside the point.'

'I'd like you to leave now,' I said and turned away from his kiss goodbye.

After that I refused his visits and David, needing to return to work, flew back to the US. When I came out of the hospital, I kept our contact minimal.

We exchanged the basics – work's fine, life's fine, fine, fine, fine. But compared to where we were before, I let a ravine form between us and he, I think, found the whole thing so bewildering that eventually, it was a relief to let it happen.

With my parents, I was even more extreme. There were phone calls to the hospital and later, when I got out, emails, but I was stoic in my coldness.

Then a letter arrived.

We won't give up, Harriet. You're our daughter. We will give you time to calm down but in a month or so we are coming over, or we're flying you home.

I considered calling them so many times, to say sorry and to explain and to say yes, yes, yes, please bring me home. Look after me. Feed me chicken soup. I looked at flight prices myself, thinking it may be better to try to explain in person. If I went all that way, they would know then that I was remorseful, good. But in the end, I was too ashamed. How could I explain to people who had invested years in raising me, teaching me morals and how to live, why I had done that to another human? And how could I take back everything I had hurled at them? How would we recover?

I thought of David's speech to me, adult suddenly and superior.

And I knew I couldn't be told off again, eye to eye, by someone who I adored. It was better just to let them go.

I wrote back.

152

Do not contact me. Do not visit me. I've moved flats now anyway, so you would have a wasted journey.

Lies, harshness, whatever was required to make sure I didn't have to answer to those faces who loved me so very much.

37

Lexie

February

I have been thinking about speaking to my mum and dad about my fertility issues since Kit brought it up. But they FaceTime before I get chance to call them.

'Have you got a job yet?' my mum asks.

There are minimal pleasantries, no chit-chat. My mum has little patience for small talk. She allocates that to my dad, who's only marginally better at it than she is. Sometimes I genuinely believe she comes to the phone armed with a list of bullet points.

'Yes. The freelance one. My job. That's my job.'

She points out that I am wearing pyjamas and it is midday and that there is no real job you can do in which that is acceptable. I start explaining bloggers, influencers, coders and how actually the world is being run in pyjamas, but she is glazing over.

'You're in your *thirties*, Lexie,' she says. 'It's been ages now since you left the other job.'

'Yes, but I left it to do this job. This isn't the in-between job. It's the *new* job.'

She starts talking about pensions and healthcare.

'If you have children, you'll need more security. And you'll barely get any maternity pay.'

Silence. Is it more awkward or less when you can see each other's faces?

I crack first.

'Well, I'm not pregnant. So maternity pay isn't an issue for me.'

It's not something I hadn't gone over the impact of losing. But in the end the financial security came second to my sanity.

'Yes, not *now*,' she pokes. 'But maybe one day. Is that in the pipeline? Something you and Tom talk about?'

She says it hurriedly, like she can rush conception along if she just speaks a bit faster. Save me some time since I seem to be squandering so much of it. I consider telling her I think Tom is cheating on me, just to change the conversation, but I don't have room in my head for her thoughts. I don't have the brain-power to balance out making her not hate Tom, but not blame me, either – not get defensive, not become overwhelmed and distraught.

I don't trust myself to speak. I realise that she wouldn't think my fertility was an issue because she presumes I would tell her if it was. But I don't believe that's an excuse for storming any conversation in your boots and leaping around, stamping. People should take more care with others' hearts, especially the ones that belong to their own children.

It spirals, then, because I don't do anything to stop it. Mum quotes a piece she read the other day about fertility versus careers. I barely have a career to prioritise, we've just established that. So now we are clear: I have no children and I have no career. I have nothing. Except for a fake pie, which I tell her needs to come out of the oven before biting my lip through goodbyes.

I cry for a good few minutes when we end the call before I decide to try to run it off; although the tears keep flowing even as I jog. Is that *normal*, to run and cry at the same time? No one seems to look at me. Maybe they just think it's sweat, streaming down my face. Or maybe half the people out there are running to chase away today's sadness.

The tears are finally starting to dry up and I am heaving my way around the park to a cheesy dance track, when a No Caller ID pops up on my phone and I answer in case it's some much-needed work. Perhaps even a *real* job. Or at least someone offering me a bloody pension.

I am leaning up against the wall of a Thai restaurant, inhaling shots of lemongrass in swift, sharp breaths as they speak.

'It's the nurse from the reproductive medicine unit,' she says. 'Confirming your appointment for an ultrasound tomorrow.'

My breath speeds up and my heart races like I've just powered into a sprint.

What?

This is the first I've heard of any appointment and I panic. Did I miss a letter? A call? There isn't a chance in hell that I would have and yet this is what I do: I focus instantly on how it could have been my fault.

I always presume that over a belief that it could be down to anyone else. If I sat back to analyse that, it would say some terrible things about my self-esteem.

'I didn't get the letter,' I say, panic rising in my voice as my breathing gets even shallower. The lemongrass suddenly makes me gag. 'But yes, I'll be there. What time? Where? I'm so sorry.'

I'm babbling now, imagining what would have happened if they'd never called, whether I would have been blacklisted forever and never had a baby, all because of my own idiocy, even though there was no idiocy, but, somehow, still, my brain is saying there probably *was* idiocy.

I go home to calm myself and get an early night before tomorrow. A date that is now not another non-event Wednesday but a major marker – the start of something huge.

But sitting on the sofa in a towel with a herbal tea cupped in my palm, I feel sick.

Because what I didn't tell Tom, when we decided to go to the doctors, was that I was already in the system. That a few months ago, frustrated by Tom's refusal to get help, I had booked an appointment with the GP to tell her that I was having trouble getting pregnant. Tom wasn't ready, but I was so very ready, and I did it on an angry whim, knowing the whole process would be long and drawn-out anyway.

I had blood tests and checks – all clear – and I was referred for more detailed investigations. Warned there would be quite a wait. I felt proven right: all I had done was get us a head start, so that when Tom was ready, we had skipped a stage.

I planned to tell him when the letter came and we had moved up the queue. Now, with the letter never arriving, the news was too late and too fast.

There is no option for cancelling – or of Tom getting here in time – so the only option is to go alone and deal later with admitting that I had gone behind his back. As he had gone behind mine recently, too?

The next day I leave a ridiculous amount of time to travel the twenty minutes to the hospital and despite my guilt, I feel good. Finally, I get to nail this, to be proactive, the definition of which is to act, not to stay stagnant, waiting, complaining but doing nothing. I have done far too much of that.

At the hospital I am in a frenzy writing lists, replying to emails, sorting the nights out I have planned, and I think I look happier than the other women in the room, heads buried in phones, Kindles or simply staring at walls where there are statistics I am trying to avoid looking at.

This won't be me, I think, disassociating from what I cannot stop thinking of in my head as Fertility Club and pulling out a Tana French with enough raging Irish crime in it to distract me. I'm always grateful when I'm reading the right book for the moment I am in; this is one of those times.

Because what is happening here is a blip, not a long-term problem, and I'm on the way to sorting it. I am not in Fertility Club. I'm a bystander. A visitor. They'll find a small, surmountable problem and then they'll fix it.

Except, they don't. When I have my ultrasound, there is no obvious problem. No reason why I haven't got pregnant again in the two years since our miscarriage. Instead, there is a whole load of nothing.

'That's *good* news,' says the doctor, smiling gently at me, and I smile back, politely.

'Is it, though?' I ask her inside my head. Because it feels like an anticlimax. Because without a problem, how is there a solution? Do we go back to just trying and failing, trying and failing? And because despite trying not to look, I saw that chart in the waiting room with its big 'unexplained infertility' chunk of pie. No problem is still a problem and it's a harder one – surely – to fix.

'Let's get you booked in for a follow-up appointment to discuss what's next,' the doctor says to me and I nod, try to look enthusiastic.

In the hours between that news and Tom's key going in the door, I become bleaker and bleaker, picturing a life that awaits me without children. I hear Harriet opening doors and walking across the floor and playing the piano and being fine.

Harriet hasn't been for an ultrasound today. Life is strolling along nicely for her. It's okay for you, Harriet, I think, feeling that out-of-body rage towards this almost anonymous recipient again. It's all so fucking okay for you.

38

Harriet

When Tom first got home, I could hear anger, despite Lexie and him having been apart for weeks. I knew he was coming back today from a social media picture of a beer he was drinking at the airport, so I cancelled my meetings, staying in and composing. Composing is a fake verb. The real verb was waiting.

At 5 p.m., Lexie opened the door and that was when the voices became raised; though they quickly subsided and then I could hear Lexie crying, the sort that says someone is inconsolable, like the cries I had in the days and weeks after breaking up with Luke.

But then I could hear the gentleness in Tom's voice and the effect of whatever had caused the row earlier seemed to have dissipated. It pissed me off. Was that it? Instant forgiveness? When I, who had never picked fights, flattered Luke, didn't criticise, had my life ruined out of the blue one day? Ended up not only alone, but also contained, in a bed in a psychiatric hospital? The universe is unbalanced. Sometimes all I want is just to balance it out.

I consider my tactics carefully then and check my emails, just in case. But the one that makes my stomach lurch doesn't do it in a good way.

My mom writes:

Harriet, now I'm even more worried. Please, get in touch.

And that irritates me, too. Because why is it my responsibility to make her feel better? Who's making *me* feel better? If I reply to that message, how does this work? She feels relief, gets on with her life and, meanwhile, nothing changes in mine – I'm still without Luke, without Tom.

But maybe I don't have to be without Tom. I can see, realistically, that it will be difficult to find a way back for me and Luke, but the more the relationship between Tom and me develops, the more I can see how I could move on. Tom is the fresh slate I've needed. The future hangs on Tom. With just one obstacle to shift out of the way.

Now, I am so fixated that I can't work or sleep. I just roam around the flat listening for clues. On Sunday, I sent Tom another topless picture. On Monday, I went to a club on my own and got thrown out for being too drunk. I don't remember writing it, but my phone tells me that I sent Tom a long and graphic email about the life-changing sex he was missing out on by not meeting up with me, Rachel.

Now, I hear him go out and I follow him to the bookshop.

My stomach contracts as I watch through the window and see Tom browsing the shelves. Sure, we are having a tricky stage with this Rachel thing, but he doesn't know that I am her. We can start again; I can disown Rachel, ghost her like a boring school friend, and make this work.

Tom and Lexie are drifting apart and there is room in the gap for me to slip in between.

Tom can make me better, introduce me to his friends, take me to his places and build me a life. I've let it happen before; I can let it happen again. We could pick up from where Luke and I left off.

I go home, pour myself a drink and grab the iPad.

I'll delete the messages, I write to him. *If you meet me for a drink.* Send.

The next day, I let myself in for a morning browse at Tom and Lexie's. A special treat after I watch them go out for breakfast. Top of my list is Tom's strange old-school diary and he's left me a gift: a new entry.

Lexie isn't the only one who woke up that morning in Sweden with self-loathing. The aperitif, the wine, the special whisky someone ordered that I had to try despite loathing whisky . . . I was almost as drunk as she was. I just had the moral high ground of the person who is slightly less drunk than the drunkest person.

Funny, Tom, funny.

But I was annoyed. I want Lexie and me to be in this together; I don't want us to become people who shout at each other in the street at 1 a.m. I felt angry that she'd made us that couple. And I felt sad about the miscarriage and gutted that Anais had got there first too, actually.

My heart races because in the next paragraph, I see the word Rachel.

Which is the only reason I would ever, ever have become a cliché like this. I knew Rachel *was flirting and I didn't stop it. I even lamely, drunkenly, tried to join in.*

But what I did think is that it would pass into the history of stupid things, and I would in time forgive myself and forget about it. But she's back, sending photos of her breasts and telling Lexie that I'm cheating with her.

I am all over this flat now – I can feel myself. I am Rachel, in the diary, I am in the condoms that now live in Tom's drawer, and in the pretty knickers that I was *almost* tempted to keep for myself after I bought them. I am in Lexie's tears, when she read that nasty tweet on her anniversary. I am everywhere, everywhere, crawling all over their broken life. And I won't stop. I want to break it further. I want to stamp it into tiny pieces. I have experience, after all, of doing exactly that.

39

Lexie

February

Tom has his head in his hand on the sofa and I am sitting barefoot on the floor with my knees to my chest, and we are spent.

'We should eat,' I say.

Tom looks up, sighs and nods.

'That sounds good,' he says with a tentative smile, because as soon as I told him what the doctors had said, his anger subsided.

This was bigger than me going behind his back. Bigger even than Rachel; than unknown underwear.

When Tom walked in, bag slung over his shoulder, I couldn't hide it.

Tom, at first, worried about my tears and holding me, but as I told him he zoomed in on one very crucial part: that I had gone to the doctor to start discussions about our potential family without him, the potential father. Understandable.

'But I was moving forwards,' he said, hurt. 'I had been to get tested myself.'

'I know,' I sobbed. 'But I didn't know that *then*. When I went to the doctor. Months ago when we had had a row and I was frustrated. I just needed to *do* something.'

I tried to talk more over my tears but it was difficult because my head was so foggy from crying.

'I am trying to understand,' he said. 'But it's hard because I wasn't there, I didn't hear exactly what they said and I don't know what tests they did because you didn't invite me. To the appointments to discuss our family, our baby. You didn't even tell me it was happening.'

The hardest thing was that he sounded less angry and more devastated. And that he still hugged me, knowing I depended on it. And that in the midst of this – which was so vast in itself – we still had the other thing to deal with. I felt exhausted, spent.

I'd messed up and I knew it, but my own pain was too great to be magnanimous and apologise. Instead, like in Sweden, it all went into hot, brutal anger.

'You wouldn't have cared, Tom,' I snarked, shrugging out of the hug I still desperately wanted to be in. 'There would have been a trip to be on, or some work to finish, or some pictures to send to some woman. And way, way down the pile, the appointment. I didn't want to put you out.'

And out I stomped from the living room to the kitchen, where I stayed, tucked into a ball against the dishwasher, for an hour. In the meantime Tom, too, retreated. He went out, came back, had a shower. Stayed in the bedroom for a while.

And then he walked into the kitchen like it was normal that I was there on the floor and awkwardly got down there himself, putting his arm around me as I sobbed with relief that he hadn't gone away any more.

'I didn't send any pictures,' he said quietly, no rage. 'Let's deal with the rest, but can we at least get rid of that worry. There is no other woman. There's only me and you and a baby we really want.'

Later in bed, we talked into the early hours about exactly what the doctor had said and what there was to try. When the letter comes through, we'll go for the follow-up appointment. Together.

We'll be proactive. It will be hard to unpick the reasons why

I got pregnant once and never again, but fixing it isn't impossible. In the end, the exhaustion of sadness sends me to sleep until I wake at 4 a.m. and feel my eyes hurt, and I remember, horribly, why.

40

Harriet

I waited three days after Luke moved out for *anything* more than the texts he would send occasionally, replying to mine.

How was your day? I messaged, clawing for contact.

Fine, he would say. No questions. Nothing to open up a conversation.

You forgot your White Stripes T-shirt.

Keep it, he replied.

They were worse than nothing. There was gravitas in nothing but in those texts, I was reduced to perfunctory and I couldn't bear the idea of becoming a life footnote.

And for those three days, too, I was hit with the realisation that when everything was bleak, no one came. I hadn't told my family. How could I admit to them what had happened when they would think it confirmed their view of Luke? I needed to protect him.

As for friends, they were in inverted commas. They were in the US or they were Luke's friends anyway. Certainly, there was no one close enough to come round to my house with wine or cupcakes or whatever girls brought one another in those situations, and that realisation slammed me in the face, as well. I drank and I scrolled social media day and night, taunting myself with what Luke was doing.

How could he be at a party? How could he drink beer and pose for selfies?

I begged him, over endless messages, not to go. I begged him to come to me instead.

The ticks came up, the messages were read. But Luke stayed quiet. I thought – I knew – that slowly I was going insane.

The difference in how we dealt with the break-up meant the crushing confirmation that his life was better than mine and kept turning even without me in it, whereas mine ground, ground, ground to a halt. He had a choice. He could go out or stay in, take the photo or not take the photo, open the beer bottle, be an active person in the world.

Anyone would look at him and think that he mustn't have cared about me because if he did, how could he be there? I was embarrassed and angry that those friends who I always felt laughed at me could still be in his life when I couldn't, despite all that effort I had made. *They* should be the footnotes. And I was overtaken with the knowledge that now he could sleep with any of them, any time, and my skin felt like it crawled with the constant wondering. Was he doing it now? Tonight? This morning?

How was any of this fair, I thought, after everything I have managed and accepted, and all the work I did to be good enough? And the injustice propelled me round to his friend's flat, drunk by then, mostly on alcohol left behind by Luke. His stuff was still at our place too, so that while he could bask in the anonymity of a friend's spare room, I walked around stepping over trainers, glimpsing a photo we had taken in the Peak District, moving his mayonnaise to one side in the fridge.

I only had to open a kitchen cupboard and there were things I didn't eat, only Luke, or to go into the bathroom to see a plug blocked with his hair, or find a can of his deodorant. He had left me with all of this. It was an act of such supreme cruelty that it could take my breath away every ten seconds, and that's what I went to tell him, for once. Now, what did I have to lose? But Luke didn't answer his phone and I needed him to know he had to take his stuff, now, get it out, get out, so I could breathe.

I banged on the door and he wasn't there and that angered me more. Finally, at 11.30 p.m., he arrived back with the friend he was living with, a guy who had previously been my friend, too, and who now couldn't look me in the eye as I sat on the doorstep, shivering and with something approaching a hangover in a T-shirt I had slept in for three nights.

'I'll see you in there, mate,' his friend said to Luke, a sympathetic hand on his shoulder.

I looked at that hand, envied it. While I might have struggled with friendships, Luke – able to be that charming, smart version of himself that he'd been in our early days – made friends easily.

'Well, there's my first question answered,' I said, my neck craning up at him as the start of a rain shower dripped onto my espadrilles. 'Yes, you are okay.'

We continued the conversation back at our flat because it was more private. Despite it all, I felt excited as soon as he came in through the door because he was a presence in our home again and that was right. I felt, oddly enough, like I might even be able to sleep if he would promise not to leave until I woke.

As Luke sat down on the sofa and moved aside a chocolate wrapper, his eyes rested for a split second on the bottle of amaretto, emptied out now, in the wastepaper bin. I flushed. He did his drinking with friends, at parties, talking. I did mine alone, at home, weeping. Never had the divide between us been so obvious.

Still, I felt suddenly calmer because he was here and so he couldn't be elsewhere. I didn't have to think about him and wonder what he was doing. Was this how parents felt when their children are sleeping upstairs safely, versus when they are out there in the world and there's a relentless low-level anxiety?

'Harriet, what is there to talk about?' he said, sighing impatiently. 'This is getting tedious. You break up, you go out, you get drunk. You spend time with friends. I'm just doing what normal people do.'

He said it all pointedly, the subtext being what he had told me many, many times: that I had no friends, that I wasn't normal.

'Please don't leave me here on my own in a country I'm not even from without you,' I sobbed. 'I have no one.'

I kissed him then, which I'm not proud of, and in the end we had the most terrible sex. Sex I knew the next day that I'd kissed him into, but similarly that he shouldn't have participated in by taking advantage of my state – and that felt layered with every shade of awfulness.

I lay there at 5 a.m., awake, savouring him being there because I knew he wouldn't be again but hating how different it felt, and when he left it was awful all over again.

Something stuck in my mind that someone I worked with once had told another colleague.

'If you want him back, you've got to look as if you're not a mess and pretend you feel amazing,' she said. So I did.

A couple of days later, I got dressed, put on more make-up than I'd ever worn, tried to carry off heels and went to his office. I phoned him from outside and when I saw his face, I felt such internal self-loathing that it was physical. My chest ached and my lips went dry.

'Harriet, what are you doing here?' he snarled, guiding me away, ashamed, when I should have been the one who could turn up at his work because I was the central person in his life.

We ended up in a side street. My feet hurt. I suspected the left one was bleeding.

'I needed to see you,' I said, smiling the unhappiest smile there is, the one of a desperate person trying to make someone believe they are joyous.

'But you can't come to my work!' he shouted, disbelieving, alarmed.

169

'Well, I didn't want to come to your work,' I explained. 'But at night I know you'll be at the pub.'

'You could have texted me. Called me. Arranged to meet up with me.'

He was right. I couldn't quite remember why I hadn't done that. I was severely sleep-deprived. And slightly drunk.

'Oh!' I said, suddenly remembering. I rustled around in my bag. 'I brought your post,' I grinned, holding my haul out victoriously.

Anyone could see that most of it was junk but technically, *technically*, it was his post and I needed to give it to him. This visit was crucial.

He took it out of my hands.

'Couldn't you just . . . forward it?' he said, biting his lip. It was an expression – nervousness – that I had never seen him exhibit towards me. 'I gave you the address.'

I stared at his nerves, mesmerised.

'Oh sure, but I was passing,' I said in my best breezy voice, despite the fact I was hopping from foot to foot.

He glanced down at my shoes.

'Harriet, you can't do this again, you know? I have a meeting. I was in a meeting.'

'Oh, I'm so sorry!' I said with a high-pitched laugh. 'Noted. Point noted. But we can still be mates, right? I'll maybe drop round to the flat in a few days if work's not suitable. As mates?'

He didn't say anything, just backed away into his building.

Then he stopped dead, a few metres away from me, and turned around.

'Harriet, are you . . . going somewhere?' he asked cautiously.

Caution! From Luke. I was transfixed, again.

'Yes,' I laughed. A laugh as sad as the sad smile. 'To surprise my fiancé at work.'

41

Lexie

February

Tom and I are in one of those situations where you feel like you're playing a part, saying your lines, doing an impression of yourself.

'So, depending on your postcode, you would be entitled to either one, two or three rounds of IVF,' says the consultant, matter-of-fact, flicking between sheets of paper. 'We'll check that in a minute.'

I'm thinking about my twenties, all those nights out, drinking buckets of wine, laughing, and how this is a different world.

Those people couldn't know me now; couldn't know this. Unless they were going through things like this, too? Was everyone dealing with real events and we were all just glossing over it with flippant jokes in too-loud bars? How did I not realise that was what the world really was?

'But for now, we will try a drug called Clomid. It might just help to kick-start things for you.'

But I'm already thinking about my bank account and how much is in it, and how much IVF it could buy if this Clomid doesn't work and we need more rounds than the NHS can give us. It couldn't buy much IVF. I'm thinking about Anais and her free, accidental baby. I'm thinking about conversations I had with my parents when I was nineteen and I brazenly told them I didn't want kids. I'm thinking about years of contraceptive pills and what a fucking waste of time they were.

I'm thinking about fifteen things at once, anything but this, and I need to focus. The consultant is handing me a prescription but I can't make out the words.

'I'll make you an appointment for a few months' time,' she says. 'Then if the Clomid hasn't worked, we can talk about what comes next.'

I'm drowning. A few months' time? If nothing's worked by then, surely I'll have sunk without trace.

But Tom is being our rational arm, literally with his hand held out. He's shaking the consultant's hand, thanking her and ushering me out into a blast of cold air. I'm shocked by it and it takes me a second to remember that it's February.

When we have picked up the prescription, we go to a coffee shop.

'Well,' says Tom, being Tom. 'That was positive.'

I'm silent with the shock and it takes me five minutes to respond.

'What if we can't have kids?' I say, holding my hot chocolate with two hands but not drinking. I'm shaking with hunger but nauseous.

Tom downs his espresso.

'There's no reason why we can't,' he says. 'The doctor said that. It's just that we are struggling to get pregnant again naturally, but with Clomid, or if that doesn't work, these two rounds of IVF . . .'

My brain is everywhere again. I'm thinking of famous couples who are in their forties without kids, friends of my parents who have lots of dogs but no children. I had assumed it was a lifestyle choice, but is this what happened to them? Is that sometimes where this path concludes?

'With all of that we stand a better chance,' I say. 'But for some people it just *never* works. And we only get two chances of IVF. What if neither works? Then what?'

'You're doing that thing again,' says Tom. 'You've even quoted it at me. You're catastrophising.'

'I can't see Anais,' I say suddenly, panicked. 'I cannot see Anais. I can't go to her catch-up dinner.'

Everyone else, again.

What does everyone else matter here?

And yet they do, don't they, they always do.

An Instagram post with a scan picture matters, even though it could be sent from a home of misery and rage.

A 'baby on board' badge on the tube matters, even though it could have come after ten rounds of IVF and many more miscarriages than I have had.

I don't know how to live among all of that.

Pretending? Acting? Hiding? Acknowledging? I don't know which verbs to choose. I don't know how this works.

Tom looks at me and I'm back in the room; back in our conversation.

'Forget about the dinner with Anais. You're leaping. We can ditch the dinner.'

But then my mind is running away again.

Was it easier before social media? Or did envy poison anyway? It just came at you via a different route.

Tom has taken hold of my shoulders and I think, honestly, at this moment, I believe, he is breathing for me.

'One step at a time,' he says.

I catch a woman in the corner looking over at me from her laptop with pain au raisin crumbs on her chin and I have the same feeling that I had about Harriet the other day: it's okay for you. It's so absolutely okay for you.

I don't have the energy to get up and walk out and Tom, my partner, almost has to carry me. I have no choice but to believe him when it comes to Rachel. There is no space in my head to doubt Tom right now. No space to deal with anything else. No potential to deal with this alone. No possibility, at this moment, of being able to carry myself.

42

Harriet

After I visited Luke at work, I felt euphoric. We had spent time together and although – of course – it wasn't perfect, I had loved seeing his face, being in his life, taking up a segment of his day, so that when his hours were assessed in his subconscious at the end of the evening, I was there. I had a role.

I texted regularly, trying to observe the rule that I'd heard from the girl at work. I was good, I was fine, I was happy. It was a mantra. I texted pretending I was at a gig I thought he'd like – I'd Google what was on and check reviews – or about items of his I'd found in the flat.

I had spent so many years trying to please Luke that I was a professional. I had tricks, ideas, skills and I put them all to use. But this time, they didn't work.

I'd gone past wanting his things to go away; now, I wanted them to stay forever, because how could he ignore me then? I had his parts. I slept with his pyjamas still in the bed and sprayed his deodorant every morning. I watched TV programmes he was into, so I could message about them. Before they would have been passes, ticking his boxes. Now, he was barely interested. I was no longer being assessed; he didn't care what I did.

And then, the killer blow.

I'm going to come round on Saturday to collect my stuff. Mate's got a van.

I lied and said I was out, but the next time he was insistent.

We need a clean break. I'm coming over at 2 p.m. If you're out, make sure you leave the key in the old place.

This was boxing practice and I was floppy now from the pummelling.

I cried then. It lasted for a long time.

When Luke did come to collect his things, he brought a buffer in the form of his mate Stu, owner of the van and avoider of my eyes. I shuffled around awkwardly, pointing out obvious piles of Luke's things that no one needed pointing out and perching on the side of the sofa, wondering what specific movement I would have to do to make Luke miss me.

'Did you get the spice mix from Morocco out of the cupboard?' I said, hopping up, and Luke, now Stu's fellow avoider of my eye contact, shook his head.

'You cook more than me, you might as well have it,' I pressed.

I knew that without Luke, a life of grilled cheese awaited me. The liveners in our life, from the nights out to the spices, all came from Luke.

'It's fine, you have it.'

'I think I have some printouts of photos of Portugal if you want them?' I said.

'Keep them,' he replied, emotionless, heaving a box of clothes up onto his shoulder and calling the elevator again as Stu arrived huffing up the stairs.

He said something to Luke about trying to get fit and they murmured to each other like friends do as I laughed loudly, awkwardly, trying to insert myself into the joke. Luke flashed me a scowl to tell me to back away. I was cowed, then, like the old days.

As he went downstairs with his boxes and Stu followed closely behind, I had an idea. I was planning to snap one of the prints of us in Lisbon that I had mentioned with his phone, which was lying on the side, and set it as his screensaver. A farewell memo. A jolt.

Except that when I picked up his phone there was a message on his home screen from a girl named Naomi, which said simply:

I had a lovely night too. And yes, dinner on Tuesday sounds good x.

43

Lexie

March

I see the back of a blonde woman's head disappear hurriedly up the stairs as I get in the lift. It may be Harriet but again, I don't get a proper look. Is she avoiding being in a lift with me?

I stare at the beige carpet to avoid looking in the floor-to-ceiling mirror and think. Is Harriet elusive? She doesn't *sound* elusive when we hear the raucous parties that intimidate the hell out of us as we sit drinking tea in our slippers, or the loud singing through the wall. And the other day I swear I caught a glance of her in that fancy hotel for the meeting I never heard back about, but it's odd how rarely I catch a look at her. I guess this is just London.

My brother has always found it hilarious, the mysterious neighbour who is more real to me on Google than in real life. The idea's so incomprehensible to them in Yorkshire, where on the right there is Ruth, mowing the lawn and telling them about her back problems, and on the left there are the young parents who ask advice about their baby twins' nipple-biting habits.

Occasionally, I'm envious. I love the anonymity of London 90 per cent of the time, but lately there's a loneliness that's new to me and someone to make small talk over coffee with – someone who didn't know me before – appeals. Would it be weird to knock on Harriet's door? I shake my head, because of course it would.

I put my shopping away and log on to my email, only for my main copywriting client to have messaged me telling me that they can't give me any more work.

I go online and see Anais announcing her pregnancy with a scan picture and multiple emojis.

Tom walks in and immediately logs on to do something important for work, without even taking his jacket off, and I'm resentful that he looks urgent.

What does anyone need me urgently for?

I go to the kitchen cupboard. The nurses told me that if we do need IVF, I should lose a little weight, but that's still down the line. For now, there doesn't seem much point. I shovel in the crisps without even sitting down.

44

Harriet

The next Tuesday, I watched the door of Luke's office from my spot next to a falafel shop. Inhaling cumin until he came out wearing new jeans.

Dating! He was available for dating when I was barely available for showering. At the junction of Shaftesbury Avenue and Old Compton Street, Luke checked his phone and smiled. I felt a rage I didn't recognise in myself. I was used to burying reactions. Anger – from seeing this life that he was building without me, with its dates and its funny texts and its happiness – was a new thing.

And yet, at no point did it occur to me to walk away and stop torturing myself. To build a life of my own and exist independently from whatever they were doing. At no point did it occur to me that what Luke and I had had been far from perfect anyway, or that what Luke did to me on a regular basis wasn't kind, or good, or humane.

At no point did it occur to me that that anger I had just glimpsed would lead to me being curtailed and locked up in an institution.

All I focused on was getting Luke back.

For now, though, I had to dive behind a queue for a burger pop-up because Luke had turned around to look for something. Shit. I had just about got away with turning up at his office; he would never let me get away with following him. I pictured him seeing me and my legs began to shake. Fury was gone, replaced by the much more familiar fear.

He disappeared then though, into a tiny Italian bar. The kind that serves coffee and pastries and five signature house cocktails, and if you want anything else, tough. London loves one of those. So now, apparently, does Luke.

Then I was free to look at every woman on this busy street and wonder if they were Naomi.

The woman with the dyed pink hair in adidas trainers. Was that her? The tiny, pretty Spanish girl marching through the crowd speaking loudly with earphones in? It could be the blonde giggling on the phone or that girl, no more than twenty-two, nervously checking out the signs to find the bar that she was looking for.

In the end, though, I knew. It was the woman who walked into the bar five minutes after Luke, looking like someone I ached to be. Petite, blonder than me, in jeans and black biker boots. She had found her look; she didn't have visible trainer socks.

Instead, she looked like one of those women I always thought Luke should go out with, more than I have ever believed deep down that I did. A confidence in her walk and in her head, held high, that said she would never take Luke speaking to her, treating her, demeaning her like he did me. Meanwhile, I knew that if he would come back to me, I would take it over and over again. I found the nearest old man's pub and got steadily but quickly drunk.

45

Lexie

March

After our appointment, things spiral quickly. In the next three weeks, with little work to keep me busy and the added stress of wondering if Tom is sending pictures to other women, I put on half a stone sadly and easily. The drugs make me nauseous and give me headaches, and I avoid Anais and in fact everybody – except Tom, who is working in London; I suspect he has made sure of that because he is worried about me.

It doesn't work well, though. Alone at home with our thoughts and our worst fears, and with my suspicions crawling around the insides of my brain, we trip over each other, snapping and biting. Should I say something? I wonder constantly. Should I, should I? But I think about how he laughed about the knickers. I think about what would happen if he admitted cheating. I think about my womb and I know: I don't have room for this.

'What happened to all your running?' says Tom, faux-lightly one night, and I scream at him that he is being cruel at a time when the last thing I need is cruelty.

How dare you! I think. How dare you criticise me when you are doing what I think you might be doing when we are in the midst of *this*? But I don't believe it really. He couldn't be, could he?

'It wasn't meant to be cruel,' Tom says, chastised, and I notice bags under his eyes that I haven't seen before. 'I just thought running might make you feel better.'

But I know he's been building up to it, rolling the phrasing around in his head and debating saying it for hours. I realised when he went to the gym a few days ago that he was making a point to me then, too, and it's a horrible thing to know. Especially when. If.

I rage-eat a family-sized chocolate bar and read Zadie Smith in bed until he comes up after a late night working at his laptop.

'Sorry,' he whispers in the dark, but I am too suspicious of him now to be able to go to him and seek solace. I pretend to be asleep.

The next day I stay in bed until ten thirty and it's only when Tom sticks his head in that I'm shamed into getting up. I don't have much clarity but even I can see that I am lacking a purpose and that makes me sadder. A baby would be my purpose.

When I open my Zadie Smith I can feel her clever, feminist eyes on me, ashamed. Women: discard me.

But this is how I feel at my grimiest, deepest core.

A text pings in from Anais.

I'm worried about you, she says. *You're so quiet. Have I done something? Is something going on?*

I put my phone on 'do not disturb' and throw it across the room.

Tom comes in and glances at it.

'Is something wrong?' he asks, echoing Anais.

'I'm just over everyone being so attached to their phones,' I mutter. 'I think I might bin it so they all go away and leave me alone.'

And then I skulk past, animal, tying up my greying dressing gown and heading for the bathroom.

The worst thing is that I know I am pushing Tom away. Even before the message from Rachel. We're strong enough to handle Bad Me for a while, I had reasoned. But is that the thought that gets people and screws them over from the inside? Is that thought why he is sending these kinds of messages to strange women?

This is the pitiful and honest truth: I haven't looked any more into what this woman said, because if I did and Tom finally did admit that something happened, I would have to make a decision about whether or not to cut him out of my life and most likely to press stop on fertility treatment. And I am full of hormones and not strong enough for that.

Instead I shelve it, like one of those photo albums from the past with the funny cards shoved inside, and I shut the door on it, vowing to revisit it later at a time when I am feeling stronger. And hoping that that time does come.

46

Harriet

After that, things rolled out of control. Naomi became a regular fixture in Luke's life. Still friends with him on social media, I could see her there, even if she predominantly stayed in the background. She was being cool and it was becoming obvious – even to me in my fog – that cool wasn't what I was being.

Even worse was Naomi's own social media, which was a hotbed of nights at pop-up cinemas, cocktail bars and picnics in the park. Luke barely appeared. He didn't need to. I saw it through his eyes.

If for some people, seeing the new girl helps them close the door, then for me it did the opposite. It felt like the biggest betrayal of my life – the equivalent of my parents trading me in for another daughter – and I couldn't believe Luke could do it, after everything I had done. I had moved, I had left behind Frances, and I had drifted from my family. I had risked my career, worked fewer hours, ignored my own needs and done whatever I could to make him happy.

I questioned his sanity, wondering how a human being was capable of moving on this fast. It wasn't just upsetting – it was genuinely unfathomable to me.

I stayed away for a while and kept my interest online only, but then I saw him mention a gig on social media that was only a five-minute walk from my flat. It was too tempting, especially after I'd drunk three rum and Cokes for dinner that evening (a now regular occurrence). At 9 p.m., I pulled my trainers on and headed out. I sat in a bar opposite the gig venue and kept a Kindle in front of my face for half an hour before I saw Luke and Naomi join the queue.

I took in every detail: the way they held hands, the way she rested comfortably on her block heels, her smile.

Him, smoothing his eyebrows down, pushing his hair double-handed out of his eyes. Her, passing him a ticket. Him, passing her a tissue. They were comfortable together and seeing that was at first surreal. How had that happened? I had taken my eye off the ball, not stayed close enough. I'd have to remedy that; at that moment, that genuinely felt like my only option.

'Do you know about me?' I wondered out loud. No one heard – busy bar – and so I got louder, daring myself. 'Do you even know I exist? Or after everything I did, am I not important enough?'

A guy looked up from the table next to me and frowned.

I settled my bill – three more double rum and Cokes, still no dinner – and headed home. And I had to keep drinking, because otherwise there was consciousness, which meant all those images in my head, of this woman who had arrived in my life and stolen it, were still there.

After that it was a few days before I saw Luke again. I'd stopped taking on work – take your pick between being too drunk or too broken, but I was constantly too something – and had been stewing on my best move all day when I remembered that he played football every Thursday.

It made perfect sense, because it was a place Naomi definitely wouldn't be, and I *had* to speak to him. The longer it was going on, the more it was unbearable to me that there had never been an answer or reason why our engagement no longer existed. It was one of the reasons I still hadn't told my family; it all seemed ridiculous. I'd followed all the rules, played his game, for so long. It had to have been good enough.

At the far end of the park from the football pitches, I set myself up. Picnic blanket, book, phone, then as I saw the game finishing, I texted him.

Just in the park and remembered you play soccer here on Thursdays. Let me know if you're about – thought might be nice to have a drink as mates and get things a bit more chilled out again xx.

He pinged back straight away.

Where are you? he said – keen! – and I told him.

He was in front of me five minutes later, a sweaty shadow over my picnic blanket with its fake set-up hummus, and I looked up and did what I hoped was a laid-back grin. His face was not doing the same.

'Harriet, this has to fucking stop,' he said, shifting his bag onto his other shoulder and breathing heavily.

I pulled a bottle of wine and two plastic cups out of my bag.

'Drink?' I said hopefully. 'It's such a beautiful evening.'

He took a second, silently, and then he sat down.

I poured the drinks and he actually did take one, which was brilliant, because it meant that today we had hung out together, in the park, drinking wine. I'd tell my mom, I'd post on my social media and everything would be normal.

He gulped down his wine and I took my phone out, leaned in and snapped.

'What are you doing?' he said, sounding truly horrified, and I laughed.

I don't think I had ever scared Luke before. That wasn't how our relationship worked.

'No need to go so mad,' I smiled. 'We're millennials, Luke, we always take a selfie.'

He put his drink down and looked up.

'Harriet, you do understand, don't you, that we have broken up? That we're not getting married? That we're not in a relationship? That we are single?'

I pushed his arm.

187

'Of course I *understand*,' I said with a fake laugh. 'What are you on about?'

Again he took his time.

'Your brother texted me yesterday,' he said, grimacing. 'Asking if I had started making plans for the *stag do*.'

My fake smile got switched off at the mains and I faltered for a good few seconds before I could reply, and even then it was weak.

'I haven't spoken to my family much lately,' I said, picking at a thread on the picnic blanket and staring at the checks until they went blurry. 'I just . . . haven't got round to telling them.'

'It's been three months!' said Luke, incredulous.

'Did you tell him?' I asked. My stomach lurched at the idea of David hearing this news, passing it on to my parents.

'No, I just ignored the message. You know I can't stand David anyway. And it's not my fucking job. But you need to tell them and stop hanging around. We both need to get on with being single.'

Because it was the second time he'd said that word, I bristled and blurted out what I hadn't intended to.

Actually I didn't, I just raised my eyebrow, but that was enough.

'What? What now?'

'Dating three months after you break off your engagement isn't my definition of being single,' I said, suddenly cold because it was only early May and the sun had gone in. I was in a summer dress in a field where everyone else was being warmed by barbecues and dates and friendship.

'What?' he said, looking me right in the eye.

I had an adrenaline rush: when had I ever stood up to Luke? This felt terrifying.

'Three months later,' I said, regretting it already. My heart pounding.

I've seen an unsettlingly calm rage cross Luke's face many times. This was different.

'No, not the three months part,' he said. 'How do you know I've been dating?'

I had my answer ready to this one – I'd come up with it about thirty seconds ago, sensing danger ahead. This was how life worked with Luke. I'd forgotten how mentally exhausting it was, working to be one step in front always so that you didn't mess up.

'Oh, come on, Luke,' I said, straightening my neck and trying for a morally superior stance. 'Like I said, we're millennials. Don't tell me you wouldn't have a quick look on social media to see what I was up to, if you gave a shit.'

He took a second and looked at me intently.

'There is nothing on social media that says I've been dating, Harriet,' he said.

'You have really hurt me,' I said, about to stand up, pack up my things and storm off, except that I wanted him to be with me, even if this was how. 'I don't know how it's possible that you're dating her when we were engaged only three months ago, and that you suddenly think it's cool to go to gigs and pretentious bars and wear trainers I've never seen you in – and all just because *Naomi* says it's okay. You used to know who you were.'

He was staring at me with another expression I didn't know. Genuine shock. It *must* be a terrible shock, when you have controlled and steered someone constantly for four years, to see them take back *any* amount of power. I even thought, for a second, that I saw fear in his eyes. The moment passed quickly, though. He reset his jaw, found his footing.

'There is certainly no mention of her name on social media, Harriet, and to be honest, you're now freaking me out a bit. Which, bloody hell, isn't something I ever thought I would get from *you*.'

And it was then, trapped, that I gathered the blanket, discarded the wine and tried to run. But he caught me. He always caught me.

'What are you doing here tonight, Harriet?' he asked, grabbing hold of my shoulder. 'I dump you, I make it obvious that we're not getting back together, and you turn up at my football game. What are you doing here? Are you insane?' He moved his hand to my chin, clasped it. 'Actually, don't answer that, everyone knows you are.'

His face hated me so much it made me take a gulping gasp of air as though his hand hadn't been on my chin but across my nose and mouth, pushing hard and meaning it.

'You know what's funny?' he asked, and I shook my head the millimetres that his grip would allow.

I wondered if anyone was looking at us, taking this in. Wondering whether to intercept. But they were preoccupied. They had their Prosecco, their ice creams, their evening in the sun.

'That you honestly think that I am not only crazy enough to go out with you once but that I would give you a second chance. Do you know what my friends thought about you, Harriet? They thought you weren't pretty enough to make up for how weird you are and you weren't funny or smart enough to make up for how plain you are.'

A frisbee flew past us and I jumped. Luke didn't flinch.

He moved his face closer to mine, peered at me, touched my forehead where the lines were.

'And now you're getting older, you look even worse.'

Familiar shamed tears started in my eyes. Did I mention that Luke used to do this to me, often?

'But you know why I stayed, don't you?'

I nodded. Because he had told me this before, too.

'Because I always knew that you were too pitiful to be without me. You were obsessed, it would have been cruel to walk away.'

'But we were engaged,' I whispered, because I needed to hear him confirm it. 'You wanted to have children with me.'

He nodded, serious.

'Yes,' he said. 'This was before I met Naomi. I thought that what we had was okay. That the best thing I could have in life was someone who did what I wanted, followed me anywhere. I thought we could make a life together because it was so easy.

'I'd sleep with anyone else I wanted, do whatever I wanted but you would accept it all. If I wanted to move to Australia, you'd pack a bag. If I wanted to eat Korean food, you'd swallow it even though you hate the taste.'

I can't accept that that was it.

'But still,' I pushed, because now I needed to know. 'Why would you want to make a life with someone who you didn't love?'

He shrugged then, like we were chatting about what pasta sauce we should make for dinner.

'Different things matter to different people. For me, that wasn't the most important thing.'

The power, I thought, having a sudden epiphany. The power was the important thing. Anything else was secondary. And what he always had with me was the power.

Did I mention that I took whatever Luke threw at me, because I was so grateful to have him?

Did I mention that after we spent a night dancing with his friends – who saw none of this, only his charm, his charisma – he would be silent with me for twenty-four hours and I would have no idea why? That he told me that he wanted to have five children with me and travel with them all over the world but then an hour later shouted at me so angrily for *looking* at a man in the hotel lobby in Copenhagen. Or that someone from reception was dispatched to check everything was okay? That all this happened even though I knew, but never mentioned, that he slept with tens of other women while we were together?

There were the whispered words of rage while we smiled through dinners. If his friends thought I seemed tense, they were right. I often was. That's what happens when you're working your whole life to criteria that move and change.

Luke liked playing with me, toying. Flirting with other women then being outraged at such an accusation. Blowing hot, blowing the coldest gale you had ever felt on an exposed beach in January. Keeping me there, hoping for this idyllic future that would never materialise.

There were the times that I tried to alter my style and he would tell me I looked stupid, that I was trying too hard. I thought of my ex-boyfriend, Ray, sometimes at those moments and had a pang of regret. But how could I compare the two? Look at him! Luke was so out of my league that I would have taken anything if I got the validation of spending my life with a popular, handsome man like that.

He shrugged again.

'The sex was good,' he said with a smirk. 'I'll give you that. It worked for me, having you there and up for whatever I wanted to do.'

I flushed. But something different to usual was happening in my head. I had had a lot of distance since the last time Luke put me down like this and part of me had been wondering: he couldn't be right, that I was utterly useless, because I had a career, didn't I? I had a creative mind. I had music.

In fact, whatever Luke said, the one thing that really *had* changed about me – us – before he proposed and then broke up with me was that I was flying at work. I was gaining the confidence that a lot of women feel when they hit their career stride in their thirties. I may not have been fully formed, but I knew that I had parts. There were germs of a human being there. I no longer thought that I was the nothing he painted me to be. Deep down, I wondered, is that why he had proposed to me, promised me this future? To halt any doubts I'd had; any thoughts that I could leave him and be my own person. But when it seemed like that was happening anyway, he'd done

192

an about turn and simply ended us. Moving on to someone else.

Is that why I was no longer appealing? Because I couldn't be fully controlled?

But I wanted to hear it from him.

'So why did you break up with me?' I whispered, because when would I get another chance, now? 'In the end, what was different?'

'Because I met Naomi,' he said. 'And she was beautiful and funny and she had her own life. I was sleeping with her for months while I was still "engaged" to you.'

He put it in quotation marks.

'Don't put it in quotation marks,' I said, but where normally my eyes would be filling with tears, something else was happening. I was furious. Livid. Every bit of pain he had caused me had transformed now into hot fire that finally, as he stood in front of me, had an outlet.

I repeated myself, louder now.

'Please don't put it in quotation marks.'

He tightened his grip on my chin and held my hair with the other hand. He thought this was just like normal – because yes, there were glimmers of what therapists at the hospital later called physical abuse, too.

Who had I thought I was, trying to take the power away from him?

But Luke wasted years of my life, ruined me. He told me he wanted children with me, proposed to me, bullied me, belittled me. He built me up then kicked me hard so that I fell, and then he just . . . left. Something was building.

47

Lexie

April

Two months have passed now since we went to the hospital. I've decided to try to heave myself out of this lonely, sugary ennui.

First step: I need to lose the weight and am huffing my way through the park. I am running to Beyoncé and I am grumpy because it's not working.

Where is the adrenaline? Where is the mindfulness induced by the repetition? Am I failing at being cured by exercise too, when even doctors say it can fix all ills?

I pass a woman who can jog with green juice in her hand while simultaneously walking – running – a dog.

She looks carefree; I feel encumbered by worries. There are always worries now, ticking along in my brain and joined constantly, like a Pied Piper, by new ones. I picture the latest one, jogging sluggishly along behind me, gagging for a drink of water.

It was last night when I walked in that I saw Tom jump nervously.

He was on his phone and he looked shifty. Tom doesn't jump. I'm the jumper. I jump these days if toast pops, if the vacuum turns on, if someone walks into a room. Tom is laid-back, calm. It's not the stray hairs of the movies, is it? It's the ever-so-slight changes of behaviour from someone you know the insides of. It wasn't even an immediate assumption that it was Rachel. It could have been him texting a friend to complain about me, or scrolling through an ex's social media, but I knew that whatever it was, it wasn't positive.

I headed straight for the kitchen and he came out, too wide-eyed, too smiley, doing too much touching of my back.

'How are you doing?' he said brightly, then he hugged me tightly, despite me only having been gone for twenty minutes to the shop up the road. Ask yourself. I'm asking myself again, Rachel.

I studied him.

'Fine, thanks, why are you being odd?'

I took a tub of ice cream out of the bag and put it in the freezer.

'I'm not being odd,' he said, being odd. 'Let's put a film on, get under the blanket, eat that?'

'I thought I was supposed to be being healthy?' I said, my voice frosty ice cream, too.

'Well, it's only one night . . .'

'Tom, is there anything you want to tell me?' I bit.

I don't want to confront him again; I want him to offer up the information. Or I want it not to be true. But he's not doing it and it's making my insides burn up, so I'm pushing.

'No,' he said. 'What are you on about? This isn't about that girl again?'

I ignored him and walked into the living room, picking up the remote control.

'Is it?' he asked, more quietly. 'Is it about that girl?'

But I turned the film on and curled my legs under me and stayed quiet.

'Forget about it,' I muttered. 'Let's just watch the film.'

I sat in front of the TV making plans. I had been scared into action. If there was someone else, I had to fight her. I couldn't just step back and let Tom be lost to me. I dug my running stuff out before bed and headed off first thing.

It's now eight thirty and I've been out for fifteen minutes. I'm spent but too embarrassed to head home already. Instead, I sit down on a bench near our flat and see Harriet going out. Casual, today. Dark blonde hair up high in a bun. Big brown eyes mostly make-up free. Still beautiful. Her endless legs jump on a bus as she reads something on her phone and grins.

As I sprint home, I imagine being the kind of girl that Harriet, or potentially Rachel, is and it seems as impossible as scaling a mountain. These women are in a different bracket to me now, with their confidence and their independence. I have drifted so far from my old self that I doubt my memories of her; suspect I must be exaggerating how together she was.

48

Harriet

April

Weeks and weeks it takes Tom to respond, but of course he does, as he's too nervous that I'll ruin his relationship. Especially when I send a follow-up, threatening to do just that. He answers quickly.

That doesn't sound like a smart move, can we just leave it?

To which – heading out of the door to some social media-invite birthday party of someone I used to work with – I immediately send back an emoji of a beer. I'm more of an amaretto and Coke girl, obviously (and as he knows), but for emoji clarity, the beer did the job.

And also, leave my girlfriend alone. I know you sent her messages.

I smile. You have no idea, Tom. You think you've just met some woman who's a bit desperate. You don't know how I can turn; you don't know how when I needed to, I *did* turn.

I send another message, naming a bar that isn't near either of our flats that I went to once with some – of course – work colleagues.

God, that night was awful. All the nights, unless I am drunk enough that I can't remember them, are awful. Do other people enjoy nights out? They are different, I remember distantly, with real friends. I ache, again, for Frances and for the other women that I wasn't as close to but who I know, in retrospect, that I loved and who loved me. Frances's friends, initially, but then mine. We sipped amaretto together in bars, picking each other up, dropping each other off. We shared in-jokes, we gave advice.

When Hayley lost her dad after a stretched-out cancer battle, I organised a weekend away for the five of us. I packed board games, bubble bath and hot chocolate, and we stayed in our pyjamas for forty-eight hours. Hayley's arms appeared around me as we'd packed up the car to come home.

'You'll never know what this weekend has done for me,' she'd whispered. 'As good as months and months of therapy.'

But I knew: they'd all have done it for me. I was part of something for the very first time. Even when we moved, they were still there, on social media, on my phone – a few hours late with a reply because of the time difference but still checking in, still in my life. But when some of them reached out after what happened, I burned with shame. I thought of Hayley, hugging me that day through her grief, thinking I was good, and I felt sick. It was only Frances I could cope with and when even she couldn't deal with me, I changed my number and cut ties. Sometimes I think I can do it again. Chantal could be my friend. Some of the other women who come for dinner. But there is a chasm now, after what I did, because I will always have a secret. I'm playing a part now, an Almost Harriet who emulates the other one but will never quite fit into her shape.

I jump on the bus and out of the corner of my eye I see Lexie, sitting on a bench, breathing heavily and holding her thighs. She is in leggings and trainers – cooling down, presumably, after a run.

'Thursday 7 p.m.,' I type to her boyfriend, because I am starting to enjoy being the bossy one with all the control. He doesn't reply.

49

Lexie

April

If I had to call it, I'd say that Tom looks even more nervous when I come back from my 'run' than he did when I left. His phone is still next to him.

'My run was good,' I say pointedly.

'Sorry yeah – where did you go?'

He is forcing himself to make conversation and pull his mind from whatever it was on, but he looks so troubled that I almost feel sorry for him. Almost.

'The park,' I say, pulling off my socks and eyeing him. What is it? Has Rachel been in touch?

I walk straight into the shower, determined that whatever type of girl I had become, I will never be the girl who checks her boyfriend's phone.

But I kick the side of the bath in frustration. Because I'm lathering up my shower gel and thinking about it. Why *can't* I be that girl? Is it because I've always judged her so harshly, made the ruling that she's the worst girl?

Or is it because deep down I don't think Tom's a cheat, so whatever and whoever Rachel is, he will tell me when he's ready?

But the truth is that I simply can't face handling anything

else right now. Suspecting is manageable. Knowing and having to walk away from Tom when we are in the midst of all of this, isn't. I turn my face up towards the showerhead but bury my head firmly in the sand.

50

Harriet

April

I am simultaneously drunk and hung-over and lying on my sofa in just a bra. A man is standing next to my sofa wearing no clothes. The clock says 3.07 a.m. The man with no clothes is going home.

'You're hot,' he says, pulling a T-shirt on, when he sees that my eyes are open. 'I'll text you.'

Yeah, I think. You're about as likely to text me the next morning as anyone is to text me the next morning.

My phone beeps.

I LOVE YOU AND I LOVE YOUR PARTIES, says Chantal, and I smile, at least, at that. And the fact that she left after an hour or so again but is still obviously very drunk.

The door slams shut thirty seconds later. I get up and bolt it behind the man and pour myself an amaretto. I reply to Chantal; this is almost the same as having a nightcap with a friend. An Almost Harriet, having an almost drink with an almost friend.

51

Lexie

April

I'm not pregnant, again, and the drugs that I am on to try to get pregnant have given me period pain so excruciating that all I can do is pace up and down our tiny flat – turning approximately every three seconds – and cry silently so that I don't disturb the night time.

I am pacing and crying when I hear Harriet making what can only be described as sex noises. The sex noises are a better painkiller than any sort I have ever taken, because I am inherently nosy and distracted by them.

Harriet is having sex! Normally, the noises we hear from Harriet's flat late at night are pure party – irritating often but difficult to get too worked up about when you live in Zone One and buses and idiots zoom past your window twenty-four hours a day. We're used to noise. But this particular soundtrack, I don't hear that often.

I'm gutted Tom is away; getting back into bed with no one to whisper with about what I just heard is disappointing. Then, I think, would I do that these days anyway? Now things are different. Now there is no fun.

I lie awake and when I stop writhing with the pain, I think about my neighbour, writhing in something else. Is she with a boyfriend or a lover? A date or a one-night stand?

I lie awake and seem unable to stop thinking about Harriet and her close but distant life. I think about how imposing and groomed she looks when I catch glimpses of her on the stairs. I think about how I feel I know her and yet realise there are basic level omissions in my knowledge – if she is in a relationship, who she loves.

I think about how much money she must make to afford her flat, alone. I think about how impressive that is, especially from a creative job that lets her be – presumably – her own boss.

I think about how she is what I had hoped I would be in my thirties and how very far removed from my reality that is today.

And then, I think about Tom. Away now, sleeping in a bed that I am not in. Alone? I think so. I hope so.

If Tom *were* cheating on me, would it be with a woman like Harriet? A woman who had her shit together but was fun, still viewing Friday nights as being for pushing your way to the bar and dancing?

Part of me still believes that what Tom wants now is me, in whatever form I come in, and a baby, however long that takes.

But on the bad days, and when he is sleeping far away and I can't soak in the reassurance of his face, I can conceive of a world in which the other appeals far more.

When the period pain lingers enough to stop me sleeping still, even at 5 a.m., I Google my neighbour. I see her social media filled with pictures from a party last night. Harriet, squeezed between friends and pouting. Harriet, downing a shot with a gaggle of equally groomed women. A platter of sushi adorned by an app with the word YUM.

And then, of course, she came home with a man. She had fun, audible, late-night sex. Tomorrow – today – they will likely nip out to a restaurant on the high street for breakfast and Bloody Marys. I realise then that I am picturing Rachel and in my head, she is Harriet. Glamorous, popular, sexy. They are blending into

203

one and merging with the other women I see on the street and sit next to on the bus, who wear ironed clothes and cute boots. The ones who take their phones out of their bags and speak firmly about what they need and what their plans are. Who have signature scents and blended eyeshadow.

I am suddenly horrified by myself: a woman who is jealously googling her neighbour in the early hours of the morning after listening to her have sex. I get up to change my sanitary towel and sit with my head in my hands on the toilet. If Tom wanted a Harriet instead of a Lexie, who really could blame him?

52

Harriet

April

Tom doesn't reply to my message telling him what time and where we are meeting. And then – what took you so long, Tom? – he blocks me.

I am incensed, briefly, but I know I need to go about this another way anyway. If I had met Tom as Rachel, he could have recognised a face that looks familiar enough for it to bug him until he places it. And then he would have known I was lying. That I wasn't Rachel and had a different career altogether.

Far better that he knows me as me.

And he will.

Time for Plan B.

It came from something someone said at work. We were in a meeting, the others making geeky songwriter in-jokes around the piano while I played and zoned out. I felt my shoulders settle. I felt people drift further away. The part where there was human interaction was always the inferior bit of my job; far better to be lost, rhythmic, to feel strong as I pounded the piano keys harder and harder and forgot that my colleagues were even there. Forget the world was there.

'Harriet! Harriet!'

I was angry that this voice had cut through my playing.

'What?' I bit, fingers snapping away from the keys, turning around to them in anger.

'We're stopping for now, okay?' said my colleague Jacob. 'Just going to order some food in and chill out for a while.'

In the chat that followed as we ate our pizza, Jacob joked that our industry would make a good sitcom and I zoned back in, just long enough to snip.

'I'm not sure any of us are funny enough for a sitcom.'

Not us. You.

I wasn't jovial; I was in a bad mood after a two-hour stint looking at old pictures of Luke between 1 a.m. and 3 a.m. this morning.

Luke. Tom. Luke. Tom.

'A documentary, then,' said Steph. Steph? Sam?

These women look the same with their skinny jeans and their highlighted hair and the same trainers. People think London is the home of the unique, what a joke. I've never seen more ubiquity in one place. At any given time there is one restaurant you should eat at, one brand you should covet for your wardrobe, one book you should be obsessed with. They might as well send out a memo at the start of the month.

And yet, I'm still here. Why? I wonder. Too lazy to uproot again? Nowhere else I belong? Clinging onto something I thought I was going to be doing with Luke? Or, lately, is it more to do with Tom?

'Oh yeah, now you're talking,' said another dramatically. 'A dark documentary exposing the cruel underbelly of the musical theatre world.'

They laughed and I thought about how unfunny they are, and how much I dislike them, and how much I dislike everybody I spend time with really, and how no one who's in my life matters to me while David, Frances, my friends, Mom and my dad are outside its parameters.

And then I remembered something I saw on Tom's social media and had an idea.

When you have no one to lose and an empty spot inside you where those people used to live, you can do whatever you want, whatever you fancy, and there are no consequences. It's one of the best things about being me.

53

Lexie

May

I'm sitting cross-legged on the sofa with Tom as we watch a new TV series we're into and drink tea – wine has too much fertility guilt in its sediment to enjoy now, hurrah – but my mind's whirring, once again.

Did I get too complacent? Have too much faith in us? Was I naive to think we weren't susceptible to the things that everyone else is?

I look at him and feel enraged. How the hell am I supposed to focus on fertility drugs and babies when I am dealing with this shit too, Tom?

The oven beeps and Tom goes into the kitchen to take out the lasagne. I simmer with silent rage.

'Low-fat cheese!' he declares, like he's announcing the Oscar winner for best film, and I shoot him a look that says he has read out the wrong result and everyone thinks he's an idiot.

'I can be healthy without us having to go on about it all the time, Tom, thanks,' I snipe, a hand going protectively around my middle.

He looks hurt.

'I was only trying to be—'

'Supportive, yes, I know. Let's just watch this, all right? They said relaxation is as important as anything else.'

He kisses me. But the other . . . The thing . . .

My mind is in overdrive. I can't say it and he won't bring it up, so it hangs there between us every day. It hangs there today as cheddar clings to my fork and my tea cools to lukewarm. It hangs there as there is a loud explosion on the TV and a loud burst of song from next door. We laugh, because when Harriet does her high notes we always laugh, and that helps things. I hold on to that because I need him. I do. With all this and so many unknowns, I need him to be in my team.

Then Tom goes to the toilet and I grab my phone. I'm trying to stop myself reaching for Tom's, which is sitting balanced on the side of the sofa. Except, I see with a glance, it's not. He's taken it with him to the toilet.

And for the first time, I genuinely think: Tom is cheating on me.

54

Harriet

July

I'm home, hammering on the piano, and I have a purpose. I need Tom to have very clearly in his mind that I work in musical theatre. It doesn't matter if I annoy him or make him want to wear earplugs for the foreseeable future; I just need him to have it in his mind.

He's often posting on social media that he wants ideas to pitch, for anyone to tell him if they think there is a story.

I log in.

I scan down Tom's feed and find the message he posted shouting out for documentary ideas a few weeks ago. I reply, making my suggestion about musical theatre.

Then, of course, I need him to think: Who do I know who could get me some ins to this world? And at that moment, I need to hammer on my piano and spell it out to him.

That way, I can get Tom into my own world and onto my own sofa without it being a problem that he may recognise me.

I'm hopeful.

55

Lexie

September

Taking the drugs didn't work. I Google stats on it retrospectively and scoff: of course it didn't work. The odds were terrible, especially when I didn't have a problem ovulating in the first place. I'm gloomy, pessimistic about the whole thing.

We have, it seems to me, simply been being kept at arm's-length from IVF to keep medical costs down. I fume about it to Tom for weeks. The personal has become the political and it's a useful outlet.

But eventually, it's time to let it go. Because we are on to the next stage.

We step off the bus and crunch through leaves as we walk to the hospital. Life, the year, has moved on.

I am lying at an awkward angle twenty minutes later, with my legs in icy metallic stirrups as Tom holds both of my hands.

'Relax,' says a nurse.

Legs, stirrups.

I think about how I am half a stone lighter and how easy that was to achieve, once there was a focus. I think about how I have only shaved the bottom eighth of my calves – ankle-skimming jeans – and how there is a bead of sweat on my inner thigh. I think about how this, now, is the start of things.

Today, we are having something called a dummy embryo

211

transfer, which is a practice run for what, in two months, all being well, will be a real embryo being implanted into my uterus. But I am newly superstitious and – not new – I catastrophise, imagining that I will probably be struck down with cancer or run over by a bus. It's not my possible death that worries me in these imagined situations, just the delay to IVF.

The nurse looks at her piece of paper.

'Oh, it's your birthday!' she says with a little smile that's also sympathy, then she reaches for the speculum.

'Yes, I meant to ask – afterwards, is it okay if I have a drink?' I say when she returns. 'Only, because it's my birthday . . .?'

I qualify it quickly, in case I get bumped down the list to make way for the people who want this enough that they'll drink green tea and eat a cake made of spinach on their birthdays and not make a fuss.

'Well, you'll be on antibiotics to stop infection,' she says. 'But perhaps one won't hurt . . .'

I feel disproportionately sad, because fertility, gradually, has infiltrated everything. We are only going out for dinner – I'd have had three glasses of wine, max – but now there are restrictions. Again.

'It doesn't matter,' says Tom when she goes out of the room to get a smaller speculum (relax, relax, relax). 'We'll still have a nice time.'

But he looks drawn, like he always looks drawn these days, and he looks different to me, like he always looks different to me these days.

Something happened in the spring, I think, as I lie there in silence. Tom stares at the wall. I don't know if I'll ever ask him again or whether I will just file it as strange behaviour we both exhibited during fertility treatment – alongside my going running and drinking liquids made of kale – but maybe that depends what happens next. Whether or not something comes along to supersede it.

The nurse comes back in, tells me to cough and inserts the new, slightly less daunting speculum.

I know all of this is a positive, but my eyes fill with tears because there are still no guarantees and fuck, it hurts.

But soon it's done and I can leave – I walk fast, even though I'm throbbing and bleeding between my legs, because I want to put distance between me and this hospital; between me and fertility issues.

I want to leave behind the two couples who come to the hospital together – one woman the surrogate – and talk loudly and smugly about their successful pregnancy and how relieved they are that it wasn't twins. Like they are so good at getting pregnant that they can afford to hope for fewer babies, not more. Other women sit next to them, sadly, unable to move, tortured.

I don't know about anyone else, but I need to be treated gently at the hospital. My skin is at its thinnest and it cannot deal with a lack of tact or a punch in the gut.

I speed up again, Tom trailing behind. I look around me. I want to be that girl, walking along the street opposite on her lunch break, with no hospital visits, just deciding what burrito to eat and whether or not to get a coffee. Or that girl, who's been on a binge in Topshop. That girl, that girl, any girl but this girl.

'Slow down, Lexie,' says Tom, but I don't and then suddenly, as we walk quickly along a busy road, something in me snaps.

'What happened in the spring, Tom?' I ask, spinning round to look at him.

And he looks genuinely blank and asks what I am talking about.

I backtrack.

'I'm sure it was just me being hormonal,' I say, unable to cope with this conversation now and regretful that I have started it. 'After that Rachel thing, I still feel paranoid that you were cheating on me.'

'Bloody hell, Lex, of course not,' he says. 'She was just some weirdo. I thought we both knew that, ages ago. God, of everything we have to think about right now.'

But he colours. His face is ever so slightly pinker than it should be.

He sighs then kisses me. Tells me that nothing happened, nothing at all, and that everything is going to be okay.

56

Harriet

September

Tom, it seems, is malleable. He likes the musical theatre documentary idea. We are in business.

Could I pick your brains? he has replied to my tweet. *Speak to you or your colleagues?*

Sure, I reply. And then I try against everything in my nature to be the cool girl. *Busy this week on a deadline but next week? Follow me and I'll DM you my email address.*

When Tom messages me, I leave that sitting there, too. I need some control of this situation and taking time, moving slowly, is the way to get it.

I pop out to get takeout noodles and on my way back I pick up my post, glancing at Tom and Lexie's box. I scan around then shove my hand in and whip out a couple of letters, adding them to my pile. Then I slip them all inside my paper bag with my noodles and jump in the elevator to my flat.

I can smell toast all the way up. I picture Lexie at home, in her slipper boots, eating her snack without a plate and licking off the butter that drips on her fingers. Brewing tea to go alongside it. I look down at my takeout.

When I get home I take off my bra and pour a large amaretto with minimal Coke before settling down on the sofa with my post haul.

I turn the first letter, addressed to Lexie, upside down in my hands and see if I can read through the envelope. I can't. The stamp, though, is the hospital again.

Things are happening.

I shovel in my noodles standing up as I make coffee, adding rum, then open the letter, which outlines all the details of Lexie and Tom's recent appointment, a successful 'dummy embryo transfer', and what will happen going forward with their round of IVF.

I have a brief pang of concern for Lexie but then I think: What about me?

She is the one who has the official problems getting pregnant. But is there any guarantee that I'll have a baby, since I have no boyfriend and I'm thirty-three, and the human being I love is terrified of me? How do I know I am fertile? Luke and I tried for a baby for a few months before that was curtailed, too, after all, and nothing happened.

Why should Lexie, who has Tom, and friends, and a life, get the sympathy?

I throw the rest of my pad thai in the bin. *What about me, what about me, what about me?*

57

Lexie

September

I see her from a distance at first and she looks the same, but then she comes round the corner and it's there: Anais' baby bump; huge now, at nine months.

I have steeled myself for this, having not seen her since it was much less obvious, and yet still my stomach deep-dives and I am aware of my armpits, damp.

There is a mode, though, that I know how to access, and it's Peak Girl.

'*Oh God*! *Your bump*!' I shriek, and she shrieks back and it's not real. It's surface. It's everything we are not.

Then we order green juice and avocado toast and post selfies on our social media, and she talks for a long time about eggs that she can have and eggs that she can't have, and I nod and it's hideous.

Right now, I hate that we must talk, talk, talk about everything. I want to be vacuous. Discuss pop culture and nothing with meaning. Not her pregnancy diet and the day they found out and what they're doing with the nursery.

When the food comes, though, there is a lull of silence as we start eating. I look up at her, devouring her toast and oblivious to my awful thoughts. And I get a lump in my throat, because I should have been organising Anais' baby shower, buying too many Babygros, messaging with ideas for baby names. I'm sorry, Anais, I say to her in my head, I'm sorry that I can't be that good, kind friend at the moment. I wish desperately that I had the words to explain out loud.

But then, she doesn't make things better.

'In an ideal world I'd have travelled a lot more first,' she says, examining an egg yolk on the end of her fork, and my heart starts thumping. Don't, Anais. Just don't.

One of my bugbears, through all the time that we've been trying for a child, is people who act like babies are a right and something you can plan for the month you want them, in between that trip to Argentina and the promotion you are after at work. How offensive to those of us who would take it anytime, anyhow.

'Mmm-hmm,' I say, then I go to the loo and take five deep breaths, like the mindfulness book I have put my Patricia Highsmith novel to one side to read has taught me. Now, I can't even read my comfort-blanket favourites. I must read books to stay sane. Fertility is like the creepiest weed scuttling all over your life.

My breaths are weak in the face of the thoughts in my head.

'What are you doing tonight?' Anais asks as the decaf coffee she just ordered arrives. 'Does it involve wine? Go on, make me envious. God, I miss wine.'

'Well, you're pretty lucky getting to have a baby.'

I can hear myself, snippy and short.

I have put my knife and fork down now. My breakfast sits, half eaten, as I leave all the fun parts out in my drive to be healthy.

She looks chastised.

'Oh, I know, I am lucky!' she backtracks. 'Just . . . if I could have planned it.' Then she reaches over. 'D'you not want that pancetta?'

Take it, take it all.

'Well, it's not something that works to people's schedules, is it?' I say, same tone, same face as she crunches down my bacon.

There's no denying it: I don't feel happy for her and I'm not magnanimous, I just think it's unfair that Anais is having a baby and she didn't – doesn't – even want one – and that we are now steadfastly ignoring that fact. And I have to go hospital and wait for someone to get a different-sized speculum and take twelve different types of drugs if I even want to stand a chance of getting pregnant.

I look at the clock above Anais' head. I want to get this over with, go and turn off my phone and hide away in my pyjamas.

I look up and Anais has stopped eating. She looks weird. I can't work out if she's sad or angry. We get the bill and leave without the muffins we normally finish with, or the stroll around Borough Market that we normally take our time over before we head home.

The hug's cold and there's no *Lovely to see you* text. And I feel more relaxed on the bus home, faintly aware of two or three strangers' body odour, than I did throughout the whole meal. This is my life now. I'm like social-event poison. It's why staying in or riding buses alone is easier; out there, I make both other people and myself awkward and uncomfortable.

I go home and I sit cross-legged on the floor, zoning out of everything except for Harriet, playing on her piano. Listening to Harriet is a version of mindfulness, perhaps. An odd one, but still – it soothes me.

After a few minutes Harriet stops and I swear I can feel it, an instinct that she is there on the other side of that wall. I lean my head gently up against it.

58

Harriet

September

It is 2 a.m. and I am here, in my unhappy place, on Lexie's social media.

Today, in Lexie's unfathomably joyous life, Lexie Does Friendship. There she is posing with green juice and avo toast – Lexie, you are perfect but you are clichéd, my dear neighbour – alongside a beautiful mixed-race friend named Anais.

I click through to Anais' page and there are similar snaps. Lexie left Tom behind and off she went to spend time with her friend. They didn't need to be drunk. It didn't need to be 1 a.m. She didn't need to give Anais free drinks to make her hang out with her. What Lexie has is genuine friendship.

I once again click through all of her previous posts, trying to discover what it is about her that these people love, what it is that makes her able to forge the sort of friendships that I have been unable to forge since I arrived in this country. I look at the smiles between them and I think of Chantal and me, awkward in Waitrose as we clutch our meals for one. I wonder what it is about Lexie that Tom loves. I wonder if it is really my secret that is stopping me from making friends, stopping any true connections from forming. Or if, more simply, it's just me. I look more closely at Lexie's pictures to see if I can work it out.

Is it her eyes, her smile, or something more subtle? I zoom

into a freckle, check what she orders to drink. I see her post a picture of graffiti in Dalston and wonder if I should look to be edgier. She goes to the cinema and I wonder if it's time for me to get into films. Would Tom like that?

I look at her family pictures, at her friends. I pick over her life. She posts book covers often of novels that she loves. I vow to visit bookshops, make this a bigger part of my life.

I screen grab hundreds of her photos and open them up together to get the whole picture, and eventually I fall asleep on the sofa, oddly comforted by the many bright, happy faces and facets of Lexie watching over me.

59

Lexie

September

And so I am back, after all, to see the counsellor.

It's the kind of thing you should do when you can't stop accusing your boyfriend of cheating on you and you want to be kinder to your best friend and you have a very low opinion of yourself, so I am doing it.

The counsellor is lovely. She has a soft, singy lilt and she appeases me of all guilt. It's okay to hate Anais for the moment, she says, it's okay to be angry, it's okay to feel bitter at the world.

But then . . .

'So, you are pregnant' I say, because her bump now is at its biggest.

'Could you not try another counsellor?' said Tom when I told him that Angharad was pregnant, and I had snapped, again, at that.

'Sure, at seventy pounds an hour, Tom. At seventy pounds an hour when we might need every penny we have to make a baby.'

He walked away; he no longer takes me on when I speak in a certain tone. I sometimes wonder if he's been reading books, learning how to deal with me.

This counsellor is provided, incredibly, by the NHS. If she were thrusting her bump in my face while laughing, I would still have no choice but to accept her and be grateful.

The counsellor's hand goes over her stretched middle.

'As I said last time, we aren't here to talk about me,' she says, school ma'am-strict.

She is the fertility counsellor. She should be a safe space. A baby-free zone. But I am a woman and I try not to make strangers feel uncomfortable, so I mutter congratulations and move on. But how, now, can she understand? And how can I speak freely? She's judging me, I think again – all of the horrible things I have said about pregnant women and their complacency, their smugness . . . now, they are about her.

She reads my mind. Of course she does, it's her job.

'My own life bears no relation to my understanding of yours,' she says. Yoga teacher replaces school ma'am.

I can't help it. Despite the politeness, I raise an angry eyebrow.

'Let's move on,' she says. 'Tell me about your partner. How are things there?'

60

Harriet

September

I am in a coffee shop two minutes from my flat. Tom is due any second. I'm wearing what someone normal would wear for a normal meeting – jeans, a top, ballet pumps – and I am trying to make my insides reflect the averageness of my exterior.

Really, they're not average. They're extreme, with a stomach that's so excited I haven't eaten all day and a chest that's hammering away and a lower back that's damp. I'm scrolling on my phone – because what's more average than that? – when he walks in.

'Harriet?' he says and when I confirm, he offers to get me a coffee, but I've necked an espresso already.

'Just a tap water,' I say. I've been practising my measured smile, speaking slowly so my voice doesn't shake.

And then, we chat.

It's businesslike, on his part, and on mine, too – like I say, exterior.

I tell the three or four musical theatre anecdotes that I've been practising.

'I think there's genuinely something in this,' says Tom when I've finished.

He looks up from the iPad he's been making notes on.

'I'm going to take this to the production company. There's

an executive producer there who I think would go for it, if I can sell it right.'

'And if they do?' I ask. 'What happens then?'

Like I give a shit.

Tom gives a wry smile.

'They'll take it to the commissioning editor at whatever channel they think it would work best for,' he says. 'They'll say they like it but "don't think the idea is quite there yet". Ad infinitum until we all lose the will to live waiting for it to happen.'

I don't know what to say. There's an awkward pause. I'm not very good with sarcasm.

'But you know!' Tom laughs, breaking the silence. 'Hopefully not. Hopefully it'll get made and we'll all get together to watch it and toast our – your – awesome idea.'

He wants to drink with me; celebrate with me. He wants to make a TV show about me then celebrate with me.

I stare at him. That *face*. Then there's another pause, and I know he's going to say it.

'So, where are you based?'

'I'm round here, just a fifteen-minute walk down Essex Road,' I say, fake stifling my fake yawn, the one I do when my voice is shaking or I'm blushing and I need to draw attention away from that.

And then he fake yawns too, and I realise: he already knew.

'How weird, me too – whereabouts?'

I tell him, taking a sip of water. 'How about you?'

'Yeah, same. Opposite the noodle place.'

'I'm in that building!' I laugh. Fake laugh.

'This is possibly odd, but I'm in there too and I always hear my next-door neighbour playing the piano. You're not number one hundred and twenty-four, are you?'

I start laughing and this is fun. And whatever else this is, I've missed fun.

'Okay, stalker,' I say, and he throws his head back. A Luke move.

'That's hilarious,' he says, pushing his too-long hair out of his eyes again, and I think Luke, Luke, Luke.

'And embarrassing,' I say. 'I bet you've heard me hit some rough notes. And God knows what else.'

'Same,' he says. 'I bet you've heard my girlfriend and me do all kinds. One rule in London, you never meet your neighbours. We're convening all laws.'

'Tell you what, if you have any follow-on questions, just hammer on the wall and yell them and I'll stop singing and answer.'

'Agreed. And if I'm playing computer games too loudly when my girlfriend's out, mention that, too.'

I think of when the noise did make it through. I think of when the shock of hearing their conversation made me think of when I lived in a psychiatric hospital. All the things you don't know about me, Tom, I think, all the things you don't know.

'Right,' he says, putting away the iPad and necking the last of his latte. 'I think that's all my questions. Thanks for that, really helpful. You never know, there might be something in it and if there is, you can pop round and we *can* all watch the final product together.'

'Sure, if that annoying girl from next door isn't playing her piano again.'

We're grinning and I'm thinking: this is almost a date. If you'd just stop mentioning your girlfriend.

He stands, kisses me politely on the cheek, then stops. He blushes before he even asks it. I know what's coming.

'This is a strange question, but did I come to a *party* at yours a few months ago?' he says.

I wait for him to continue, look blank.

'There was this really drunken night . . . I sort of stumbled into a flat near ours . . .'

226

Blank.

'A red-haired girl was kind of whizzing around in circles and then fell over?' he says.

Oh, Chantal. A class act, always.

'Not mine, I'm afraid. Wow, you must have been seriously drunk not to know where you were.'

'Oh, I was,' he says, bright tomato now. 'I even lost my flat keys; the porter had to let me in.'

Ah! So that's what happened.

I picture him, asleep.

'Ignore me,' he says, slipping into his jacket. 'Just a stupid night.'

He is stumbling.

'I guess we're going in the same direction?'

He says this awkwardly too, because it's one thing having a coffee together and another walking along the road and letting yourselves into your respective flats, where you can immediately hear each other through the wall.

I let him off.

'Actually, no; I'm going to meet the girls,' I say as though I am a person who has girls. 'But shout if you need anything else. And if not, I'll see you in the elevator.'

61

Lexie

September

'Tom is amazing,' I say to Angharad.

I am loyal to Tom, always. Even with what has been happening, I dislike those people who moan about their partners leaving towels on the bed, dressing badly, forgetting the dry-cleaning, never doing the vacuuming. It's life-draining. I am pro-Tom. And if I wasn't pro-Tom, I would leave. Would I? I think I would, but then lately – it's not quite so simple.

'He wants a baby as much as me, and he's so on board with this treatment,' I enthuse. 'I'm incredibly lucky to have him.'

Angharad smiles.

Then she stays silent.

Silence has always been tricky for me.

I get together with friends to watch a film then speak over it until it ends. Kit and I never let each other finish a sentence.

But I try for a few seconds, smiling, meeting eye contact.

Angharad is better at it than me, though, and I crack, inevitably. I can't bear it – how do people cope with the lingering emptiness of no noise?

'There was . . . I was a little bit worried that he was . . . but it's probably nothing.'

'What did you think it was?'

'Nothing. I shouldn't have mentioned it.'

'But you did.'

I try silence again. Fail again.

'It just crossed my mind he was cheating on me, but he wouldn't, it was stupid.'

How have I said these words out loud?

'Okay.'

She's doing it again.

'It was just some odd behaviour.'

'Mmm.'

'And a social media message from some girl.'

'Okay.'

'And some condoms that he'd bought, even though we are trying.'

'Mmm-hmm.'

'In the spring.'

Silence.

I literally can't do it. I am powerless to stop speaking.

'Nervous, distant, taking his phone with him to the loo . . .'

Beat. Big, silent beat.

'But it's fine now.'

Oh, the torture.

'I probably imagined it. The girl was clearly weird. I was paranoid around that time.'

Finally, she speaks.

'Have you ever talked about it?' she asks. Voice as steady as a newsreader now, she is a chameleon of reassurance.

'Kind of. I tried.'

I flush so much it stings as I think about how easily I swept this away. What kind of girl doesn't track down the other woman and find out more? But our situation is so dense, like everybody's, and so those sweeping 'what kind of girl?' sentiments: they're more complicated than that, aren't they?

'Well, it might be something to talk about, if it's on your mind.'

229

'No, it's really not,' I say decisively. 'I don't know why I mentioned it. It's gone. I mean, it wasn't anything anyway. But it's gone.'

She nods and we move on.

'Are there other people you can speak to?' she asks. 'Outside of your relationship? How about your mother?'

I resist the urge to eye-roll. Oh, here we go, in therapy and back on to my relationship with my mother.

'She's not really a talker,' I say. 'She believes in getting on with things, fixing them, buckling down.' I pause. 'She's always thought I'm a little . . . flighty.'

I think about her disappointment when it was evident that I was headed for more creative pursuits, rather than the rules and the black and white of science.

I suddenly picture telling my mum I'm in therapy. She would find that incomprehensible.

'And your dad?'

'He's a bit better, but he's a little older than Mum and he's old-school, too. We don't delve into the hard stuff. Plus, they're very far away, in Canada. There isn't much chance to talk.'

Despite our distance, I feel disloyal.

'What about when they were here?' she asks. 'When – presumably – you did live with them. Did you talk then?'

I try to think. *Did* we?

'I think so,' I falter.

But all I can picture is Kit's bed, Kit's arms around me when I was sad, Kit's kind eyes as he brought me a custard cream.

'Angharad,' I say as I leave. It's the last time I will see Angharad – if I want to continue I'll have to transfer over to somebody else - as she is going on leave. She doesn't state what type of leave, comically, even though it could not be more apparent.

'I just wanted to say that I am sorry. For going on about you being pregnant.'

She smiles.

'That's okay,' she says. 'You're human. This stuff isn't easy to navigate.'

'I'm a nice person, normally,' I laugh. 'Believe it or not.'

She touches my arm.

'I can tell that, Lexie,' she says. 'I can tell that.'

My eyes fill with tears. It takes so little, these days, and now – like a true cliché – I am leaving my therapy session and contemplating my own family. Why *didn't* we talk? Is that why I haven't told my mum about our fertility struggles? Because an open conversation about something so clunky and unsolved is beyond us? I walk away from the hospital feeling tipped upside down and shaken out.

Next, reflexology. Tom is suspicious, wary that the promises of reflexology helping fertility issues are designed to take sixty pounds a time from desperate middle-class thirty-somethings, pulling off their socks and handing over their wallets.

'I can't see any problems with your uterus,' says the reflexologist, putting pressure on my foot, and I think: What if you could?

What would we do then? March down to the hospital and tell the doctors what they missed?

I have three sessions then abandon it and Google acupuncture.

Tom is quiet this time. 'If it helps you feel better, then it's worth it,' is all he will say when pushed.

62

Harriet

September

I've just finished a musical, so work is more manageable than it has been recently. I have time to think. To plan.

Next door too, things are quiet. Tom and Lexie are visiting Lexie's brother in Yorkshire. Ugh, family. Tom and Lexie, and their family.

I picture country cottages and homemade soup and twenty-year-old in-jokes, and there is a pain across my forehead that is worse than a hangover, worse than a migraine. I look at pictures of David again. I touch his face lightly as a child, as a teenager, as the grown-up I barely got chance to know. I wish that I could explain to him where the distance between us came from. What Luke had said to me. How I had felt like I had to make a choice between him and my fiancé. How I felt like if that were the case, I had to opt for my future husband, the man who I would have children with. How I am slowly, hesitantly, starting to admit that I made a catastrophically wrong decision.

Tom has posted some pictures of him and Lexie on social media. Tom and Lexie do the pub; Tom and Lexie do walks in the country. Tom and Lexie do refusing to be broken, no matter how big the boots are that trample all over them.

I look at the images again and feel that familiar and strong desire to erase Lexie from the picture, to sketch myself in instead.

I feel betrayed, angry. Everything I used to feel when I thought of Luke being with Naomi.

I've not left the house since Tuesday. I've drunk cup-a-soups for dinner, and Googled Tom and Luke. My skin is pale and a large spot has sprung up on my chin. My hair is lank and greasy, right to the ends, and I smell oddly of damp.

I contemplate the last time this happened; where it led.

I make another coffee, more amaretto, and check Tom's social media again. The selfie of the two of them walking, the one of them in the pub probably taken by a friend, or just someone they met who liked them because that's what life is like being Tom and Lexie. I've seen the cards in their flat, the invites. People are drawn to them, in a way they have so rarely been drawn to me.

By now, Tom and Lexie have most probably finished their walk and are thinking about watching a film with a bottle of red.

I throw my own coffee cup against the wall and leave the remnants there. Because who will know? Who will care? This isn't like being in the hospital: no one cleans up my mess, no one checks if I'm falling apart.

I'm losing patience. I need Tom and Lexie to come back. They are too in control up there, too happy. I need to move things on.

I set up another Facebook account and send Lexie a follow-up message from Rachel.

Do you know where your boyfriend was on the fifth of this month? I type. *Might be worth asking him . . .*

I've done my online research. I know Tom was away that night.

I log out. Look around. What now?

It hits me then, a feeling that one of the therapists identified long ago and that comes to me in a physical form often, especially on those nights when those people are in my flat with

233

their names and their faces blurring with Pinot Grigio: I am very, very lonely.

I'm lonely alone, and I'm lonely in a houseful of people, and there is no time when I am *not* lonely. I am too lonely to reach out to people on the periphery of my life and pull them closer. I am scared of rejection, of being known. I keep Chantal half a metre away in Waitrose, make sure I don't socialise with work colleagues unless I'm drunk.

I don't have the guarantee of the other friendless; a family who will ensure that I am not lonely unconditionally, surrounding me with bickering and a claustrophobic Christmas that everyone will grumble about but never, ever want to give up. And I can't get that back now. My family are too far gone.

But Tom can fix that, I think, he can fix that. As long as Lexie is erased.

63

Lexie

November

It is November, but I am sweating. I am on the tube, squeezed up against rush-hour commuters, and in my bag are forty syringes and what looks like enough medication to cure a ward full of sickness but will actually just do me and my uterus for a few weeks. I am terrified. Not of taking the medication but of dropping it, of it being stolen, of losing my mind for a moment and leaving my haul abandoned in the luggage rack. It is the most precious object I have ever carried and when I get home, I look at my stinging palm and realise I've been holding it so tightly that it has left a raging red mark that doesn't fade for an hour.

'Oh my God!' Tom says later as I chop an onion and lob olive oil into a pan, then I jump again.

'Nothing bad! Nothing!' he says quickly. 'I just realised that I forgot to tell you that I met Harriet from next door for that musical thing.'

'What?' I laugh, but I hear it and it's disingenuous; the laugh Tom's envious friend Adam does when we tell him something good has happened to us. Adam is awful.

'Everything had been so busy and so rushed that I just forgot to tell you,' he says.

'How could you forget to tell me that?'

Harriet and her singing is one of our best gags, and the idea that he could cross the line to real life on one of our best gags and not tell me is, he concedes, inconceivable. Perhaps I wouldn't react so strongly if it didn't feel like this came on the back of other omissions, other gaps.

'I just can't get my head around how you could not tell me that you met Harriet,' I say, doing an Adam-esque smile. 'Are you mates now?'

I laugh. Again, it's not real and I hate it.

'No! Not at all! It was about twenty-minutes long and just nothing. That's why I forgot.'

'But you met Harriet,' I point out, again, throwing the onion into the pan. 'It's like me meeting Madonna and telling you it was nothing.'

'That's ridiculous,' he snaps and opens the fridge for the garlic.

'It's not, though. She's like a celebrity in our world and you had coffee – coffee? – with her.'

He's nodded at coffee and thank God. Because I think if he'd said three vodka and Cokes and a chaser, I might have lost it and this risotto might have been left abandoned to a row. Harriet, Rachel, Harriet, Rachel. Could this be something?

'So, what was she like?' I ask, and he glances nervously at the way I am opening a bottle of wine – cooking-purposes only for me now, of course – quite violently with a corkscrew.

'She was exactly like you'd think Harriet would be,' he says. 'Bit awkward, geeky. Sweet enough.'

I frown.

'That isn't how I would think Harriet would be,' I say, pouring the wine into the pan and feeling slightly calmer. 'I would think she would be loud, and confident, and this statuesque goddess with five of her colleagues in tow.'

We've heard the same woman existing through the wall and come up with such completely different impressions of her.

'All those evenings that she's entertaining and they're doing karaoke . . .'

He blushes, and I note it.

'Did you fancy her?' I ask.

'No! Of course not. Why did you ask that?'

I look at him closely. Shit. What if he was – is – sleeping with Harriet? But now, I think, I *am* losing it.

'I think I'd be intimidated by her in real life,' I say, finally.

'Seriously?' he says, incredulous. 'How could you be intimidated by our jolly singing neighbour?'

But I am nodding. I mean it.

I leave him to the cooking and I go into the living room to check my phone.

I have another message on Facebook, from Rachel. A different account but same face, same accusations, except this time she has upped the ante, implied that she and Tom slept together.

I walk into the kitchen and stare at the back of Tom's head. My mouth opens but I can't do it again, I can't. He's denied it, claimed that she's a psycho, and I know he won't say anything different now. So what's the point? This is my parents' influence coming out in me now. Bury it, ignore it, stop harping on about it.

Instead, I lock myself in the bathroom and sob silent, heaving tears about how I am now so desperate to have a child that I am potentially letting Tom cheat on me without saying a word.

64

Lexie

December

Today, Tom and I are at the pre-Christmas wedding of one of my old school friends – the kind who I bond with over oft-wheeled-out Nineties nostalgia and love dearly but haven't actually had a conversation with in about ten years.

Relations between Tom and I are frosty. Tom doesn't know why, but I have an internal monologue of rage that I cannot say out loud to him, so I am playing it out in my mind. I have come close to asking him again if he has been unfaithful so many times, but I cannot. I don't have space for this in my mind. I need to get through IVF and then we will deal with it, as incongruous as that may seem.

I watch our friends say their emotive vows in front of a crackling fire with tears in my eyes and glance fleetingly at Tom. We've planned to do it ourselves. Quietly, with good wine and bad dancing. Children were – are – a priority over a wedding, but we intend to get there, eventually. Tom looks back at me, tries to read me. He is bewildered, I know, by my distance and my mood. If pushed, I blame hormones, the many, many drugs I am taking. And then I simply retreat.

Am I making a mistake? Am I attempting to bring a child into the world with a man I don't trust? Or *do* I trust him, deep down? Do I know we will sort this and is that why I can shelve it? As he looks ahead, I stare at him again, trying to see, trying to reassure myself.

And today, there are more practical things to deal with. Inserting, for starters, some vaginal gel that involves, according to the packet, as this is my first one, lying horizontally. That's okay, I thought, before we came. Someone I know will be staying at the venue and I'll ask if I can use their room for ten minutes.

Except, because I have been a little distracted and thought of little but IVF recently, I know nothing about this wedding other than the train station we need to get to and what time we need to be there.

I look properly at the invite for the first time on the train. The wedding is in a tent. No guests will be staying 'at the venue', unless they pass out behind the pop-up bar and no one notices.

So 8 p.m. comes and the alarm on my phone goes off, and a minute later I am in a Portaloo, doing what looks like a yoga move to make myself as horizontal as possible. Despite my best attempts, I have always been shit at yoga. The gel insert, a bit like a tampon applicator, can't go where it needs to go because I am too vertical so it keeps hitting bone – bone? Wow, I am clueless about my own body – and that brings tears to my eyes.

I am also nearly naked, because I wore my jumpsuit to this wedding, the leg of which is now trailing in some Portaloo wee.

I give up and run back into the tent crying to tell Tom that we need to go home *now* so that I can do this there instead, but as I walk in all faces turn to me and cheer.

They were waiting to do the speeches. Everyone else had returned; they were just holding on for me. And now I am here, with tears streaming down my face, a packet of vaginal gel sticking out of my bag and the wee of one of my fellow wedding guests on my trouser leg.

Fertility issues: drainers of energy, thieves of dignity.

We leave for home after the speeches and my vaginal gel finally reaches its destination as I lie on my own bed. I exhale.

We missed a large chunk of the wedding but my medication has been done within the ideal time slot and that's the important thing. Swoony first dances, boozy last dances: they, like the rest of the wedding and the rest of life, don't come close to mattering at the moment.

'I'm sorry I didn't realise you needed help,' says Tom.

'There's nothing you could have done anyway,' I snap, cold.

Tom sighs. Gives up trying to speak to me. We might have left early but he's still had enough free wedding wine to pass out on the duvet.

I can't sleep though, so I sit up scrolling Harriet's social media and noting her poised, together pictures. Is Rachel like you? I think again, glancing at Tom snoozing in his suit next to me. Is she poised and together like you? And I think about the fact that Harriet would never end up with wee on her jumpsuit or naked in a Portaloo, let alone doing both at the same time. And I think about Tom, and I picture them, again and again and again, together.

65

Harriet

This, then, is my story.

For three weeks after I left Luke in the park that day, I neglected to function.

I grieved. I knew it was over and I had run out of energy to try to fight it. I stopped working.

My family phoned but I deflected them with the odd text, and that was enough.

And I realised then that no one knocked on my door. No one even smiled at me kindly in Tesco, or gently touched my arm as I became teary on the bus.

And I did, often.

I became teary walking across the green holding a coffee and in the elevator, where a woman my own age stood staring straight ahead and pretended not to notice.

How could you be here in Zone One, in one of the biggest cities in Europe, and be so adrift from the world?

I saw myself through Luke's eyes and I was hateful.

And then I stopped waiting for someone else to invite me to get drunk and got drunk by myself.

I got so very, very drunk for a long time. Weeks, maybe. The world was cloudy, and my lips begged me for balm and in the kitchen there was no food but many empty bottles. Finally, someone did interact with me, in the loosest sense, the newsagent's eyes pitying me through my blur as I bought more own-brand vodka.

And that spurred me on.

One day I got dressed, went to Luke's recently rented house – he had finally moved out of mates' places and into his own home with a flatmate – and I watched from over the road.

I was there for hours, and I was angry.

Luke had made me a person who people pitied and cringed at, when I should have been a happy bride, dancing in a crowd with champagne in my hand and euphoric. I had worked hard for that moment. I had tried more than any other woman would. How could he deny me it?

I thought about my friends, distant now in Chicago. I thought about how Luke spoke to me, how I tiptoed around him, how I had tried so hard and how it wasn't enough. I felt shaky and leaned up against a wall, still watching and waiting.

I was starting to sober up, because it had been a while and I hadn't come prepared, and now I couldn't leave my station. But still, I was drunk enough.

I was drunk enough that when I saw Luke come out of his house and kiss Naomi goodbye, leaving her in his home without him, it took me three seconds to decide to speak to this woman who'd ransacked my life and taken the best part.

The world was cloudy but Naomi was vivid.

On the doorstep she wore a neatly ironed shirt with tiny doves all over it. Her jeans finished just above the ankle. She had bare feet with toenails painted carefully in a vivid orange. I stared at them.

Her hair was loose and she had on no make-up except perhaps for a tiny bit of mascara and, if I was being hopeful, some concealer.

'I'm Harriet,' I said.

I stood still and she did, too, and then she turned briefly to check something inside, probably where her phone was, and in that third of a second, I slipped past her.

She told me to get out, of course she did, but I walked into the living room and sat down. She stared at me and I stared at her doves. They wanted peace; I didn't.

66

Lexie

December

I am lying face down holding the outer edge of my knickers between my fingers while Tom draws up some liquid into a syringe. We are amateur doctors, taking on big tasks with small knowledge but making up for it in how much we care.

It is winter, a couple of weeks before Christmas, and for over a month now I have been immersed in the process of IVF.

I have gone from someone who is terrified of having blood taken to someone who can inject myself in the toilet of a pub in between my soup and my salad.

'Have you got it all?' I stress. 'Make sure it all goes in.'

Get in, progesterone, make a baby.

In it goes, to my bum cheek.

'Now massage!' Tom shouts at me, panicked that I may miss my post-injection massage window.

I furiously knead my bottom.

I stop and stand to take six tablets ten minutes later, my hand cramping, before inserting a suppository. Then I lie on the bed, still, for it to 'stay in' for the next hour. The last part isn't on the instructions and were I to have a normal office-based job – seriously, how do people do this with a normal office-based job? – it would be impossible, but it makes sense in my head, so I'm doing it. I need to exert some tiny hint of control.

Work has ground to a halt. This is it. Making a baby is my job and I'm treating it more seriously than I have ever treated any job in my life. The biscuit habits of before have gone, the cupboards full of lentils and seeds and oats.

I go to 3 p.m. yoga with a teacher named Izzy and three fabulous retired Londoners, as we are the only ones available to do classes at 3 p.m. and the only ones who want a class that involves no sweating and is really just a bit of lying around and breathing.

They all know why I'm here. I treat it less like yoga, more like group therapy.

In my last class before the embryo transfer Maurice, who is seventy-three, has hair down his back and can do a headstand, puts a gentle hand on my shoulder. I turn to smile at him.

'I'll light a candle for you,' he says and my eyes are wet. 'Namaste.'

His hug is grandfatherly and warm and I wish I could pocket it so I could have it again later. We wave goodbye, yoga mats tucked under our arms, and walk in opposite directions.

The hope is that I won't be back at class but instead will be heading off to big school or, as we know it, pregnancy yoga. To rub my bump and bounce on a ball and practise breathing for the birth. We all hope this is goodbye.

I take vitamins, and I call the hospital with facts and figures. I sit for half an hour twice a day and I meditate to an app on my phone. I watch, smiling, as Tom fills in my chart for me, to make sure we do every bit of medication at the right time, that we don't miss a beat. I grab more blueberries because what if, what if, it's the blueberries that make the difference? I drink more water. I go to bed early.

I don't even consider Rachel, because there is no room in my head to consider Rachel. Unless Rachel is some form of progesterone that I need to inject myself with twice a day, Rachel is of no consequence.

Things are better with Tom. I decide to trust him and be loyal to him because I need him. I remind myself again that Rachel is no one; she is words on a screen. If injecting your own bum cheek is difficult, coping with the gruelling emotion of hormones and terror without someone who you love is harder. Sometimes you have to take a punt. I can deal with this later if I am wrong, but right now I am taking that punt.

Tom, too, takes a break. 'This is the bonus of being freelance,' he says. 'Though on the other hand, kids do cost a lot of money . . .'

He winks. No irony. Because now, we are newly optimistic. We aren't fatigued any more. This isn't the twenty-fifth try but the first one. The odds are far, far better for this than they are for what we have tried before. In fertility terms, IVF is the big gun. We're excited for what might be about to happen. I'm stoic about the bad bits. Tom tells me I'm brave and I feel it, like I could take on the world for this imaginary baby. I haven't achieved much for a long time but this, actually, this I am acing.

And finally, all there is to do for two weeks is wait.

We wait asleep and we wait awake. We wait while we eat Christmas dinner at Tom's parents and we wait while we talk about the news, or our Christmas presents, or what is coming back on TV in January. We pretend we are doing other things but really, we are always waiting.

We have a date, a Tuesday just after New Year, when we must call the hospital with the test result.

Until then I rest and relax, but not in a hot bath because I'm too scared that could damage the imaginary baby. I can walk but not too far, because what if that hurts imaginary baby? I can eat, but nothing risky, because food poisoning is the enemy of imaginary baby.

It's a fortnight that doesn't exist in the real world, which is going on around us as our imaginary baby does or doesn't develop. I see people lifting heavy gifts or drinking champagne with their Christmas dinners, and panic for a second, before I realise they are not me. It's okay. They don't have to follow the rules.

And then, finally, it's time.

I wake at 6 a.m. having dreamt of children and heartache and joy and everything.

I get out of bed and walk to the bathroom, shaking all over, to my knees, to my neck.

'I'm going to do it,' I say over my shoulder to Tom and he sits bolt upright. He's not slept, either.

My hands shake so much that I wee all over my fingers, but this unpleasantness fails even to register.

Because already, I can see the result coming up.

There is no baby. We did all of that, we tried so hard, but there is no baby.

67

Harriet

'I'll call Luke,' Naomi said, but for whatever reason, she didn't.

'Luke is my fiancé,' I replied, staring at her.

'No, Luke used to be your fiancé,' she said gently, but her voice shook.

'You can't go out with someone who was about to marry someone else a few months ago. You can't do that.'

I believed it.

She sat down. And she actually picked up her phone and moved it away from her, onto the mantelpiece next to a picture of Luke skiing.

'I was on that holiday,' I said, disbelieving. '*I took that picture.*'

She looked at the picture then shrugged.

'Well, that happens,' she said, and now gentle sounded more like irritation. 'I have pictures my ex probably took. But you move on. You need to move on.'

'Were you engaged?' I asked her, glancing round the room at the other pictures in Luke's living room.

Luke graduating. Luke with friends who I knew. Luke after a bungee jump I booked for him. And there, in a gold frame, Luke and Naomi, dressed up, grins, wedding guests, plus-ones.

'No, we weren't *engaged*,' she said slowly, a verbal eye-roll, as though she is putting the word in inverted commas.

It wasn't in inverted commas. It existed.

And so whatever has happened now, the idea that this wasn't

real, that this didn't happen. Don't tell me that, Naomi. Don't fucking tell me that.

'Then it's not the same,' I told her, snapping back to reality, hands shaking like it was a year ago and I was back on that beach in Norfolk, saying yes to Luke.

A pause.

'Whose wedding was that?'

'A friend of mine. Esra.'

'And Esra and her husband presumably said vows. Promised things. Meant them. Presumably, it would have been quite shit if Esra's husband had just bailed on that and abandoned her, right before their wedding.'

This time she didn't speak. She just stared at the picture.

'Do you want a cup of tea?' she sighed and it threw me.

Magnanimous? Weird? A ruse to get to a phone to call Luke? An attempt to sober me up, if she can tell I've been drinking?

But I said yes. Who the hell else did I have to drink tea with?

'Milk?' she asked and the mundanity of the conversation was bizarre.

I thought.

'No. No milk. But two sugars, please.'

She nodded and brought us both in a glass of water while the kettle boiled. I need the sugar, I thought. I was shaking. Weakness? Or rage?

Once again, there was no one else to look after me, so I had to do it myself. Have some sugary tea, Harriet, sit yourself down.

I couldn't remember, thinking about it, if I had taken my antidepressants today. Or yesterday. Or at all, lately, despite the fact that I had been on them for years. See, I told you – no one came to help me. My mind was half there and half on that beach, and I was feeling it again: untethered, adrift.

Maybe that was why Naomi looked so relaxed; so obviously not scared of me.

You should be scared though, I thought through my haze,

you should be scared, because I have never hated anyone more than I hate you, life thief, Luke thief.

'Look, woman to woman, human to human, you don't look in a good way,' she said, cocking her head to one side like a dog's leg as it pees.

I looked away from her, disgusted, and scanned the room. She went into the kitchen to get the kettle that had just boiled.

Actually, I thought, there are many things I recognise here.

The David Hockney picture on the wall. The mug that came all the way with us from the States. The framed Chicago vintage postcard, the jacket slung over the back of the sofa, the photo frame. I stumbled as I walked between them, the room getting hazier, too.

Fuck, fuck, she did steal my life. This bitch stole my fucking life. And the worst thing: I suspected she would live it better than I could. Exist on an equal footing to Luke. Answer back. Deserve him.

'I recognise them all,' I muttered to myself, and she asked 'What?' and set my tea in front of me before beginning her speech.

'Harriet, look, sometimes relationships don't work out. Sometimes they just come to the end of the line. There will be someone out there who suits you better than Luke, anyway. Someone perfect for you. Someone who . . .'

And it's then that I did the thing.

I picked up the cup of tea and I threw it, scalding Naomi's perfect, make-up-free face.

68

Lexie

January

I sob in Tom's arms after the negative pregnancy test. I take another one and it says the same, and again the result comes up so fast that it felt like these tests work on a percentage basis: 0 per cent pregnant. You have failed the test. Did you even try? Are you sure this is the subject for you?

For weeks, I am reclusive.

I veer between comfort eating and starvation, and punish my body for not giving me what I wanted. I had done everything that was expected of me, and I have lost and I am devastated.

'You can tell me now, *did* you cheat on me?' I bark at Tom, because now there is no reason not to ask, is there?

I tell him about the other messages Rachel sent me too, the ones I never mentioned, and he denies it all again and says he doesn't know who Rachel is, or why she would send me such awful messages. I laugh in a nasty, disbelieving way and raise my eyebrows because I want to hurt him, or hurt me, it is unclear which one.

I won't let it go.

'This girl said you slept with her,' I say coldly.

He swears on his family's life it isn't true.

'Have you done anything to piss anyone off? Anything to make someone want revenge on you? Because otherwise, *why* would she say this if it's not true, Tom? You're not a celebrity, you're not in a boy band. It makes no sense.'

He shakes his head.

'I genuinely have no idea,' he says, and now he is crying. 'All we have been through and somebody does *this*. Of course I haven't cheated on you, of course I haven't.'

Where do you go from there?

I ignore calls from family and friends, then I turn off my phone so no one can infiltrate my world, because I hate the world, all of it, and I am on an angry lockdown at home.

Which means, of course, that there is a lot of the one person in my life I cannot shut out: Harriet.

Harriet becomes the recipient of much of my rage.

'*Fuck you, Harriet!*' I shout when she is singing loudly enough that I am confident she won't hear but later, I say it when she is quiet, too. '*Fuck you and your happy fucking songs!*'

I throw a lamp against the wall and it breaks, leaving a tiny scratch mark in the plaster. I convince myself that leaves a gap for her music to get through and only serves to make her louder.

I go online to see what she is doing, who she is socialising with and just how perfect her life is now. I become convinced that she knows about my existence and pities me. I consider the possibility once again of her and Tom. I fixate on her, as someone who is everything I am not, who has everything I don't.

69

Harriet

After the liquid hit her face everything moved fast.

Suddenly, I felt lucid and I could see terror etched on Naomi's face where her neat and subtle make-up normally sat.

'Get out!' she screamed, hysterical, as she clutched her reddening cheek. 'Get out, get out, get out!'

I thought, briefly, how good it would be if her social media audience could see her now. Not nearly so composed, are you, Naomi?

Then I ran all the way to the tube and jumped on a train, amazed that no one looked at me when I sweated, panted, and when it was written all over my face that something of some magnitude had just happened to me.

'Do I look weird to you?' I remember asking a stranger in a daze, but she just looked up from her book then moved seats.

I stared at the cover across the carriage, longing for the woman reading it to come back. All I ever wanted was for people to connect to me. To touch my arm. To stroke my hair. To tell me it would be okay.

I've never been sure if a person could survive with so few connections to the world, on such meagre touch rations as I seem to have been allocated. I've read studies about it, Romanian orphans, rocking, rocking, side to side, and somehow that's how I picture my life. It doesn't move or progress, it just rocks slightly, left to right.

I bought a bottle of wine and I went home until they came for me, and then I sobered up in a police station.

And then someone asked who my next of kin was and I couldn't bear to call my parents, so I called David, who arrived only after I had spent a night in a cell because it takes a long time to get from Chicago, even when your sister has been arrested.

The cell was rotten, and bleak, and I had the distant, drunk feeling of coming home. I wasn't a person to exist in the world, I thought, self-pitying. I was narrow and isolated, and this made more sense for me. It was a relief, actually, not trying to work out what I was supposed to do to make friends, or how to fit in, but just to close my eyes and accept now that I was on the other side, the bad one.

70

Lexie

January

I am naked except for a towel, holding a showerhead and aiming it at the bath plughole, but it is beating me. The clot from my period, which I am chasing around the plug, veers from side to side.

It's laughing at me, like everyone is laughing at me, because I'm weak and I'm also so unpregnant, unpregnant, unpregnant.

71

Harriet

When my trial came, the worst thing wasn't the sentence – which after evidence was read out from a psychiatric report about my drinking and my depression and my coming off my drugs too fast meant a stint in a psychiatric hospital. It was the fact that Luke was there, looking at me across the dock from where the good people stood.

We had switched roles now and he didn't like it. He stared at me, daring me to look at him, and I, shaking all over, avoided his eye contact.

Even after my outburst at the hospital, my parents tried. My mom wrote long letters, sometimes asking questions, sometimes filling me in on the neighbours' sweet granddaughter and the new recipe she had started making with English cheddar cheese. Had I tried it? It really was delicious. Wittering, across an ocean. I never replied.

She called too, every week I was in hospital, but I stayed resolutely silent as she spoke.

'Please just tell me you're okay,' she would sob. 'And if you're not, let me help.'

I stared at the wall. Finally, one day, I replied.

'I am an adult,' I said, working hard on not crying once again. 'I told you, this is what I want. If you want the best thing for my recovery, you will leave me alone.'

My mom's tears rung out in my ears before I buried mine

in my thin, sad hospital pillow. After that I refused all of her calls.

It was rage mixed with shame mixed with nostalgia mixed with love and that combination was too much for me to handle. It's easier to cut off your family when you live in another country. It's easier to cut off your family when you are locked away in an institution.

I stayed in hospital for three months, and then I had intensive therapy and a higher dose of antidepressants.

When I came out, friends fell into two camps. The ones who had in the meantime blocked me, deleted me, cancelled me from their worlds, and the ones who tried, but who I pushed away anyway. But there was one I needed. One I couldn't let go.

'Do you think you could still be my friend?' I said quietly, hopefully, on the phone in bed to my dear, dear Frances.

We were no longer as close since I moved, since Luke, but she had written me a postcard once, when I moved out, saying 'You will always be my bestie.' I kept it in a book of Emily Dickinson poetry next to my bed. It was one of the only things I took with me to hospital. It was the one and only time anyone had called me their best friend. And Frances had no ties to Luke; unlike everyone else, first and foremost she was mine.

'I love you, Harriet,' she sighed. 'But I'm sorry, I have to go now. I need to put some dinner on for the kids and feed the dog. I'll call you though, yeah?'

The noise of her family chaos sneaked into our line and she went back to her packed world, while I went back to silence. She did call but it was awkward, dealing with such huge events over the phone when so much distance had been created between us. Over time that distance stretched and grew. I always had the sense that I was putting her in an awkward position, just existing. Eventually, I stopped contacting her and made it easier for my Frances to move on.

I know Luke went back to the States, from one rogue social

media site he left public accidentally, but I know nothing else. After the trial it felt like Luke cancelled himself; Naomi, too. I couldn't find a trace of them online, no updates, no pictures, no signs of life. They went off the grid, in social media terms at least.

So I was left only with my barely there contact with David and with me, knowing that I wasn't that drunk, and I didn't trip, and that I picked up that mug and I made that decision.

72

Lexie

March

I thought stress was mental, internal, but it has written itself all over my face and it's making moves to travel further.

There is a rash over my forehead, over my cheeks, inflamed. I get migraines now, which are new. Last month I skipped a period and had what doctors think was an anovulatory cycle. This, too, is new. But the stress, the anxiety, it turns out that it is powerful enough to freeze nature.

And now I am lying here at 2.30 a.m. and Tom isn't home. He went out for a quick drink after work and last checked in around eleven to say he was having one for the road.

I never want to be that girl – another 'that girl' – who nags him about being out drinking, but right now, I need him to be present. I need him focused and available. I need him to reassure me even further than he has done that he isn't cheating, has never cheated, would never cheat. I need not to be lying awake worrying about him. I also need him not to develop new habits because they are disconcerting. Until a few months ago he hadn't been out until the early hours in years. He was slowing down like all of us, preferring his alcohol to be slow-cooked with a shoulder of lamb than chucked down his throat like urgent medicine. But then, this.

I start writing him a message but when I've rewritten it five times, I stop. This is ridiculous. When did Tom become someone to whom I had to edit my messages? I decided to stay with him and to trust him, didn't I? Then that applies, still, whether it is 2.30 p.m. or 2.30 a.m. And also I know, of course, that this is Tom's way of coping. So I try to be patient. And I try even harder to sleep.

But my mind is whirring with the knowledge that he goes to anything these days. We have turned him into that man. He goes to the birthday drinks of someone from work who is twenty-two and whose surname I suspect he doesn't know. He texts me at 6 p.m. about leaving dos, thirtieths, twenty-ninths, engagement parties, impromptu beers. Sometimes he invites me, but mostly he doesn't.

He needs to be drunk, alone in a crowd. He needs to throw beer — and Jack Daniels often, which is new — at his insides until he has flushed away any weakness and he can return to me stronger. I know all this, of course, because I know Tom. And because I have done it myself, when work has been hard, or when not being a parent has been hard.

Tom carries the weight of not being able to make me feel better. He carries the pressure of not crying when I am sad, or shouting when he is angry at the world, too. He is heartbroken and grieving, but his heart and his grief are not the priorities. In this situation, he doesn't know which man he is supposed to be, and so he has reverted to the trope of the man who hides in the pub under a cover of beer and makes sure he gets home too late to talk. That man.

73

Harriet

March

Out of the blue, I get an email from my brother.

Please call Mom, it says simply. And then: *And call me. I saw Luke.*

I know that it is most likely a trick to get me to call, my family dangling the only carrot they know is irresistible to me. And for a moment, I think about not replying.

I have Tom now, don't I? I don't need anyone else. I don't even need Luke. Though it is sometimes like they are on a seesaw. Eventually, Tom will sit down firmly and throw Luke off course perhaps, but right now, they are balanced against each other, both existing as equals in my mind, thrusting forwards, sitting back, depending on the other's movement.

Luke is Tom, Tom is Luke. The lines are blurring and the two are starting to fuse. It feels sometimes like they have to co-exist, like one couldn't be real without the other.

Of course, I call David back.

'Harriet, where have you been?'

'You said you saw Luke.'

David sighs and despite everything, it is beautiful to hear his breathing and his life. See, Lexie. I have a brother, too. One who worries about me and cares.

'So?' I push.

'It's nice to speak to you, too,' he says.

But I have no sense of humour about Luke and I need this. Once he's given me the drug I'll be able to have a normal conversation, but until then I am shaking, desperate, with a fissure in me that needs fusing.

He knows it.

'Okay fine, Luke. It was at a bar and brief. Awkward, unsurprisingly.'

I want to ask if he was with anyone but I am too scared.

'He was with a friend,' David fills in. 'Male.'

'Bradley? Andrew?' I need more.

'A guy I didn't recognise; I think they worked together.'

'Where? Where did they work?'

There is a pause.

'Harriet, you know that's the kind of thing I couldn't tell you, even if Luke had let it slip to me, which he didn't.'

Because psychotic me might board the next plane to Chicago and storm his office.

But, suddenly, I can hear Luke laughing, not scared.

Tom.

It is Tom, through the wall.

Things are in the fog, again.

'Harriet, there's something I only wanted to tell you if you sounded like you were okay. Like you were moving on.'

My heart plummets. Luke. Luke. Luke.

I speak fast, reassuring him, because that seems to be what will get me more of the drug.

'I'm okay. I've moved on. I told you, I'm busy with work, with friends. Life's good.'

Short sentences. Speed this up.

'Is Luke okay?'

'Yes. Naomi isn't.'

He is so stilted saying her name, the one word in the world that has made us this distant.

Okay, Naomi. I can deal with whatever has happened to Naomi.

But then.

'Naomi killed herself,' David says gently. 'Luke told me that Naomi killed herself a few months ago.'

I laugh, at first. Because Naomi irons her shirts and paints her toenails bright orange. Naomi isn't dead. I stumble, where I am stood. Naomi is utterly alive.

'Are you okay? Do you need a minute?' comes David's voice.

I make a noise, small but affirmative.

We sit in silence for that minute, for two of those minutes. Then David speaks.

'Naomi and Luke moved back to Chicago. It's not your fault that she did this. It wasn't because of what happened with you.'

There is silence, end to end.

'Harriet, do you understand what I am saying to you?' David asks.

I am dizzy. I need sugar, or an arm around my shoulder.

'No,' I whisper, childlike.

Silence, again.

'Do you hear me, Harriet? It's not your fault. This is way bigger than that. Bigger and longer-term.'

I don't know what he means. I think I might vomit.

'Harriet, I spoke to some mutual acquaintances after I saw Luke. I did some digging.'

I can't speak and cradle the phone to my ear with a shaking hand.

'That day I saw him, when he told me Naomi had died, Luke tried to blame you.'

'He was right,' I said quietly, tears rolling prolifically down my face. 'I did this. I did it.'

'Harriet, listen to me. I'm not saying what you did wasn't bad, but it didn't do this. I found a friend of Naomi's on Facebook. I met up with her one night, we talked for hours.

263

Naomi's injuries were quite bad, yes, but they weren't life-ending. They were fading, slowly. She covered them mostly with make-up. They weren't something that makes somebody kill themselves.'

Still, unclear.

'What, then?' I whisper. 'What did?'

'Harriet,' David says very softly. 'Naomi's friend told me that she was in an abusive relationship.'

I frown. Had Naomi and Luke broken up? Had Naomi moved on?

'Like you were.'

Me?

My heart starts pounding because yes, it has been suggested to me in therapy that Luke mentally – and sometimes physically and sexually – abused me. But it isn't real, is it? That wasn't what that was. I still know that most of it was down to me. Luke wasn't a monster.

'Luke abused Naomi, too. "Gaslighted" her, her friend called it. Stripped her confidence. Charmed her and then turned on her, belittled her, blamed her. All of the things he did to you. And Naomi was his type from the beginning: already depressed, low self-esteem, vulnerable.'

I think of myself when Luke met me. Depressed, low self-esteem, vulnerable. The words sounded familiar. Yet, how could they apply to confident, pristine Naomi?

Normally, I love the anonymity of non-face-to-face contact. Now, I wish so hard that David were here, in person, so that I could rest for a minute on his shoulder and absorb this.

'By all accounts, his abuse and his taunts got worse and worse, and Naomi couldn't cope with it. She took her own life. *Because of her depression and because of Luke*. It might have started rosy, but you were seeing it through a lens, Harriet. He did to her, what he did to you, especially by the end. He got bored and he played with her.'

'No,' I say, tears falling so fast now that my eyes hurt. 'She did this because of me, I caused this.'

'Are you still fucking defending him?' David shouts, exasperated now. 'Even now? I'm telling you that this guy is an abuser, that he did it to two of you – at least – and you still blame yourself. Look at what he has done to you. Look at what he has done to our family. Jesus, Harriet. Come *on*.'

But I ring off and mutter goodbye, and then I roar and yell, clawing at my sofa. It doesn't matter what David says, my brain can't compute anything other than Naomi's death being my fault.

But how can I bear that? How can I have done this? How can I be responsible for this? I cannot even have *contributed* to this. I am not a bad person. I'm a bit much, and I'm weak, and I have done bad things, but I am not bad, I'm not, I'm not. Frances loved me. I write songs that make people feel things. I care deeply about David.

But I am so appalled by myself now that I throw up over and over straight onto the carpet.

When I am empty, I lie prone next to the vomit on the floor. When I am hungry, hours – days? – later, I gnaw stale bread standing up in the kitchen and I bring that up, too.

And it's only then that somehow I can think a little more clearly. Were the words that David – and my therapist – said, true? Was I abused? And was Naomi, who I thought was so different to me, so together, Luke's next victim? Did he flirt in front of her, criticise her doves? It seems impossible that I can have read a situation and another woman so inaccurately and yet, doesn't it happen every day, all day? Skewed perspectives, everywhere. Look at how I used to view Lexie.

The next day, I finally reply to the text my brother sent me after our conversation, concerned about my reaction, hammering home his point.

Don't worry about me, I type. *Just off to meet friends for drinks* xx

My favourite thing about text and email and any communication that doesn't involve eye contact or time sensitivity is how unprecedentedly *fine* I can be all the time.

No one can ever catch you at a bad moment or take you off guard or make you blurt something out or read your eyes. Even I can be a woman, heading into Soho to drink one too many amaretto and Cokes at an old friend's birthday do. I can be breezy and happy, enough to reassure even the people who know me best. I can fake it and omit things. I can build a picture of something that isn't happening. I can present an existence-sized lie.

I'm fine, David, I continue. *In fact, better than fine . . .* I message. I add a wink emoji. Then, for good measure, because David's never been one for subtlety and indeed, neither have I, I add the little picture of the happy couple and the words 'new man'.

Oooh! says David, and I can virtually hear the relief tinged with terror and his breathing through his message. *Name??*

I reply.

Tom.

74

Lexie

April

Time has passed, slowly, with a distance between Tom and me, and a sadness, and we are here again.

Even though I've been through the IVF procedure before, the part on embryo transfer day where I have to drink enough water to give myself a full bladder but not wet myself next to the coffee machine in the waiting room hasn't gone well.

'Have you drunk any water at all?' asks a nurse, harsh, and I am so prickly that I am defensive about this, the most ludicrous of things but also, not. The bladder affects the uterus affects the embryo affects the baby affects the life.

This is the most important thing in my world. Does she think I wouldn't follow the rules?

'Three more cups of tea and two water,' she prescribes, opening the door, and Tom heads back to the drinks machine, hands me my first cup.

I walk, up and down a corridor, as this will apparently make the liquid reach my bladder faster. Sip, sip, sip in time with my footsteps.

Here we are, again.

There is nausea and discomfort but I welcome them. They are physical and right now that is what I need: to be distracted from the mental. People pay big money for mindfulness as effective as this.

Every time I pace, I pass a woman, glamorous, beautiful, mounds of blonde professionally done hair, from another London world to mine.

Her bag, her demeanour, everything says Kensington and private members' clubs and oligarchs. My bag, my demeanour, everything says northern comprehensive school, cheesy Soho nightclubs and a massive dose of imposter syndrome.

But here, we're equals. We have taken the same drugs, placed our feet in the same stirrups, and we have the same chance.

We pace past each other. She sips, I sip.

We don't look at each other for a while because is that offensive? Invasive? Is there anything to smile about here? Isn't this far too serious a situation to smile in? But in the end, we do. Because we are human, and no human couldn't think that this situation warrants a wry smile. I think of hugging Shona close and I fight the urge to take this woman – struggling, hoping, desperate, whatever handbag she has – into my arms, too.

In she goes to the doctor – and out again, more tea.

Sip, sip.

In I go – and out again, more tea.

'More tea,' we say, brandishing our polystyrene cups, hoping this one will be the one that tilts our bladder to the right angle to make our uterus right, and receive the right embryo, and make our lives and our futures right.

We think – or I think – about the women who become pregnant by having sex in their beds. The ones who suddenly realise their period is a week late. The ones who didn't plan it, who necked four shots of tequila then accidentally conceived.

And then there is us, the other women, who become pregnant – we hope – by injecting hormones and inserting suppositories and drinking enough tea to feel like we might be sick. And by pacing. Sip, sip, sip.

This woman and I are relay racers, teammates but competitors.

I look at her and wonder – who gets the good news in two weeks? Could it be both? Could it be neither? Is good news for her bad news for me? Has she done this before, too? How many times? One? Sixteen? What an odd thing, that we will leave here today and I will never know.

Tom is sitting next to her partner, a large, scowling man in his fifties. Tom has started to scowl as well, as though it is contagious.

A nurse walks by and I grab her.

'I'm about to wet myself,' I say, crying now – this is true torture, though it may sound comical. I am rocking front to back, I am in pain.

She takes Tom and me into a room.

'D'you think you can just let a little bit out?' she says and I grab the pot from her hand, yank my jeans down and wee in it standing up and in front of Tom and a small Asian nurse, who looks alarmed.

'I meant in the toilet,' she says at the same moment that Tom says: 'Lex, I don't think you took the pot wrapper off.'

On the floor, there is a small puddle, sitting there neatly alongside my dignity.

75

Lexie

May

It's 10 a.m. on the date that a nurse scribbled on a piece of paper, two weeks ago, next to the words 'Do test/call hospital'. Again.

Tom has booked the day off work. Again.

And still, we haven't done the test.

Because what if it's not worked again? What then? Our NHS tries are up and we will need to gather something like five thousand pounds and the emotional energy to go private.

We will need to consider how many of those tries we can afford – if any – and at what point we draw a line and stop.

Right now, I feel like I have no resilience or ability to dig deep. So it's safer, I conclude irrationally, not to do the test.

By 11 a.m., though, still in bed hiding behind an Elena Ferrante novel, Tom leans over from his space next to me on his iPad and whispers: 'We have to do the test.'

He rests his nose on my temple. 'Come on. We can do it together.'

And so, we head silently to the bathroom. I wee in front of Tom, on the stick, hands shaking into the liquid. Again.

Tom sits on the bathroom floor, holding his knees and looking transfixed by a tiny bit of mould next to the shower. After I wee I immediately look away, panicking that a negative result will show up any second and I might see it and then it will be real, like last time.

I leave the room and lie face down on our bed and wait there instead, a child myself.

76

Harriet

May

The weeks after I left the hospital were some of the best of my life.

No one expected anything from me.

I wasn't working, I had no friends, I had no hope any longer that maybe there was something I could do to change Luke's mind. I had wiped the slate so clean that in it, I could see my solitary face.

My mom and dad still called and emailed endlessly, so I switched my phone off, deleted the messages.

I didn't have the restrictions of the hospital: I could sleep from 2 p.m. until 4 p.m. but lie awake playing games on my phone at 3 a.m. I could numb my brain with noise and pointlessness. I didn't have to *talk* or *think*, as I had had to do incessantly for the last few months.

I could get drunk and fall asleep and not worry that I might have missed an appointment or a pill. Because really, did it matter? I knew now that I was bad, and I had accepted it, and it was simple.

I didn't work, as I had been in hospital for long enough that I had fallen off the radar and had no ongoing projects to pick up and focus on. I didn't touch my piano. Again, what was the point?

Instead, I lay face down on my bed for large portions of the day, dressed sometimes, naked others, and I saw white noise TV come and go in front of my eyes. In retrospect, it's obvious that I was waiting for somebody to find a way in to help me. And no one did.

Now, as I think about Naomi's death, as I know – really – that I must be to blame, it is like being back there. Sometimes I drink until I black out at 11 a.m. Sometimes I vomit until my chest hurts. Sometimes I cry, terribly, and I dream about her blonde hair and her bare skin and always, about her doves.

And I wait for somebody to find a way in to help me. Nobody does.

77

Lexie

May

Hour-long minutes pass and I know I need to deal with this, whatever it may bring. I know I need to be brave, but I am made of jelly and terror.

I heave myself up from the bed, shove my feet into my slippers and walk slowly to the bathroom. Tom, who had followed me back into the bedroom, is behind me. Steeling himself for what his role may need to be today. Supportive partner, rock, voice of reason, mental punchbag, simply a shape on which I can cry.

I breathe, trying for deeply, but it's shallow and raspy with nerves.

I think of Maurice from yoga. I picture his lit candle.

And then I push the bathroom door open and look down.

Next thing, Tom and I are wrapped around each other and again, I am a child. I cling to him, I cry, I heave, and he now does the same.

But this time it is different.

This time, I am being told that there are presents downstairs, Father Christmas has been. This time, something magical has happened. This time, it says yes.

I'm doing heaving sobs, every tiny part of me shaking as though it is minus twenty. This is the biggest influx of emotion

I have felt in my life and already I am thinking: Shit. Calm down. Is this much shock good for the baby?

Because there is a baby.

Tom is smiling at me and hugging me and whispering one word: positive.

The test is positive. I feel positive. After so long of negative, there is positive.

And just like that, there is a new reality.

I think of last time, when our baby didn't stick, and every time I go to the toilet it is like sitting in front of a doctor and steeling yourself for the worst news.

But it is impossible to block it out and pretend it's not happening, because this Almost Baby is there, in all its physicality. I am only five weeks pregnant, but I am so bloated from all of the fertility drugs that my normal clothes no longer fit comfortably.

Days later I am opening a parcel containing a pair of maternity jeans. I stroke them. My pregnancy is tangible and it feels like size 14 super-soft denim.

I meet Anais for lunch, determined that I will keep this baby – this barely a baby – a secret. Until we've had a scan at least. Until it's safer.

Anais looks nervous of me, wary. I know she is thinking before she speaks, tiptoeing around me like I am her sleeping child, just off for a much-needed nap. It's understandable, I think, I don't blame her.

'We could get the goat's cheese?' she says, looking at the shared small-plates menu.

I look at her son, Dexter, who *is* sleeping next to us in a pram. It is only the third time that I have met Dexter. Dexter has been my enemy. Dexter is seven months old.

My eyes spill with tears, but then there is more than that and out of nowhere I am sobbing on a shared table, as people try not to look at me and focus on their charred broccoli.

Dexter stretches and yawns.

Anais springs out of her chair and hugs me, and I think of how it used to feel, in the months when her bump was in the way and I wish we could go back. Do it all again. To a version of events where I don't resent her happiness. Where I can be kind. A friend.

'I want to explain some things,' I start, pulling away, but Anais stays where she is and clings more.

'You don't need to,' she says, speaking through her own sob as it catches in her throat. 'I knew. I always knew.'

Was it so obvious? Did *everyone* know? I feel oddly relieved at the idea that that might be true.

And then we stay there until we have calmed down, the rest of the diners possibly thinking Anais has fallen asleep on me through baby-induced sleep deprivation.

I know I shouldn't tell her, I know it's too soon, but it's impossible now not to complete the picture.

'I'm pregnant,' I whisper into her hair, and she pulls away with her eyes wide and then kisses my head over and over, crying herself. Then she hugs me again.

'I don't think I can have goat's cheese?' I say through tears that keep coming and aren't slowing.

Dex stirs; cries lazily, half-heartedly.

Anais pulls away and says softly as she wipes a tear from her own face and then one from mine: 'Goat's cheese is fine when it's cooked, my love.'

She takes Dex out of his pram and hands him to me, and I sit him on my knee while he giggles. When she takes him back, I look down at my stomach. I still feel the anxiety. But surely. Surely. Nothing can hurt us now, can it?

78

Harriet

June

It has been months since David told me about Naomi. How long exactly is hazy. I'm drunk, now, as I often am. Sometimes I don't sleep for days; other times I sleep for eighteen hours. I am barely working; my bank account is in the red.

I picture Naomi's soft cheek, I hear her telling me to leave the house. I think of her, sitting the tea down in front of me. I picture her in the photo from her friend's wedding framed on the shelf, smiling, no worries.

'Was it me?' I ask out loud.

I did that to her; she ended her life. How can anyone but me be to blame?

On Monday, at the time Tom usually comes home, I stumble downstairs and I hover, checking my post, checking my phone, checking the menu outside the restaurant next to our flats, checking with the porter to see if any parcels have come for me. Check, check, check, check. I need something to take me away from Naomi, something to shift the focus.

I don't see Tom. But three days later, going through the same routine, check, check, check, I do.

'Hey!' I shout, run-walking across the courtyard, past the bench and the shared garden that everyone who lives here feels too self-conscious to use.

Instead, we pay the service charge to have access to it and then walk half a mile to a park. The water feature sounds beaten down, drip dripping despite no interest or admiration from the hoards of residents who hurry past it to the tube every day.

Tom turns, his bag falling off his shoulder.

'Oh, hey,' he says, shrugging it back on.

'I'll jump in the elevator with you, if that's all right?' I say, heart pounding. 'Sorry, I know everyone hates getting in with someone else.'

He laughs.

'It's all right; we know each other now so it's less awkward. It's the ones where you have to stand facing forwards and not acknowledging each other's existence that I struggle with.'

The elevator cranks into action.

'Actually, while I have you, I had an industry book I thought might be useful, if you were still thinking about a musical theatre documentary,' I say, as I have planned to say.

Confidence comes in the form of rum, drunk before dinner-time.

Tom looks embarrassed that he never followed up.

Whatever. I just need to get him inside. Bury Luke under a layer of Tom newness. Get these thoughts about Naomi out of my head. Move on.

'But you probably decided it wouldn't work or you need to get home or . . .' I ramble.

'No, no, it's still a potential, just on the backburner,' he smiles. 'I'll pop round now, shall I? The book would be great. Hey, also, I meant to ask ages ago – did you ever have any issues with post? We've had a couple of bits go missing. Hospital stuff. I mentioned it to the porter in case someone was stealing it for identity theft or anything.'

I avoid eye contact.

'Huh, weird. No, nothing from my end.'

The elevator opens and Tom and I head into my flat. Tom, Luke, Tom, Luke. Blaming me for Naomi's death. Tom, Luke, Tom, Luke. Getting on with your lives. Leaving me behind. Tom, Luke, Tom, Luke.

'It's Lexie's, mostly,' he says, carrying on the conversation as we walk into the flat. 'Her post seems to go AWOL the most.'

Bloody Lexie, here again. Stop interfering, Lexie, leave us the hell alone.

I head into the kitchen and faff around with teabags, sending snippets of conversation over my shoulder into the living room. Tom is in there, studiously examining the spines of the handful of books on the bookshelves to give himself some-thing to do.

I take a breath and pour Tom's tea. The one in the G mug – sure, my name doesn't begin with G, but a colleague bought it for me for a Secret Santa once and told me it stood for 'Great'. It was clearly the only one M&S had; this is the effort I inspire in people.

My own drink is alcoholic, of course.

'There you go,' I say, handing the mug to him. 'Milk, no sugar.'

I glance at the suspicious white dots floating on the surface; the milk almost certainly off. It's certainly been a while since I made it to a shop. Tom doesn't notice.

He holds his drink in two hands but looks too distracted to consume it and I can tell he's building up to something.

He sits down and puts his cup on the table next to him. I sit down on the other side of him, too close.

He looks around.

'I could have *sworn* this was the place I came to that party,' he says, shifting ever so slightly to put extra millimetres between us.

This tortures him, evidently.

'It feels so familiar. And you have a lot of parties here, don't you?'

I do a look so blank that it is hammy, to toy with him more and because this way, there is more distance between his lost keys and me.

'Sure, I have a few. But I know quite a lot of the other flats on this floor have a lot, too. Maybe it was one of those?'

I can't make eye contact and my hands dart around like they are playing an imaginary piano. It's a tick that helps me to remember my place in the world, remember that I have a role. Remember that I am good at something. Though right now, it's not working well.

I think about how unsure I was that I could rebuild a career, when I changed my surname after what happened to Naomi. About how easy it was, in the end. A new website, with the same information and an ability I could demonstrate when I turned up to interviews. Beyond that, nobody checked too much and I cried with relief. I could carry on. This part of my life – such a fundamental one – could keep going, after all.

I look at the clock. We've been here ten minutes and once Tom finishes that drink, I don't expect him to stay for much longer. I need to up the ante. Move things along.

I touch his arm when I speak, I fling my head back and flick my hair, I open a button on my shirt, I copy all of the most clichéd flirting moves there are and I hope that he is battered over the head by my intentions.

'Another drink?' I say, moving my hand to his thigh.

I point to my own glass. 'We could upgrade you to an amaretto and Coke?'

An odd look crosses his face. He shifts his leg away from my touch.

'So I definitely didn't come here to a party?' he says, ignoring my question.

The word 'party' strikes me as funny, suddenly. There are parties here, sure, but they aren't the kind you picture when people say the word. They are the bad kind, the kind no one feels great about in the morning. The kind filled with strangers and sadness and people who want to drink away their day. They wouldn't inspire smiles, years later, at their memory. They wouldn't lead to in-jokes or nostalgia or true friendships, people who bonded at 2 a.m. singing loudly with their arms around each other.

And in the mornings, when the people and the whisky bottles are gone, I can see the reality. There are no photos here and just a few books. No life, either – not a plant, not a voice from a radio, not a cut flower.

The rooms feel as sparse as the wine rack, until I stock it again for next time. There are no framed prints, no old vinyl, no handmade card from a glitter-obsessed goddaughter. The piano is the only hint of art – at parties, I cover it with a table-cloth, because it is the only item I truly care about. Everywhere smells airless and stale.

'Definitely not here,' I say vaguely, the room rocking slightly now. 'Maybe your next-door neighbour on the other side?'

Tom glances towards the piano and frowns. Then he remembers my question.

'I'm all right for a drink,' he says.

My hand, I realise, is gripped to his thigh.

'I'll just grab the book.'

'Are you sure?' I say, leaning over.

And just like that, I kiss him. Slip a hand under his T-shirt. Knowing that my iPad is recording this across the room.

'Just the book,' he says, pulling away, taking my hand firmly from under his T-shirt. 'Then I'm going to get home. To my girlfriend.'

I pause. Consider. Then I decide to do it.

'You weren't in such a rush to get home last time,' I say, flatly.

He turns from where he is about to head out of my front door.

'What?'

I smile.

'You know? When you came here, partied and then slept with me?'

79

Lexie

June

Tom isn't home when Tom should be home and that's making me anxious.

I am in a yoga pose in our living room. I have one hand on my heart, one hand on my baby, and I would be in total peace if I couldn't hear the sound of the number thirty-eight bus pulling in at the stop outside – and bloody Harriet, of course, whistling and talking to somebody next door. I exhale slowly, counting to eight.

But then something stops me.

Suddenly, I can't breathe slowly any more.

Suddenly, I am not at any sort of peace.

Suddenly, I feel sick.

I press my ear against the wall and I know who the other voice that's talking to Harriet through the wall belongs to.

He comes home twenty minutes later.

'Sorry,' Tom says, pale as he walks through the door. 'We got delayed. I accidentally told Dan about the baby and he bought some champagne. It felt rude to leave before the bottle was finished.'

Luckily, I have my back to him as I sit on my yoga mat. He cannot see my face. Or my now ineffectual breathing. Lies, I think. I've suspected them before but this time, I *know* that what you are telling me is a lie.

There are no long exhales, when you are thinking the thoughts that I am thinking. Because what reason would Tom have to be at Harriet's that he couldn't tell me about? Other than he is having an affair with her. Or have I gone genuinely crazy?

I stay silent then, wait for Tom to speak more to see where these lies go.

But that's as much as he can be bothered with.

'I'm going to jump in the shower,' he says.

I hear the water running and the door close behind him, and I take my hands away from my hammering heart, from my oblivious baby.

Only three more weeks until our scan and then the hope had been that we could begin the next stage of moving on. Buy weird toy sheep that keep children asleep. Book courses. Learn to be ourselves again too, without injections and denials and suspicions. But I know that voice. I wouldn't get that voice wrong.

And my heart, now, won't slow down. It won't slow down even though I am panicking about what this surge of anxiety will do to the baby; even though I am willing my body to calm.

Lately, Tom and I have been optimistic and celebratory, giddy with the newness of all this and with our secret. We have been getting our closeness back, slowly.

But, really, did I ever leave the other stuff behind? That feeling that someone had been in the flat, the condoms, the underwear and Tom, behaving just oddly enough to mean that niggle about his fidelity felt valid. To mean that I think about those emails from Rachel sometimes and I can't quite file them away as nothing. Ask yourself, she said, and I do, all the time. Especially when I hear my boyfriend's voice next door speaking to our pretty neighbour, at the same time that he tells me that he is in the pub with a friend celebrating my pregnancy.

As Tom gets out of the shower, we hear the sound of glass hitting the wall on Harriet's side. It's loud. We both look at the wall, but neither of us acknowledges what has happened. What is going on here, Tom? What the hell is going on here?

80

Harriet

June

I throw an impromptu party. As usual, the subtext is this: come if you're heartbroken, come if you're lonely, come if you want to drink until you cannot remember who you are. Come if you don't want to be with people close to you, come if the people close to you have hurt you, come if there is no one who is close to you at all. Come if all you can think about is a dead girl named Naomi.

I welcome the misfits and the broken, the drunk and the debauched. I want no surnames and no platitudes. I don't get token texts the next day about what a great time they had because they barely know where they have been. The whisky bottles are as empty as we are and we like it that way.

I do it deliberately, to get under Tom's skin and cause him to itch. To punish him for turning me down, when I had needed him to fuck me. When I had needed him to fuck me to bury the thoughts of Naomi and Luke and what had really happened next running laps around my mind.

The door's open, Tom, feel free to come in. That should help you to figure out what happened last time.

But he won't, I know.

I had thought that there was a spark. I knew Tom and Lexie's relationship was rocky. But he didn't kiss me back and he couldn't wait to leave my flat. I look at my too-tall, clunky shape in the mirror. Was that it? No physical attraction? Would he have liked me more if I had, say, Naomi's body? A wave of nausea comes over me again. I think of Naomi, bodiless now. Is there a percentage, perhaps? A percentage of her death for which I am responsible? And will I ever know what it was? Is there a number I could live with, and one that would cross the line to too much to bear?

Perhaps Tom's rejection was nothing to do with physical attraction. Maybe some men are just more loyal than Luke, with his multiple affairs, ever was? I kick the mirror, putting a small crack in the bottom.

I should have known: from the second Tom arrived at my flat, he had the aura of a man who had turned up for a job interview but known straight away that this wasn't a place he wanted to work. He kept his jacket on, nervously turning the bottom of his sleeves up and down, over and over. He didn't kiss me back, even for half a second.

It's why I grasped at something else. Did he believe me that we had slept together? Did he believe he could have been drunk enough to even forget *that*?

He left my flat and I drank and drank and crashed down to the floor.

Because: *after all of that*. After all of my hard work. I slung a wine glass against their wall and hoped he'd hear. I didn't bother picking up the glass, because who am I protecting from being hurt? It's a bit late for me. Why, when I do this much for these men in my life, do I never get rewarded?

I sit in the corner of my party, alone, with a large amaretto and Coke. If Tom thinks that rejecting me means that I will bow out of his life, I think, he is wrong.

It's addictive, bitterness.

It multiplies inside you so you begin by resenting the people who have it all, life's lucky ones. And then you go further. You resent the guy in the shop who smiled and seemed okay. You feel hostile towards the people in the pub buying a bottle of wine to share slowly, not down alone. You detest your neighbour, who has a life you want and hears somebody say I love you.

And all of these people, they are characters in your mental play. The play in which you make them pay, and punish them, for having parents they speak to, and brothers who visit, and partners who stay with them. For not having an image of sweet Naomi who stumbled into this, unknowing, sitting in their mind. For not having to think about her orange toenails.

And sometimes, the play crosses over and you find that it's not enough. And that you want to punish them for real.

If Tom thinks I will sit and listen to what I could have won through the wall, he is wrong.

If he thinks that I will leave them alone and let them be happy, he is wrong.

If he thinks that once again, I will work and work for something, only to be dropped, he is wrong.

If I learnt anything from what happened with Luke, it is that even if I can't have him, I can still reach into the insides of his life and pull at its bones and tear it to shreds. I can still destroy them, even if they think I am no one.

At midnight, Chantal walks in.

'Harriet!' she says, kissing me on the cheek. 'How are you?'

She has brought a man with her. She seems somewhere approaching moderate. I am disgusted.

'You're so sober!' I shout at her, grimacing. 'Have some shots. Do some dancing.'

She smiles at me.

'I'll definitely do some dancing,' she says, calm, happy eyes, red hair loose and wavy around her face. 'But I'm all right for shots. I'm actually trying to cut down.'

Then she glances at this man, who is looking around the

room and taking in the fact that he is ten times more sober than any of us. He pushes his hair out of his eyes.

When I walk away I see him whisper to her and frown.

Half an hour later, she mimes 'we're leaving now' across the room to me and heads off with her new boyfriend, holding hands and feeling loved. Even Chantal. I want her lying on the sofa weeping, clinging to my parties as the only bit of fun in her life. I can see the appeal of being a drug dealer sometimes: what a feeling, all that control.

81

Lexie

June

There is a large black nurse who works at the hospital and calls me pet. She has a slight Caribbean lilt, but the pet reminds me of a friend I had from the north-east at university and I think it has a nod to Geordie.

I've never asked her why, whether it came from a Geordie partner in her life, or a flatmate, or a brief stay, or is nothing to do with geography and just feels like the right word when you're looking after crumbling women every day?

I have never asked her because we speak about my egg count and when my period came and the girth of the speculum and whether or not I'm comfortable. I answer my mobile to her on train platforms and dial her number on the bus. Once, I sat on the floor on the pavement outside a chicken shop in King's Cross and sobbed down the phone at her because my appointment had been moved back.

'I can't take one more thing,' I cried, and she stayed patiently on the phone to me while I emitted all of my frustrations. She did that though she had back-to-back appointments, an already-long day, and though she wasn't my friend, or my partner. She did that because she is good at her job and because she is kind. Life is a lesson. Be more Norma.

Now, when Norma puts her hand on my arm and talks to

me gently, it's a massage. When I hear her calm exhale as I brush past her on the way to our three-month scan, I am reminded that I have forgotten to breathe myself and take a huge gasp of air.

She smiles, kindly, and gives my belly a light touch. I don't mind; it's not invasive. She's been involved in making this child, all of these brilliant NHS staff have, and if there's joy to be had in among their long days and their bad news, I want to cut them a slice of it and give them a fork.

We wait twenty minutes and then we go into the room, Tom and I, and she's there again, standing in her blue uniform next to the doctor who'll perform our scan. Both of them have such generous, knackered eyes.

I go, automatically, to take my jeans and my underwear off in one movement, and the doctor laughs.

'Not for this one!' she says. 'The baby should be big enough to see without an internal scan.'

Maybe this is when it starts to become like the poignant scan moments you see on TV, instead of the grim ones so far with their internal cameras and their mystified conclusions. Is this when we become average about-to-be parents? Is this where people stop giving me the sympathy eyes?

'Don't worry, it's an easy mistake to make, no need to be embarrassed, pet,' says Norma, but I laugh.

'Oh, I'm not embarrassed,' I say, thinking of the time I weed into the pot with the wrapper on in a room with three people and one jean leg around my ankle. Thinking of the time that in my efforts to prove how determined I was to do my best at IVF, I accidentally suggested that I enjoyed rectal suppositories. 'I'm way past embarrassed. I'm just relieved those ones are over.'

On the bed, jelly is rubbed on my belly and Tom has his eyes trained on the screen already, my hand encased in two of his like it is the plastic inside a Kinder Surprise chocolate egg.

My stomach lurches as the scan comes up on the screen and

suddenly, all my newfound positivity evades me. I pray to gods I don't believe in to back up the superstitions I know are non-existent and it's like the pregnancy tests again. I'm back there. I can't look. We have had an early scan already, the one that confirmed the baby, but this is the big one. Can we really hope for *more* luck? For *more* good news? I leave this one to Tom.

But the doctor speaks quickly to reassure me.

'One baby,' she says. 'And one healthy heartbeat.'

I look at Tom, at Norma, and only then at our baby. This baby who all of us made together.

Now it's not theoretical, something else has moved from cliché to real fact: this *is* a miracle. Tom's sperm and my egg, and medical science's years of study and work, and a National Health Service clinging to life, and now this human growing there with this flashing red bit that is its brain (I think).

'Thank you,' I whisper and once again – whether it's hormones or gratitude or just me being me – I cry heavy sobs of relief.

The tests we need come back clear and we sit on the bus home staring at the scan picture. Tom leaps if anyone stumbles, or trips, or leans too near us. By us, I mean me. I can see how his protectiveness might lose its sheen in a few months but right now, it's delicious.

'Next stop,' says Tom and then he – and it's not a verb I use often in the passive form, and never with such joy – escorts me off the bus.

When we get home I text the scan picture to my brother, who calls straight away. We don't have a conversation; we simply weep down the phone at each other. Noah weeps too, but that's because he's three and having a tantrum about not being allowed to eat only sausages all day long so it's not really the same thing.

On FaceTime, even my unemotional parents look like they have feelings. I told them I was pregnant when we first found out, along with the true history of what had been happening to Tom and me. I cried in front of a screen for the lost baby, for my sadness, for the distance that had been between us throughout it all. And while they are never going to be criers, they felt it, I could see.

They apologised for being insensitive. Mum told me that she felt bad for being so far away when we needed help. I tried to be gracious: I could have made it better, could have helped them to understand. Now, I felt like we could move forward, to a new stage where I could let go of my anger towards them and write cards to my mum made out to grandma and filled with glitter. She is coming to visit next month. I'm looking forward to it.

Later, I download the social media that I had deleted back onto my phone because I can bear it, now I am not consumed with envy. I don't see smugness and ingratitude. I just see people, living their lives, celebrating their good days and trying to get through their bad days.

For me, I don't post anything. I can't ever, now I know what that can do. But I can look, I can be in that world again. Until the next thing comes, of course, which makes other people unbearable again. And it will. That's the nature of it.

For now, though, everything is sunshine, and we order a curry and drink non-alcoholic beer and talk endlessly about this baby, who will live here in the world, with its vests and its socks and its heart, beating.

In the back of my mind there are still questions, unanswered, about Tom. But it can't be real; can't be bigger than this.

82

Harriet

June

It is 4 a.m. and, as has happened a lot lately, I have taken strong painkillers, given to me by a stranger at 2 a.m. rather than a GP with a prescription pad. Concepts, reality: they are vague.

The good news, though, is that I am not stuffed full of pills. It's all about balance. While I have *started* taking these pills, a few weeks ago I stopped taking the others: the high-dose anti-depressants that I have been on since I was in the psychiatric hospital. Do it slowly, they said, we will come up with a way for you to cut down gradually. But I'm just not a gradual kind of person. Slowness frustrates me. And! I have a plan. A good, solid plan.

First, though, I need to sleep. But I cannot sleep, because there are too many images and too many thoughts. I'm writing them down, drawing a complicated diagram to show where they all fit in. It's actually extremely clear. Luke, Tom, Chantal, smug with her new boyfriend. Naomi, Naomi, Naomi, Naomi and her doves.

I have been messaging Tom, not as Rachel this time but as Harriet, his real-life neighbour and friend who he met for coffee but didn't want to have sex with. His real life neighbour who he thinks he *might* have had sex with. He doesn't reply. I simmer with anger.

I close my eyes and think of Naomi, as I do often. When that happens, I get another drink or another painkiller. It helps.

I see Luke, telling me that he wanted to have children with me. I feel cold, cold hands holding mugs of hot chocolate. I see the Little Mermaid statue, hiding away from us under that thick wedge of snow.

I don't know now if I am awake or asleep.

I sit next to Tom and Lexie's wall and listen. I hear Lexie's warm laugh. I hear a radio playing pop music. I stay quiet. I am noise, I have always been noise, but now I have to be silence.

I imagine Lexie sitting in the same position that I am in now just centimetres from me, our heads but for a bit of plaster resting against each other, bearing the weight and taking some of the other's burden. We could have been friends, Lexie, I think, if things hadn't become quite so complicated.

I think of how Tom wants to be there and how he doesn't want to be here. I scrape my fingers down the wall again. When I look closely, I am surprised to see there are other nail marks, hundreds of them. If I do this enough, I wonder, will I eventually dig my way through to them?

My thoughts shift.

I hear the voice of Iris, standing right outside my own home and declaring me 'a bit much', and I see Chantal, happy, happy, happy with her new man.

I think of being fifteen and playing the piano at the front of my class. I think of overcoming shyness and fear and feeling something approaching pride in myself that I had been asked to play. And then I think about the hum, quiet at first but then louder, of the usual names, all coming at me from my peers and drowning out my piano, no matter how hard my shaky hands tried to pound it.

I think about Frances telling me she had to see to the dog, and about Luke's friends, smirking across the table at each other over dinner when they thought I wasn't looking.

I am in and out of sleep and not sure if I am messaging David, or dreaming of messaging David, and if I can hear Tom and Lexie laughing, or if that, too, is happening in my mind.

I picture Luke again. This time he is holding wine in a plastic cup as I sit across from him on a field. I have a football baby bump. Things become hazy and he fades and finally, finally, I drop off, only to be woken by a knock on my door what feels like seconds later. Naomi. I leap up, fling it open, try to focus.

'No major thing,' says a porter, who looks like he has come to discuss a major thing. Not Naomi, I think, as reality dawns on me. Not Naomi, because Naomi is dead.

The porter scans past me to the bottles on the floor, the remnants of lines of coke on the tablecloth that is draped over the piano. He thinks this is mess and disorder. He should see inside my brain.

'We've had a few, erm, complaints about your parties. Just a quick mention to be considerate of other people in the block. Maybe chuck them out earlier. Turn the music down a bit.'

He's practised this. I nod; open my lips to make them feel less parched until I can escape to a tap. Things are spinning.

'Thanks, Harriet,' he says. 'Appreciated.'

I see him wince as he walks off and I vow to shower and tidy the flat today. Especially since I am lucid about one thing: there is someone I plan to invite round soon. I cannot have the place looking shoddy. Not for such an important visit.

By 4 p.m., both the flat and me are clean, and I am in the pub and drunk again.

Today, I was sacked from a musical I was writing a score for after not turning up for a meeting for what was apparently the sixth time.

But it's difficult getting to work on time when strangers fill your house until the early hours and you have to scrub traces of drugs off your piano. I got particularly drunk after Chantal left, holding the hand of her real life and waving her sad, old one goodbye. Her sad, old one was my present and my future. My reality. It turns out that for her it was just a small diversion.

I shrugged when they sacked me, put the phone down and went straight into a pub. Since then, it's just been top-ups.

Except now, maudlin, drunk, something is dawning.

Without Luke, I thought I was nothing. Without Tom, I thought I was nothing. Without friends and family, I thought I was nothing. And yet, I was always something, because I wrote songs and someone sung them, and people heard them and hummed them on their way home with their theatre programmes sticking out of their handbags – and that was real. I could hear it.

If I get a reputation as someone who shouldn't be relied upon for work and I lose that? Then I really will descend into nothingness.

I picture everyone with their roles in life. Naomi, strolling into her office wearing her shirt with the doves all over it. Luke, at the centre of a gaggle of friends in the pub. My mom and dad, at home, toasting their retirement with Californian red on the terrace, relieved, probably, to be rid of their troublesome daughter. Tom, lugging his camera around the world with him. Lexie, typing, typing, typing, through the wall.

And just on the edge of all of those images there is me: aimless, centreless, pointless.

This is how I feel when I compose: I feel sharper and like I have a place in the world. When I am at the piano, it is the only time that I have ever felt like I was enough. That I have something to bring to the world.

I gave up my contacts in Chicago to emigrate with Luke. But one good thing was that I *did* get work here. Lots of work. Better work. And since what happened, with Luke gone, work has been all there was left to anchor me.

Now that is over, potentially. And if I can't create any more, the only thing left to do is destroy: my liver, my flat, my bank balance. My neighbour.

Lexie looks different when I jump in the elevator with her a few days later. I've been waiting for the opportunity, hanging around. Now, here we go.

Lexie meets my eye then gives me that warm, generous smile that I have seen in so many pictures. Lucky me: finally, the recipient.

I am breathing heavily; I had to run to catch up with her.

'I'm Lexie,' she says. 'I think we live next door to each other.'

For once, I am okay with someone starting a conversation in the elevator; it saves me a job.

'I'm Harriet,' I reply. I try to mirror her smile; after all, I know it well enough. 'That funny thing with London when you live so close but never interact.'

She laughs, just as the elevator shudders to a standstill.

'My brother thinks it's so odd that we don't know our neighbours,' she says.

That smile again.

'It's probably good to meet you now anyway. I'm pregnant, so I should apologise in advance for 3 a.m. crying.'

I look at her belly and there it is – her rounded verge.

I'm following her out of the elevator now as I issue the obligatory congratulations.

So, I think, it worked. That was your only problem, and it's fixed. You're having a baby. You have the friends, the family. Tom doesn't even want to cheat on you with someone who is offering sex on a plate. You really do have it all.

I smile at her, heart hammering with rage and, suddenly, without warning, filled with grief for Luke and where my life should be.

That's the one I wanted, I realise. I wanted to recreate what family felt like. I wanted to live in a bubble of roast chicken and movie nights, and that is another thing that I'm grieving. Being part of a team. Why should Lexie be part of a team when I cannot be? Why did Lexie choose well when I chose a man who played games with me, taunted me and then, finally, abandoned me?

'Do you want to pop round?' my voice is saying. 'Cup of tea? Your brother will love it.'

And she laughs again, head back so that her untamed, curly hair falls around her shoulders. She's nice, I think, likeable. The kind of person I'd like to be friends with if I didn't know that she would never have the space in that full, bursting life of hers. The kind of person I'd like to be friends with, if I didn't want to destroy her more.

83

Lexie

June

An offer of a cup of tea in a lift and as easily as that, I end up inside, on the other side of the wall. To speak to Harriet, to look at her, to maybe put to bed once and for all the idea that she has a connection with Tom that is something more than the one I know of.

'Ah, your piano,' I say, stroking the top of it like a cat. 'I've got to admit, I've heard you on it and wondered what you do. Do you play professionally?'

'Yes, I write songs for musicals mainly, bit of TV work,' she says. 'It's hard work but rewarding, getting to write music for a living. I love music.'

Her voice is softer when she talks about her work and if I didn't suspect her of sleeping with Tom, I would almost feel guilty that I know about her job already, that I have to lie about not knowing before. I feel creepy; imagining if somebody knew all about my life before they met me. I shudder at the thought.

'It sounds great,' I say, keeping it brief, but I mean it. It does.

I hear a cupboard open as she goes into the kitchen to put the kettle on.

When she comes back into the room, something about her has changed. Instead of being relaxed in her own home, she's stiff and awkward. The softness that I heard briefly when she spoke about her career is gone.

On one shelf are ten or fifteen books and on the others – all of the others – is nothing. Rows and rows of dusty nothing. I think of the stuff, the endless stuff in our flat, how I am constantly bagging up things for the charity shop and trying to curb the flow. Is she an eco-warrior, vowing to live a life without things? Or is this something stranger?

There are no thank-you cards, no wedding invites. No fancy bottle of champagne being saved for Christmas. No thirty-something version of pretentious art that is actually the cheapest thing you could buy this year from the *Frieze* art fair. No flowers, no plants, no candles. No scent at all, I realise. And no joy.

There are no discarded theatre tickets or loyalty cards from one of our many local coffee shops. Perhaps the most notable thing though, especially considering that she is an ex-pat, is that there aren't even any framed photographs of parents, siblings or much-missed friends. I feel cheated. Where is the anatomy of my neighbour? I came here expecting to see the pieces that made up the woman I listen to for hours each day. And here, there is nothing.

She shouts from the kitchen to ask what I do and what tea I want.

'Copywriter! Camomile!' I shout back.

I look down at my tummy. Even normal tea is out now.

I glance at the other shelves. They are just as sparse, but there is something on one of them that's of note. It's my own name on an envelope with an NHS stamp on it. On top of a pile of other letters. I frown. Did it go to her by mistake? Is she going to pass it on to me? The thought crosses my mind that the other letters underneath it could be all of my missing post, but of course not. Of course not.

Harriet appears next to me silently and I jump.

'Sorry,' she smiles. 'Did I startle you?'

She is holding two mugs of steaming tea.

Then she follows my eyeline straight to the letters and puts the tea down close by them. Yet still doesn't acknowledge their presence.

'Sooo, when are you due?' she says, suddenly animated, my best rom-com friend with an arm linked through mine. 'Will you find out what you're having? Do you have any names in mind?'

She's grilling me but barely giving me time to answer as she steers me to her Ikea couch.

I sit down tentatively. I glance back at my post, then think about what's happening on the other side of that wall.

Is Tom home? Can he hear us, like I thought I could hear him? It sounds silent through there, but then Harriet is loud.

'I'm so sorry, all I've done is talk about me and I haven't let you get a word in,' I say.

That's not strictly true, she did ask a lot of questions, but still. Talking too much is one of my major self-flagellation trigger points, so I instinctively think it's me who's to blame. And even though Pregnant Counsellor talked through this with me count-less times, I've warped my mind so much that I can't see this scenario from any other perspective.

Harriet smiles. Her mouth is closed. It's the smile of the together person. The one who doesn't need to give a barrage of 'No no no, not at all, it was definitely me,' rambling.

She just sits, smiling, and it's me – of course – who does the barrage.

I've always struggled with people who aren't warm. How do you get to them? How do you make this interaction real?

I think of another question.

'So, do you . . . have a boyfriend?'

I have no idea why I have just said that. Except that I was flailing. And there aren't many things to start conversations about round here. Except . . . why do you have my post, Harriet? And are you sleeping with my boyfriend?

'I don't,' she snips.

'Sorry,' I say, the blushing getting worse and now, I suspect, even pink armpits. 'That was a massive assumption.'

Mark it up as my latest feminist fail: making women feel awkward for not adhering to the relationship status quo.

I take a bobble from my wrist. I am too hot suddenly to feel my hair on my neck.

I try to breathe calmly. The post is probably just an error. The man, somebody who just sounded like Tom. The baby needs calm. Focus on the baby.

I look at Harriet and once again, I realise I have no idea of anything. Of Harriet's sexuality, of her relationship history, if something horrible happened in her life last week. I feel like I know her but it's 1 per cent, it's nothing.

We are human beings, Harriet and I. We are sad. We are anxious. We panic. We judge ourselves. We turn on ourselves. We loathe. We are competitive. We edit. We get bitter. We feel envy that we wish we could banish. We are jealous. We rose-tint others and post a horror-filter on ourselves. We think we know, but we know nothing. We judge through walls and apps, and we do it constantly, all day, all the time, forever, and then we wonder why we are unhappy.

Somewhere in my mind I am seeing the ludicrousness of this. Of middle-class women thinking they comprehend one another despite never having sat in a room, hugged, shared a meal, revealed secrets. Of feeling jealous towards someone whose life is so unknown to me.

'Sorry,' I mutter, draining my drink.

She is silent. She asks me if I want another tea ten seconds later and it seems so awkward to leave at this juncture that I accept.

'Yes, please,' I reply. 'I'd love one.'

As she leaves the room to make it, I stand up again, glance in a flash through the post pile. Lexie Sawyer. Lexie Sawyer.

Lexie Sawyer. It wasn't just one letter. All of this post: it's mine.

'I'm doing a pot, if that's okay?' she says, appearing without me noticing. Making me jolt. 'I'm having camomile too.'

I have the post in my hands. She glances at it but her expression doesn't change.

Instead, she laughs. Talks about tea, of all things.

'I think it's an American thing,' she chatters. 'Wanting tea to be proper and serious and formal. My ex and me used to do it all the time. Go to those old-school London places for afternoon tea with scones.'

I laugh, forced.

I'm being crazy. The post thing is odd, but Harriet must have meant to pass it on to me. She'll probably hand it over shortly, apologising that it's taken her so long.

'Well, I'm not American and it's not novelty to me, but I still love a scone,' I smile.

But then I think of that voice again; of how sure I was that it was Tom. Here for work, perhaps. Though in that case, why lie?

The kettle hits the boil in a rage and I think I see the tiny hint of a smirk creep over Harriet's mouth as I jump.

A minute later she brings the pot in, sets it in front of me. And then she looks me right in the eyes.

'There's no easy way to say this,' she says.

She crosses her legs and puts her hands together, primly, in her lap. She looks at them.

I wait, an eyebrow raised in readiness for her revelation. My heart has speeded up because I know, don't I, what's coming.

'I've been sleeping with your boyfriend,' she says. 'I've been sleeping with Tom.'

And there it is.

I feel my legs begin to shake. Tom, having sex with Harriet while I lay counting on my yoga mat. Tom, having sex with

Harriet in between injecting me with hormones. Tom, having sex with Harriet on this sofa, maybe, where I am sitting.

I remember hearing Harriet have sex through the wall, when Tom was away. But was he away? Did I hear the man's voice? Ask yourself if he's been acting differently. Think, Lexie.

This isn't out of the blue. Because I've been adding up, and working out, and this: this always felt somehow like it would be my final answer.

She looks at me, the smirk again.

'You don't have anything to *say?*' she asks.

I look down at my legs and find it odd that that is the part of me that is shaking so violently. But this revelation is too much for a hand, for a sweaty palm. This revelation is making the biggest parts of me vibrate and shudder, like an earthquake to tell me that the world will look different after, a physical announcement that nothing will be the same again.

I think of the social media trolling, of the condoms, of knowing what her underwear looks like underneath those jeans.

I think of that feeling that someone had been walking around, breathing, being in our home. I think of the months that Tom was acting oddly and of the messages from Rachel. I think of every odd conversation and of every sheepish expression. I think of Tom and me and our baby and our family and my heart breaks, my stomach dives back to that place under the sea that it went to during the months, years of trying.

All of that time when I thought we were submerged together, Tom was swimming up to the surface and betraying me.

'Do you love each other?' I hear myself asking.

Harriet looks taken aback.

'Of all the questions!' she chirps joyfully. Throws her head back and laughs. Then she looks thoughtful. 'I wouldn't have thought so,' she says, hand stroking her chin, revelling in her role. 'Not yet. But there are feelings there. It's more than just a shag.'

The word sounds funny delivered in her accent. I think of the late nights, of the times Tom said he was in the pub. Could he genuinely have been here, just next door?

I retch. Then I look up and assess Harriet differently. Look at her, really look at her, this woman who has taken my joy. Who is collecting my post and collecting my life.

She is tall and that isn't normally Tom's thing. But what is normal, now? Harriet's hair, like mine now, is tied up in a bun on top of her head. She has pretty brown eyes, pale skin, freckles. Maybe these are all Tom's things now. Or maybe Tom's thing is convenience. Maybe I don't know what Tom's thing is. Maybe I don't know Tom.

Couldn't we have just held on, I think, for a little longer? We didn't have much more to weather. But he left our team and now, where does that put us?

I stand to leave in shock and feel my legs tremble, but Harriet blocks my way, looks down and then touches my bump, gently at first but then pressing, forceful, with both hands. She looks up at me and smiles.

I jerk away.

'It's Tom you want, clearly,' I hear myself saying. 'So why the fuck are you coming near my baby?'

Have I underestimated how much Harriet wants to take from me?

She smiles, serene.

Everywhere in my body I can feel my heart hammering. I sit back down, complicit now in whatever she wants.

She sits down next to me – too close – and hands me a pile of pictures. The top one is of Harriet, in my living room. The second is Harriet, topless in my bed.

I look at her.

She hands me the third picture. Her and Tom, kissing, her hand feeling its way up his T-shirt.

I think I am going to vomit.

'What?' she says, eyebrow still sky-high. 'You didn't think I was telling the truth? You can't imagine that your loyal Tom looked elsewhere when sex was a chore during fertility problems?'

I've fallen down a lift shaft.

I glance at the wall – I know what noise carries through it and it's not enough to get that information.

'So,' she says, jolly. 'Lots of surprises today.'

And then her eyes travel, with mine following. On the other windowsill – placed there carefully like an ornament in among the nothingness – are Tom's lost keys, with their cheesy camera keyring making them unmistakable.

And my brain allows in the worst thoughts.

I'm scanning through memories, dates, times, opportunities, all with Harriet squeezed next to me, invading my space, invading my life. My arm stays across my middle. In my pocket, my phone beeps. I look at it instinctively, the message coming up on the home screen.

Flora just told me your news, it says. *Huge congrats to you both xxx*

It's from Tom's mate Dan. The one he said he spilled our pregnancy news to weeks ago, before the scan. The one he told me he had been with on the night I thought I heard his voice through the wall.

I reply, quickly, as Harriet stares at me.

But I thought you already knew? I say to Dan. *Tom told you?*

Dan is typing.

Nope, not a word. He can keep a secret, after all. But seriously, you'll be great parents xx

Tom definitely wasn't with Dan, toasting our news. And I wasn't losing my sanity. Tom *was* here, in this room, before he came into our home, told me a lie then walked past me on my yoga mat to wash our neighbour off him in the shower and get straight into our bed.

Harriet is holding out her phone to me.

She shows me a screen grab of an email from Tom's address and a weak attempt to flirt with somebody called Rachel. I think of the evening Rachel asked me where Tom had been. How I knew the answer straight away because he was away for work that night: the same night that I had heard Harriet having sex through the wall.

Rachel. Harriet.

I look at her, suddenly understanding. She's been infiltrating my life. She's Harriet but she's someone else, too.

'You're Rachel?' I ask as the dots join, as the sums compute.

She smiles again then leans down. I flinch instinctively, but this time she doesn't touch my stomach, just moves her head close to it instead.

'Uh-oh, looks like your dad's been naughty,' she says, singsong to my baby.

I retch again and put my hands across my middle, shifting away from her as much as I can in this tiny space on the sofa. Harriet moves with me and reaches out. My body spasms.

'Relax,' she laughs. 'I'm only taking my phone back.'

She swipes a few times then holds it back in front of me.

On the screen there is another picture of Tom, on the red sofa that I am sitting on now. I thought the bricks between our flat were Seventies Berlin, were the Great Wall of China. In reality, they are made of Play-Doh – he has been here, she has been there, and the movement has been fluid and constant. It is only me who hasn't known. I feel faint and clutch my hands instinctively to my belly. But I need to keep going. What did I come here for, really, if it wasn't answers? You can't stay in denial forever, Lexie.

The next image is Tom on the sofa, eyes closed, with Harriet draped – there is no other word, she is draped – over his lap. Tom knows Harriet well. He hasn't just been to her flat but he has been relaxed here. Drinking, probably. Kissing, I now know. Sleeping, definitely. And all the while I have been going for internal scans and taking myriad drugs and thinking that he was as tunnel vision about our end goal as I was. Thinking that yeah, things weren't great right now but we were in this for the long haul. Thinking that Tom wouldn't have room in his brain even to contemplate someone else, let alone spend time with them, relaxing with a beer, dozing off on their sofa.

I glance at the date on the photos and I try to think back to when Tom went out, when he was behaving oddly. It's easy to remember, because days have taken on huge significance since I've been pregnant, as we made it through another one and another one and crawled towards that Mount Everest three-month mark. And we're finally here, then this happens. If I weren't so terrified, I would be made of fury.

The date on the photos is the one when Tom claimed to have food poisoning. When he lost his keys. When I knew, really, that he was lying to me. When I know, now, that he was cheating on me.

And that worse, it wasn't with someone anonymous. It was with Harriet, our neighbour. I thought we laughed at her, but really, they were just through the wall, laughing at me.

84

Harriet

June

The world is cloudy again but Lexie – like Naomi was all that time ago – is vivid.

Lexie doesn't have doves. Lexie is sweet.

Embarrassingly sweet, at times, with her endless questions and apologies.

I hate it.

It is another thing that reminds me of Naomi, the capacity to be gracious and self-critical because you have it all.

Everyone can be pleased for other people when they are even more pleased for themselves. It's those of us who've lost at life who struggle to be as eternally kind as the world expects that we will be. I picture Naomi now, in the moments after it happened, holding her cheek, shrieking, screaming at me, grabbing at a towel, at a glass of water, at her phone. Shock, I guess. I was shocked, too.

Thinking of Naomi and what happened gives me snapshots of another time and suddenly, Lexie standing here with her tiny baby bump, they are lucid.

I hadn't thought much of myself but I was starting to. There was the odd scribble to my brain: I was in a relationship with a man who had chosen to be with me, I was doing well at my job. Having someone like Luke, who people admired and liked, was erasing the notes that were made that day when I played the piano at school, scrawling all over them with new ones.

But then, the ending. A message in block capitals to my mind that it should forget all previous memos. That as originally thought, I was too awkward and too tall. And that these were all the reasons why Luke, seeing the possibility of a future with me, decided that wasn't what he wanted. It was time to make his choice and he saw that he had chosen badly. He sent me back, demanded a refund.

I messaged Luke over and over, begging him to tell me why he had swapped me for Naomi.

You want the truth? he replied, in the end. *Because she's cooler, prettier and smarter than you. And that's just for starters.*

Now, I know the version David has told me of their relationship, but back then I believed what he was saying. I saw only an upgrade. And I tumbled backwards so quickly that it was impossible to get a foothold, to put a brake on or to take a breath, and the next thing I was there, holding the empty mug, looking at Naomi's eyes and her face, reddening.

Next, the police. The blurriness of their arrival, seen through alcohol and shame and drug withdrawal.

A trial, a verdict, a stay in hospital – and time to spend in my own mind and my own body. Afterwards, lonely weekends with too-long limbs, evenings out with the wrong-shaped friends, and a constant, constant feeling that this wasn't right. I fitted badly, everywhere, all the time, when all I wanted was to slide into my slot.

I read stories of people who were trapped in the wrong gender and wondered if that would fix it. But no, that wasn't it. Mine wasn't a gender misalignment. It was a personality misalignment.

And then I met Tom and it seemed again like it might be possible to clamber my way up to the surface. I could get to know him through my work and he would see the best me, the one who had talent and knew what she was doing and was respected. My hands dart again across that imaginary piano.

I look up, focus on Lexie.

I can't have Tom now. But what I can have is the knowledge that I won't have to hear her, living the life that I wanted through the wall every damn day. That I won't have to listen to their unbearable joy.

'The alternate me,' I whisper to her.

'What?' she says quietly, shaking.

'Perhaps the important part was always you,' I mutter, looking her right in those eyes that I know so well.

She holds her arm taut across her middle now, finally as scared of me as she should be. I move her arm away, put my hand to her stomach again. Focus.

I look at her baby bump closely, trying to imagine the human being in there. I cannot stand the idea of her thinking that she has beaten me. It reminds me of Luke's friends, those looks, that mocking. It reminds me of those girls at school. It reminds me of colleagues, party guests, glancing at each other when I try to get them to stay longer and I'm slurring my desperate words. It reminds me of the next day, when we are working together and I see them head off to lunch together while I eat alone.

I'm still not taking my antidepressants and my thoughts are fuzzy.

I try to remember the Harriet that Frances knew all those years ago, but she's as inaccessible and distant as a character in a novel I was ambivalent about a decade ago. She's the Harriet with the heart and the soul who was touched and loved – and she's long, long gone. I think of Chantal and how everybody moves on eventually, and how I am still here, waiting for somebody.

I look at Lexie, manifesting everything that I used to be.

I move my hand, gently, across Lexie's middle. I look at her face, devastated, betrayed. I wonder what her brain is doing, whether or not it has scanned forwards to single-parenthood, to custody battles. Whether or not it is still computing the part where she has been betrayed at her most vulnerable by the person she trusted the most, just centimetres away through this wall. Or whether, now, it can only rest on her baby.

'Stay there,' I say, my hand clamped firmly to her stomach. 'And I'll tell you everything.'

85

Lexie

June

I stay. I am thinking of Tom being here, through a thin, barely there wall. I think I might vomit in a way that feels so different to morning sickness. I gag and she feels it, her hand sticking close to my insides. It feels like she is crawling around them.

Thoughts dash across my brain briefly and urgently. I will fight, I think, I will fight.

I am desperate to claw her off my baby but know that I need to move gently. I know now that Harriet won't let me leave. I know now that Harriet wants to ruin my life, just as my life is making me happy again. Just as my life is precious. I retch again at the thought of Tom being naked with her. At the thought of Tom laughing at me as I asked him why he had condoms, whose were those knickers. He is worse than a cheat. He is an abuser. He has lied to me, laughed at my valid questions, made me think I was losing my sanity. He has made me doubt all that any of us have in the end: our own mind. Cutting through my terror, I feel a surge of rage.

Fertility issues alter you. They've altered me, in ways from which I am sure I will never come back. And this is the way they have managed to seep under the skin and change Tom. Fertility issues have turned Tom into a person who betrays, who lies, who plots. Who watches someone he loves think they're going insane and allows it to happen.

I knew something happened in the spring. I knew – and I chose to let him get away with his denials. How fucking pathetic does that make me?

And now, even though she has taken Tom and ruined us, Harriet has come for more.

Then, just like that, she moves her hand and walks slowly and deliberately into the kitchen. I pick up my phone again, to tell someone – anyone – to get me out of here but she is over my shoulder behind the sofa, yanking it from my palm before I have even realised she is back in the room.

'I'm having an amaretto and Coke!' she says, Party Harriet coming into my line of vision with a huge grin. 'Want one? I'm sure just a single won't harm the baby.' She cocks her head to one side. 'And it might help with the shock?'

I ignore her and try to breathe now that the baby and me have been left alone for a few seconds. I will try to give you anything I can that could help you, baby, shore you up. Breath: that is all I have to offer.

'Just more tea, then,' she yells, a statement of fact this time. I will be staying, that isn't in question.

'Do you miss not drinking?' my neighbour asks, re-entering the room and swishing her ice cubes around her glass. She dabs a drop of Coke off the side of her glass, licks it off her finger.

She asks her question casually, as though we are friends, chatting about pregnancy guidelines. I think of her, pawing me, pawing my baby. My skin crawls.

I shake my head, glance again at the door, inhale and give the baby more breath, more breath, more breath.

There's a pause.

'I suppose you drink a lot, socially,' I try, to calm things down. 'I hear you often, with your friends having parties.'

She smiles a weird smile, puts her drink down on the coffee table on top of a copy of *The Stage* newspaper.

Then she leaves the room and comes back with another pot of bloody camomile.

'Sooo, Tom told me about your fertility problems,' she says, singsong, next to me on the sofa again, too close.

She puts both hands back on my stomach, mimicking an over-familiar colleague invading your space in a meeting. But this is something far more sinister. Get off my baby, I am screaming internally. Touch me, hurt me if you want, but get off my baby.

I understand the meaning of breathlessness for the first time. I need to gulp air, like it is water on a hangover.

'Right,' I gasp again, inhaling the word. 'What did he tell you?'

She waves her arm around dismissively.

'The hospital trips, when you took that drug that didn't work.'

It's a feeling of betrayal that I have never even come close to. Her hands press more firmly on my stomach. And I think, you put us here Tom, you slept with this woman and this is what has happened. I feel weak, when I need to feel strong, and I focus everything on not passing out. I cannot. God knows what Harriet will do if I can't fight back.

When I look at her eyes, there's nothing there, and I know I can't make a human connection. I can't get out of this by making her feel empathy, or even sympathy.

86

Harriet

June

I look at Lexie and continue to speak.

'The decision to do IVF, how that would affect you both, if it was really what he wanted?'

I'm making it up now but it doesn't matter. I have enough from the hospital letters I intercepted to mean that when I fill in the gaps, it's convincing. I'm riding on a wave. Lexie looks weakened, frail.

'And of course, the effect that it had on sex. How you were doing it to order. How it was mundane. How he didn't enjoy it.'

Lexie looks at me for a long time before she takes a deep, audible breath, like someone has taught her at yoga or at therapy, and goes to speak.

'Oh God, Lexie, shut up,' I say before she can get her words out.

'What?' she says, sounding shocked that I would be so rude.

It amuses me that she thinks rudeness is the worst I have to give.

My last drink was about 80 per cent alcohol and it's hit me now. Lexie, in her jeans and her cosy, friendly jumper, is blurry.

'I said shut up,' I say, louder, the room swaying. 'Your yoga breathing, your baby. You're smug. I hear you, with your boyfriend and your friends and your family. You are so fucking smug.'

'You don't have family?' she asks, closing her eyes briefly, putting her hands to her temples, to her face. 'And I know . . . I know you have friends.'

Her voice shakes. I take my hands from her belly and stand up, I see her body un-tense. Too soon, Lexie, too soon. And oh God, she's pushing me now with words.

'I don't have family.'

The room spins and she pushes, pushes harder.

'Parents?' she says, gathering her focus, like Naomi with her head to one side, giving me advice. 'Maybe you could call them if . . . things are hard? My parents are abroad, too. We're not the closest but we FaceTime.'

'I speak to Tom when things are hard.'

I see her hand shaking. She closes her eyes again.

'You speak to Tom?'

'Yes.'

She nods, slowly. And then she does that breathing again, holding on to her stomach.

A familiar wash of rage is coming over me. Don't patronise me, Naomi. Don't steal the life I should have had, then pity mine. I rip her hands from her belly.

87

Lexie

June

I think, in the second or two that Harriet's face changes, about what she might do to me. To my child.

I am on her sofa and she is standing over me, muttering to herself, ferocious. Then suddenly she is focused again.

'All that post of yours over there?' she says, proud. 'I took that.'

Do you want congratulations? I think. Feedback on your work? But I am too afraid, too weak, to say anything close to this out loud.

'I played the baby noises through the wall, put the fertility leaflets in your postbox.'

I nod, accepting. What does any of this matter? It's the past. I have lost everything else now. There's only one thing left to keep hold of.

'I sent you messages online.'

I sit as still as I can and keep my eyes down. She still stands. Hands – for now – off my baby.

'Why?' I whisper, feeble – buying time. But also, because I genuinely want to know.

'Because I wanted you gone, wanted you out, so that Tom and I could be together,' she says. 'I know Tom wanted that, too. We were developing feelings for each other. I thought if I could drive you insane, that would speed things up.'

I think about seeing her that time in the hotel when Leo didn't turn up and I suspect that she was even responsible for that, the puppet mistress of my life at a time when I was easy to wiggle into position.

Grinding me down, down, further and further when I was low anyway and easy to bury. Making me more undesirable for Tom, more self-pitying, more unappealing.

The room becomes blurry and I cling to the sofa, trying to stay alert. Trying to stay on guard for my baby.

Think, Lexie, think. I need to get out of here, somehow.

Now, Harriet is saying snippets of words – Mom, Naomi, Luke – as she stares at her hands.

She looks at me, sits down and takes my hands away from where they had gravitated to – across my baby again. Less gently this time, more force. I can hear my body screaming; she has walked into the hospital ward and I am fighting with her for the Moses basket.

I glance at the door but I know she has locked it; I heard the click, the familiar sound the same as my own door, earlier. Except my click keeps me safe. Harriet's click does the opposite.

'I want you to read a story,' she says, wide-eyed as I feel sweat pouring down my back. 'About what happened the last time somebody stole a man from me.'

And then she instructs me to Google her.

'Come on,' she laughs. 'We all know you've done it before. Don't pretend you don't know my surname. I certainly know yours.'

I enter in her full name on the iPad she passes to me, hands shaking, fingers leaving damp on the keys. The first page is her professional website, a few work interviews I've already seen.

I look up at her. And?

'Keep going,' she instructs, looking down.

It's like being with my kidnapper. I would do anything she said, anything she wanted.

'Keep going,' she says again.

Nothing of note. I look at her blankly.

'Oh! wait,' she sighs, theatrical. She throws a hand to her face. 'You're probably searching for my *other* surname.'

She takes the iPad off me. Types. Hands it back.

'Young woman charged after scalding love rival.'

I read the story and in the background, her voice is muttering words again. Naomi, Luke, stolen, life.

This Harriet is American.

This Harriet is in her early thirties.

This Harriet lives in London.

There is no picture, but I don't need it.

This Harriet is our Harriet.

I lose my footing as I try to stand, stumble to run and leave, and Harriet blocks me so that I am up against a wall. Sorry, wrong pronoun: I am up against my wall. Any hint of gentleness is gone now, and she is firm and strong as she slams me backwards into the hard surface.

'Why do you get to be the one who is happy?' she says, pinning my hands above my head and smirking that now familiar smirk. 'Why do you get to be the one who has *everything*?'

She thinks I had everything and she is taking everything back. She came for Tom, my love, and she got him, and now she has come for my baby. I scream now, loud and animal.

I look at the keys again and know it was her who has been crawling all over our home.

'Did Tom give you keys to our flat?' I whisper, head back against the wall as she holds me there. I am feeling faint, vague, just when I need strength.

She nods.

A shiver runs through my whole body as I think about them having sex in the bed in which we tried so desperately to conceive a child.

I thought that our flat was just a shell, a place we would

eventually pack up and leave. But in this moment it feels like when she walked across the floor of our home, she stripped me naked.

'Look at the rest of the pictures, if you like,' she says and hands me a pile of photos, stepping away from me so I am leaning now, catching my breath alone against our wall.

Anything to distract her, anything to appease her, and so I do, slowly sifting through forty or fifty pictures of my home, my things, my clothes spread out on my bed and worse – Harriet wearing them. I think of all the moments that it has crossed my mind that the pillows looked odd or the toaster in a different place to normal and thought, Lexie, get a grip. Who would bother stalking you? Who would bother making a play for your life?

She takes the pictures off me as I get to the end of the pile. She looks again at my stomach.

88

Harriet

June

Once something is done, once you are something, does becoming it for a second time make any difference?

Sometimes I wonder if what I did to Naomi was a desperate attempt to show Luke that I could do *something* independently without him, something he would never have signed off on. Or maybe something snapped when he left me and I found some fire. Enough to take something from him, after he had torn so much from me. I wonder if his biggest anger afterwards wasn't what happened to Naomi but simply knowing that I had taken some control. Well, I learnt from the best, Luke.

Because he knew he could dominate me; that he had the power. He always had it and he was so unused to handing it over. When I wouldn't let him go, it scared him, and when I went one step further and scarred Naomi's right cheek like that, it enraged him. How could I have taken on his role? Started navigating our story, instead of riding along in the back seat flicking through a magazine, grateful that I had been asked along?

But now I know what it's like to have the power, it's kind of addictive.

I want to take the best bits of Lexie's life away. I want to dilute the perfection.

Then I could bear to hear through the wall, if I knew it wasn't idyllic; if I knew that she was struggling and stumbling, too. She could keep her friends. If I could take the rest away.

89

Lexie

June

It's in that moment, as I am looking through the pictures that Harriet gave me, that something changes. Because Tom may have changed through fertility treatment. Tom may now be a cheat, and a liar, and an abuser, and he may even be unfit to be this baby's dad.

But on what planet would Tom let Harriet have his keys? At a push he may have cut her some, but to give her his, crap keyring included, then to have to tell me that he had lost them? My mind may not be at its most lucid, but it can cut through this particular piece of bullshit.

And once it does that, other questions seep in.

Could she have learnt about our fertility problems from the post she stole, rather than from Tom?

And why would Tom let Harriet wear my clothes and pose for pictures in them? That's not what you do when you're having illicit sex with your neighbour. Instead, that is the behaviour of a stalker, acting alone, gathering evidence she'll use in some way, somehow, some time. Because if she went to our flat to see Tom, where the hell was he as she slipped her too-long legs into my jumpsuit?

It's enough: there's doubt. I am unsteady and vulnerable but this isn't over. My family might be salvageable; my baby certainly is. I look around and suddenly I'm awake.

Our flats are small, Harriet's a mirror of mine. I take in everything. There is nowhere to run, nowhere to slam a door behind me and ride out a few minutes until I can yell loudly enough for help or get through to someone on the phone that's in my bag.

We are in this together, Harriet and me, as we have been really all along.

I feel my own heartbeat, hammering, terrified, inside my chest and think about the tinier, calmer one that is beating alongside. This baby can't be harmed now. This baby has worked too hard to get here.

And what if Tom is still Tom? I need to get to him, at least, and ask questions. We have been through too much for me just to give up on him, if there is any doubt. Think, Lexie, think.

But suddenly, there is no room for thought. There is nothing but Harriet, flinging her body on top of mine so that I fall backwards into the sofa. I cry out. Since I've been pregnant I have barely allowed myself to graze up against a work surface. Now, there is Harriet, a whole large human, holding me down with her arms. Her eyes are fire and she started this and knew where it was heading so she has all the power. I try to move but she has the advantage and I am frozen, too, with terror. This baby, this baby, this baby that we worked so hard for.

'Hurt my face,' I beg. 'Like you did with her. With Naomi. Hurt my face, hurt my face, hurt my face.'

Because my face doesn't matter now. Only one part matters.

But she isn't interested in my face. Instead, she raises her knee to my stomach. That's her focus, her knee attempting to go into my belly with its tiny curve, over and over, and I am bending, arching, so that it is as unreachable as possible.

This is what she wanted, I realise. She wanted Tom, yes, but she also wanted to make sure that I couldn't have a life that I was happy with; to make sure that she didn't have to hear any

326

more happiness through the wall of her joyless flat. Harriet is fuelled by pure, nasty envy. I know because I've felt it, too.

I glance around for a key, but in that moment Harriet finally meets my eye and I know, don't I, where Harriet's and my story goes next.

She says with no emotion, 'She didn't have any make-up on, either.' Naomi.

I know then, too, that this has been a long-term campaign. That she is a sociopath – perhaps even a psychopath – and that Tom has more than likely been a victim, too. Fuck, Tom. Be home. Hear this. Do something.

'Please!' I shout, desperate, words turning into sobs. 'Don't hurt this baby.'

But Tom isn't home. And now it is probably too late to apologise for doubting. Too late for anything. I think of Naomi and I know Harriet won't stop.

I have no idea how I will escape, no idea how my tiny foetus and I will get away from my feral neighbour.

Except then, I see something out of the corner of my eye. One hand across my baby, the other starts to reach, reach, reach for what I need.

My fingertips, the edges of me, are reaching hard to help my deepest parts. They claw and they stretch and just in time, like a baby rooting to suckle, they latch onto what they were going for. The handle of a china pot. I knot one finger around the edge.

And there is power. There is unlimited power, unknown, unexpected power. Suddenly, I am a person who can aim to hurt somebody. I am a person who could do anything. I could snarl and I could scratch. I could kill and I could maim. I could do anything for this baby. Anything she drove me to. And I wouldn't regret it, wouldn't feel anything about it, other than to know that it was a necessity. At my weakest, it turns out I am at my strongest.

Because it isn't Harriet who picks up the hot tea. It is me.

It isn't Harriet who is the attacker in the end, it is me.

It isn't Harriet who screams a guttural, feral scream, it is me. She isn't the only one who can act.

I get a purchase on the teapot and I throw it as hard and violently as my weakened body can manage. The lid flails open and the liquid hits her, and I hear a noise from Harriet that I have never heard, in all of my time of hearing Harriet's noises. And then, I grab the keys that I saw for Harriet's front door a few minutes ago – the ones she locked me in with – and I run.

90

Harriet

June

I feel pain that I have never felt and I cry out. The focus is on my scream and on my agony, and Lexie, suddenly, has escaped me. She bolts past, grabs the keys from the shelf where they were badly hidden. I didn't think they needed to be. I never expected it to be about whether or not Lexie could get out because she was never going to get the chance.

I scream, but she doesn't glance back to check that I am okay. She just bolts, back to her perfect life.

'Bitch!' I yell, but she has gone now, the door flung open.

I go to race after her but the pain is too intense. There won't be a second chance.

All I can hear are my own cries and I look down to see my forearm, where my skin is burning.

It is reddening, deeper and deeper. I feel faint.

I sit down on my sofa and look up at the camomile tea now splattered across my wall. I try to focus on where it hit the paint as well as me, as the pain gets worse.

When he left, Luke took all the pictures from the walls and I painted everything beige. Luke took the imagination, along with everything else. Lexie and Tom's walls are, of course, in colour.

Now, though, Lexie's weak camomile tea adorns my wall, shaped like a map.

Art, in a sense, I think in a daze, like a tattoo showing off the defining part of my life. The first art on my walls since Luke took all the pictures away.

Maybe this is what the scar that is starting to come up now on my arm will be. Art too, in a sense.

I think about Luke sitting there on our sofa where Lexie was sat and I think, through an agony that is making me nauseous, I want desperately for you to be back. Whatever that comes with. I need someone to make this a real place again and to make me a real person. I close my eyes. Is that right? Is that what I want?

I want him to brighten the walls and colour me in.

The pain is making me delirious. It could, I think, be a good thing.

I thought that if I replaced Luke with a man who looked like him then I could squint and convince myself that things were the same. I thought we would move on and have a family and a sausage sandwich in the pub, and that the picture would be so close to being the same, I wouldn't even notice the oddity. Like a Spot the Difference puzzle, of my life.

I gasp, once more, as another shot of pain runs through me. I should get some ice, call an ambulance, call Chantal, perhaps, but I can't. Instead, I just sob in agony and wait, once again, for someone else to come. And once again, nobody does.

91

Lexie

June

I am sobbing so hard that it sounds like I am laughing, but I am not, I am not. I worry about my mental health, because surely what has just happened is a mirage. I was never getting out of there. My baby was never getting out of there.

But it was real; it has to be, because now I am no longer pinned underneath Harriet but running up and down the hall hammering on doors. My neighbours come out but they immediately inch back inside again, looking alarmed, like it is me they need to fear. Sticking their heads out of the door is the token amount of effort they must make so that they feel like good people, people who don't ignore what's in front of them. Anything more is beyond their neighbourly remit.

Don't ruin the anonymity, for God's sake. This isn't a borrow-a-cup-of-sugar kind of place. We aren't living in the suburbs. I'll put your post in your postbox and pretend I don't see you in the lift. Let's keep to the status quo.

'I need some help!' I shout to one of them, begging.

I don't have my phone, Tom isn't home and I need desperately for somebody to do something. For somebody to bring me biscuits and call the police and order me a cab to the hospital. For somebody to touch me kindly, not violently. For somebody to check that my baby is okay.

But the woman I am looking at has kept the chain on the door.

'What is *wrong* with you?' I yell, but it only serves to confirm her fears about me.

She didn't move here to be part of a community and get involved. She moved here to lock the door and know nobody's name. And in truth, hadn't I been happy to do the same?

Finally, I get it together enough to make my own way in a cab to the hospital, where I shriek at the woman on reception, my hysteria alarming people in the waiting room.

'I was attacked,' I say, out loud, in shock at what I am saying. 'I'm pregnant and I was attacked by my neighbour. She has a history of violence.'

They call the police for me, then they take me into a scan room.

I hold my breath and stroke my stomach rhythmically, like a mantra.

I weep like I need to emit something and I tell it – her, I have suddenly become sure today, her – that I am sorry that she should have had to have gone through something like that, when she hasn't even had the chance yet to gasp some air and drink some milk and relax for a while in the world.

The sonographer speaks.

'The baby is fine,' she says.

It is a fine baby.

I lie there then, longer than I should, longer than NHS waiting times allow. But I cannot move. I just watch my baby on the screen. While Harriet and I speeded up and became louder, the baby carried on steadily and surely, drumming a beat inside me that tells the doctors and me that she is safe.

92

Harriet

June

After Lexie came over, the police arrived. I felt awfully popular; I've never had so many visitors. And now, a few weeks later in the psychiatric hospital I have been admitted to, Chantal.

Chantal knocks on the door of my room in the middle of the afternoon. She takes in the starkness of our surroundings, the reality of a scene that so far in her life has only featured in movies and books and nightmares. Not like me, of course – I've been here before. It's a home from home.

I see her take a deep breath.

Still, she recovers quickly. She kisses me on the cheek and slings off a rucksack, from which she busies herself unpacking biscuits, chocolate bars, sweets, magazines, fancy herbal teas. Like girls do! And this moment, that I have wanted for so long, wrecks me and I am sobbing in her arms. She strokes my unwashed, greasy hair and I relax into her touch.

'I wanted to see you in person,' she tells me as I eventually pull away and she moves from the bed to the chair alongside. She crosses her legs, prim. Uncrosses them. Tries to get comfortable in this place where there is no comfort. 'Because I feel like over the years we have become friends, as well as neighbours.'

If only I had known that, before. I ask her, mumbled, why she ran away from me when I saw her during the day in the supermarket. Why she didn't stay and talk. Why she had never come over clutching biscuits before.

'Because I was embarrassed!' she laughs. 'I thought you must see me as the awful drunk who turned up at your parties and made an idiot of herself. I've been a bit of a mess these last couple of years, to be honest, Harriet. Bad break-up.'

Everyone is focused on themselves, aren't they? It's all about me, me, me, whoever we are.

'Meeting Archie has really turned things around for me,' she says, gesturing to the door when she says her boyfriend's name.

He is there, waiting for her, the man who made things better. The man who came to my party, looked horrified and left. The man who saved her from me, from my world.

'I'm applying for jobs, cutting down on the booze. I'm feeling a lot healthier.'

I nod, distant.

'I didn't want to harm her baby,' I say quietly when she stops speaking. 'Not really.'

Chantal looks down, awkward. But I need to get this out. And Chantal needs to know this, surely, if we really are going to be friends?

'I felt so jealous that she had all the things I should have had with my ex, Luke, in my old life,' I continue. 'It overwhelmed me.'

Tears spring in my eyes as I picture David, the last time I was here, sitting where Chantal is now; avoiding my eyes in the same way that she is. Soon, Chantal will leave with Archie for a sofa and some sweet-and-sour chicken and contentment. And I will stay here in this desolate place, alone.

I look around, bewildered. How have I routed so off course that I have ended up back here?

'I was lonely,' I say, and I am sobbing, desperately and with no restraint. 'Every time I heard them being together through the wall, I felt so utterly alone.'

I reach for Chantal then. My friend, my Frances, my friend. She moves onto the bed and stays there until I am spent.

'Shall I get you a cup of sugary tea?' she says eventually, laying a hand on my arm.

And it feels like being loved. It feels like being human.

'Tom and Lexie have moved out,' she says a few minutes later when I've calmed down and we clutch our mugs like hot-water bottles. There isn't much cosiness to be found in this place; you cling to it where you can. 'To the country, the porter told me. Fresh start.'

Her cheeks are red; I know she has been building up to this.

'And how are you feeling about everything?' she asks then.

I take a deep breath. Lexie would be proud.

'Well, they keep telling me again that it sounds like I was the victim of domestic abuse in my past relationship,' I say. 'That that may be what led to everything that has happened.'

That was always confusing last time I was in here because it sounded right, but I loved Luke. I adored him. Now, though, I think I'm finally starting to get it.

I look up at her.

'I'm not trying to excuse it,' I say, panicked, ashamed. 'But I had stopped taking my antidepressants. I hadn't slept in weeks. I was just . . .'

'In a bad, bad place,' intercepts Chantal with empathetic eyes. 'I get it. Trust me, I get it. And we want to help. When you get out of here, spend some time with us, with Archie and me.'

She looks shy. We.

'We've actually just moved in together. He's great. I've told him about you. He wants to help, too.'

Charity work from Saint Archie. Excellent. I murmur congratulations.

'We'll cook you dinner, we can all hang out,' she carries on, on a roll. 'We can make sure that you're not alone this time.

That's what friends do. It must have been awful being here in another country and feeling so solitary, Harriet.'

I go quiet. So much kindness and yet — is smug creeping in, too?

'The good news is that I think I'm finally over Luke,' I say, changing the subject.

Chantal nods. Smiles gently.

'That's great,' she says. 'Really great.'

I take a Hobnob, and another.

'Someone used the word "toxic" to me,' I say thoughtfully. 'And I suppose in retrospect that's what Luke was. Messing with my thoughts, putting me down, making me think I was insane.'

She puts out a hand, squeezes mine.

'God, you've been through it,' she says.

It feels good to talk. Especially to somebody who isn't being paid to listen.

'Apparently it wasn't just me, either. He's got a history of it, a university girlfriend who was in rehab for a year after they split.'

I sip some water.

'They even think he abused the girlfriend he had after me, Naomi. Naomi! I can't compute that. She was smart, beautiful. She had a career and friends and her own mind.'

Chantal smiles, leans over and touches my face. I flicker at first because she has her fingers on my chin, as Luke used to do, often.

But this is different. A soft version of a hard move.

'Do me a favour,' she murmurs. 'Look in a mirror one time.'

I'm too embarrassed to respond and tuck my chin under so she has to take her touch away. Then I miss it, of course, instantly.

'I wrote a letter to say sorry to Tom and Lexie,' I say and Chantal raises an eyebrow. I see her glance towards the door.

'Don't worry. I didn't send it. I just folded it up and put it in a drawer. It was mostly catharsis.'

I lean over and take another biscuit.

'Anyway, you should go.'

I know what that glance was about. Archie out there in the waiting room. Real life. Priorities.

'Get back to your boyfriend,' I say. 'He must be bored out of his brain waiting outside there. Their magazine selection is particularly bad.'

She leaves and promises to come back soon. And she does, regularly.

I don't tell Chantal that I miss Tom and Lexie and their role in my life. I don't tell her that our lives were so interconnected that it seems a shame to have nothing. I don't tell her that it seems a shame to me, too, that just as we had connected and hammered down this wall, they have left.

That they were in a way my flatmates; my family. The closest I have ever had. Until I'm sentenced, when I will very likely go to prison, or stay in hospital, in which case – maybe that's really the time for me to make some friends. They can't turn down my invites, can they, when they are locked up in there and prevented from leaving?

93

Lexie

July

I have a baby bump now and I feel simultaneously obsessed with it and guilt-ridden by its existence. Is a baby-on-board badge for the bus smug? Am I ruining people's day just by walking into a room? I won't ever not be self-conscious about pregnancy. I try hard not to shout about it.

For Tom and I, there is a fresh start with all of the new baby clichés that you would expect. Off we are headed to the outskirts of Essex, where people tell me there are good schools and we can just about afford a tiny square of garden, with Tom's parents helping. I know, we break the mould.

We'll be near Anais, too, and I feel a little like I'm starting to build a life again. To build myself again.

I see a counsellor every week – a different one to Angharad – and now I am out of the fog I have realised that seventy pounds an hour is a bargain to remake myself and to remake Tom and me.

Because we have struggled. Tom with the guilt, me with the thoughts of what if, what if, as my belly begins to swell and make tiny movements.

I have struggled with dreams of Harriet, with jumping whenever anyone enters a room, with the wondering of who will live next door to us in our new house, and of how I will keep them at a distance.

With Tom's betrayal too, despite it being a far watered-down version of the one I at one point thought we were dealing with. I had thought it was possible that he could cheat on me. *Tom* had thought it was possible that he had cheated on me, he has told me since. Harriet told him that they slept together and he wondered, for a time, if he could genuinely have forgotten something so big. Until Harriet attacked me, when he knew this had just been part of her menace.

But if you can both believe that? Things have changed between us, immeasurably.

'I'm sorry,' Tom says to me every night in the dark.

'I'm sorry, too,' I say and I kiss him as we lie, closely entwined with our Almost Baby between us.

Am I right to forgive him for the messages, for the lies? That's an unanswerable question. But for me, Tom is my baby's father and he is my partner. He is a human being who made a mistake during a time when we both lost ourselves. The intention was there, at the time I needed him to be fully in my corner. But he didn't touch anyone, didn't sleep with anyone and that's a distinction for me, even if it isn't for some. His was a forgivable mistake and now we move forward, flawed. But loving each other, still.

Today, we are back at our flat, emptying it out and packing our things in boxes with ridiculous names like 'Alcohol, sieve x3 & Xmas tree lights'. Somewhere in the back of my mind I remember people talking about packing boxes only with things that belong in the same room. I remember this when we are 95 per cent finished with our packing.

'Charity shop?' Tom asks occasionally, but I cling to it all.

I'm nostalgic. We're ending a life. I want to remember it and out of the bubble of what I now see clearly was my depression, I value it. I want to remember our life here as more than Harriet, too. I want to remember laughing and eating and reading one word on a urine-covered stick that changed our lives.

There are three items sitting lonely in the bin bag marked for the charity shop while the rest of our life is coming with us to sit for a couple of hours in angry East London traffic jams.

Tom goes out to get more boxes.

I am sitting cross-legged on the floor sorting through a box of clothes. I pause. Hear a sound that makes me think of all the other sounds I heard, all the other times that I listened in.

It's impossible to be here and not to think about Harriet.

I know she isn't there, I know she is in hospital, and that the noise I just heard came from downstairs or outside, not next door.

I feel her presence anyway.

I shuffle up to the wall, close, still sitting down. My hand rests on my protruding belly.

And I lean my head gently against the wall.

Epilogue

Present

I sit, listening to the drip, drip, drip from a shower that only runs for a short time to prevent me from trying to drown myself in it.

There is a loud, unidentified bang at the other end of the corridor. A sob that peaks at my door and then peters out like a siren as it moves further away towards its final destination.

I slam my fist down on the gnarly carpet in frustration. Pick at a thread. Trace the initial that is in my mind: A. A.

I press my ear against the hospital wall again, so hard this time that it hurts. But since when did pain bother me?

Somehow, I am back here. Through the wall is the only way, again, and it has been awfully convenient, my room being the one next to the waiting area. It is convenient, too, that he comes along with her when she visits, *every single time.*

I listen to his voice, try to make out the words and garner some clues. Because whatever he says, *is* he genuinely happy? Is she? I have the experience to know now that what they project may not be the real picture. I know about the filters that people put in place, about the omissions, about the gaps that are there, if you look hard enough for them.

For Tom and Lexie, their fertility issues. For Naomi and Luke, their imperfections: a relationship that was no healthier or more stable than the one between Luke and me.

Another patient – suicidal, I think – screams loudly and I curse her for masking this conversation that I am trying so hard to tune into, as I do every time, to help build up my picture. Work out where the holes are that I can squeeze myself in between. Just because something doesn't work once, doesn't mean it won't work the next time.

'Shut up,' I whisper. 'Let me hear.'

But in this place, even my own head makes noise. A buzz that I am forced to listen to because I cannot drown it out with endless scrolls, messaging and updates. I am banned from the distractions, banned from the nothingness.

A notebook sits by my side and I flick through notes taken every time I have done this, every time I have listened in to what they say while they wait.

The notebook sits side by side with a special violence-free pen. A privilege, apparently, as I haven't yet killed myself, despite weeks in this wailing, barren place.

Despite many of those weeks, unbeknown to my doctors, being medication-free, again. I glance down at my mattress, under which my latest lot of meds are hidden.

I hear a few more words as they wait patiently, him set to read the out-of-date magazines for an hour, her to come in here once again, holding out her biscuits and being my friend.

I flick again through the notebook. Archie, it says on it, over and over. I whisper it to myself, to test it out: this new name now, in my life and ready for its possibilities. Archie.

Acknowledgements

Before I start my acknowledgements, a warning: I haven't been given a word count, I had a baby a few months ago and I'm still in shock that I have written a book, so this could get emotional. And long. It could get very long. In fact if it seems to come to an abrupt end, Avon probably changed their mind about the word count and decided that I needed one last edit. If I've missed anyone off, erm, that'll be why too. There was a gushing paragraph about you in my original draft, honestly.

Firstly, thank you to my agent Diana Beaumont at Marjacq. I lucked out when Diana became my agent. *Through The Wall* would be a far worse book without Diana and her smart suggestions, notes and edits but, on a personal level, working with somebody who is so understanding and kind when you are juggling writing and parenting has been invaluable. There aren't many people that, when they phone to tell you you have your first book deal, wouldn't flinch that your response is 'Just hold on one second while I whack on *Paw Patrol* and turn the bath water off.' You made me feel like it wasn't unprofessional, it was just reality and you're right. Workplaces in 2019: you should all try to be more Diana Beaumont.

Thanks also to everybody else at Marjacq, but especially Leah Middleton for your early input and Sandra Sawicka for your eternal patience in explaining complicated foreign tax forms to me. *TTW* being sold to foreign territories makes all the clichés about wildest dreams apply.

Thank you to the lovely and hardworking team at Avon, especially my editor Helen Huthwaite. We haven't been working together long but I find that 24 hour stomach bugs speed up the bonding process. Thanks for holding my champagne and not laughing too much when I said, green faced, that I didn't want you to take it away because I might magically feel better soon. I'm not very good at giving up drinks. Aside from drink holding, your tight edits have made *TTW* a better book and your flexible approach to my, erm, slightly chaotic schedule (see above re: *Paw Patrol*) has also made the whole process joyous and unstressful. I appreciate that so very much.

Phoebe Morgan, who was *TTW*'s first editor before she headed off to pastures new. Phoebe, it may have been short but you were fundamental to *TTW* being out in the world and deserve a giant thank you. How lucky was I that my manuscript landed in the hands of such a talented editor/author/multitasker extraordinaire? Especially one who has made me seriously rethink my garlic storage habits. Even now you have left Avon, you champion the book from afar, which is a lovely thing. I have high hopes that we can get our timings right and do some literary festivals/eating together soon.

Speaking of eating, a massive thank you to the side dish ordering legend and publicity machine that is Sabah Khan. I think we share the same terrier-like brains and so thank you for not minding when I send you 35 emails a day all with some small random thought I have had. I can't imagine anyone with more energy, ideas and creativity working on my book and I'm incredibly happy that our paths crossed again. Not least because you never let me eat a meal without five different types of carbs on the side and left me the last Hawksmoor Rolo.

Thanks to the people who helped me with research, including James Ross, who told me all about working in TV, and those who answered my questions on police procedure.

Thanks to every editor that's let me write for a living as a journalist, especially my unofficial mentor, Susan Riley from *Stylist*. I'm ridiculously lucky that I get to do it and that it's carved out a path for me to live out a 30+ year long dream of writing a book.

When I read tips on how to do book acknowledgements, Google said to group them. It seems odd to do a hospital group but sometimes *Through The Wall* was written and edited in hospital waiting rooms and, once or twice, beds, so for that and a few other reasons, here goes.

Thank you first to UCLH and CRGH. Fertility treatments are something that Lexie and I have in common and both hospitals are the reason that my family exists and that my present and my future look like they do. There is rarely a chance to go back and say a proper thank you after treatments ends so I'm taking this opportunity. Thank you.

And then to the other hospital that changed our lives. Arrowe Park on the Wirral, maternity and neonatal units. You didn't just save my son's life, you saved mine, and we are working on ideas for how we can repay that in a more practical, fundraising way. In the meantime, remember how, one hazy January night in the neonatal unit, I said I would write you into my book acknowledgements? It's nowhere near enough but here's that mention for starters. Long live and protect the NHS (and give blood, everybody give blood).

Next, Rachel Tompkins, Sarah Bush, Francesca Brown. Where to start? You are the epitome of friendship: loyal, utterly in my camp, full of compassion. Fran, I would be friends with you even if you didn't review books for a living. Sarah and Rach, taking on unofficial marketing roles even when in dressing gowns at a spa really was above and beyond. And to all of the other friends who've been supportive of the book since I started harping on about it years ago, I am very lucky to have you.

Lucy Vine and Daisy Buchanan, co-authors of our creepy "Diana" WhatsApp group where we share details of Diana B's movements and track her location at all times. Kidding! Diana, really we just geek out over how brilliant you are.

Daisy and Lucy, thanks for:

A. Hooking me up with the (did we mention?) brilliant Diana. It's a big thing to "share" your agent and trust in my writing enough to inflict my manuscript on her and I will forever appreciate the gamble.

B. The wisdom when I message about book terms or acronyms

that I think I'm supposed to know but I don't. You're such pros and you never make me feel silly.

C. The "we all feel like that" solidarity. Working alone in your pyjamas is the best but, at times, it can breed the worst paranoia. I always feel calmer when I speak to you two. What brilliant, funny women you are.

And then a thank you to the biggest champions of *Through The Wall*: my family.

Mum, Dad and Gem, AKA The Originals, you've done some very crucial babysitting while I've written/edited but, much more crucially, nobody believed that I could write a book more than you did. Nobody is more excited every time there's any update, nobody is prouder and nobody is keener to celebrate and cheer me on with every win. Mostly with a bottle of champagne. It's almost like you're looking for an excuse, Mum?! Gem, thanks for doing my Facebook marketing for free too with your lovely proud sister updates. Thanks to my best chum Luna, to Blake and to Gibbo for reading a book that wasn't about a player at Liverpool Football Club. And to the Turner/Sharps for being the best in-(non)laws. Dad, I'm sorry I didn't write about the Tudors.

To my favourite people in the universe: my hilarious and smart boys. You can't read this yet but one day you will and that'll be pretty cool. Though ignore the swearing! Swearing is bad! They made me put that in, I don't swear. Oh and by now, you might have figured out that I didn't write *Room On The Broom* after all – sorry about the, erm, 'confusion' around that.

Lastly, to the hardest bit. Simon. For someone who writes for a living, I always run out of words when it comes to you, but I will try. Thank you for the support, the championing and for juggling things so that I am always able to write or edit if I need to. You told me once when I had a low moment that this book would get finished no matter what we needed to do and you were right. But only because I had you in my corner. You are the definition of a teammate. The biggest thank you of all is for you.